The Hero

Louise Le Nay was born in Melbourne. She studied acting at NIDA in Sydney, and spent fifteen years working in film, radio, commercials and television. In 1994, Le Nay gave up acting to study literature and the classics at Melbourne University. Over the years she has worked as a waitress, motel cleaner, kitchen hand, receptionist and supermarket demonstrator. *The Hero* is her first novel.

The Hero

Louise Le Nay

ALLEN & UNWIN

Publication of this title was assisted by The Australia Council, the
Federal Government's arts funding and advisory body.

First published in 1996 by
Allen & Unwin
9 Atchison Street
St Leonards, NSW 2065
Australia
Phone: (61 2) 9901 4088
Fax: (61 2) 9906 2218
E-mail: frontdesk@allen-unwin.com.au
URL: http://www.allen-unwin.com.au

National Library of Australia
Cataloguing-in-Publication entry:

Le Nay, Louise, 1957– .
  The hero.

  ISBN 1 86448 157 9.
  I. Title.

A823.3

Set in 12.5/13pt Lapidary by DOCUPRO, Sydney
Printed by Australian Print Group, Maryborough, Victoria

10 9 8 7 6 5 4 3 2

Acknowledgments

The author wishes to thank all those who gave permission to reproduce the following material.

From *Rivers to the Sea* by Sara Teasdale (New York: Macmillan, 1915); an extract from *An Irish Airman Forsees his Death* by W.B. Yeats with kind permission by A.P. Watt Ltd on behalf of Michael Yeats; an extract from *The Soldier* by Rupert Brooke (Macmillan Publishers); extracts from *The Moods of Ginger Mick* by C.J. Dennis (Angus & Robertson); extracts from 'Dulce et Decorum' and 'Strange Meeting' from *The Collected Poems of Wilfred Owen*, edited and with an Introduction by Cecil Day Lewis (Chatto & Windus); lyrics from 'Pack Up Your Troubles' (Powell/Asaf) and 'Goodbyee!' (Weston/Leigh) © words reprinted with permission of J. Albert & Son Pty Ltd; extracts from *Attack*, *The Death Bed* and *To Victory* by Siegfried Sassoon, by permission of George Sassoon.

Every effort has been made to contact the copyright holders of material used in this book. However, where an error or omission has occurred, the author and publisher will gladly include acknowledgement in future editions.

To my mother
R. M. Le Nay

1

Sing a song of War-time,
Soldiers marching by,
Crowds of people standing,
Waving them 'Goodbye'.
When the crowds are over,
Home we go to tea,
Bread and margarine to eat,
War Economy!

NINA MACDONALD

Nonie lay on the ground under the peppercorn tree and watched the house. Sunlight needled her through the uneven leaf canopy. From here, she could see her new home—a side view of the big house with its bluestone foundations; the lean-to woodshed, rickety against the back wall of the wash-house; a section of the kitchen garden; the hen-house; the tangled orchard, burgeoning with summer fruit. She could see the yard at the front and the gravel carriageway. Behind her the yellow paddocks stretched to the creek, where their openness was swallowed into the bush. It had been her father's home. Now it was her home.

The property had once been a wealthy farm. *'When I was a girl,'* Ruth said. *Nonie replied, 'That must have been a long time ago,' and Ruth blushed and looked away.* Nothing ever comes out right, Nonie thought, it is better to stay silent.

The others adored Ruth. The twins and the little ones called out *'Auntie Ruth! Auntie Ruth!'* the way they might have called *'Mumma!'*. Their mother was just a word to them, really, not even a memory. This small, firm woman, Ruth, was their real mother now. Even Flora seemed satisfied with the arrangement. She followed Ruth about, chattering, telling her things. Flora

1

was a stupid sheep. When Nonie and Flora had first arrived Flora would sit on the gatepost and cry, staring down the road waiting for Dadda. *Ruth said, 'Flora, you must be patient,' and Mrs Haggerty said, 'When the war is over, all the soldiers will come home, all the heroes will be home to their wives and their little children.'* So Flora had stopped the gatepost business, believing everything she was told, like a sheep.

Elsie wanted to be a Hero after that. She and Georgie tramped around the paddocks with sticks all day, waging violent war against the twins. But Tom and Phip always won. They were older and stronger and would rather die than give in. That was the way with them. Nonie could remember the twins—sniffly toddlers with eczema round their mouths—holding onto her, one on each hand, not wanting to let her go, even for Mother. Elsie never minded losing the war games anyhow. That was Elsie.

'It's silly wanting to be a soldier,' Nonie told her.

'Why?'

'Because it is.'

'I want to be one.'

'But you can't.'

'Why?'

Then Hannibal would say, 'Leave her be, Nonie. Let her play as she wants.'

Hannibal was impossible. Nonie buried her face in the prickly grass. She could hear him in the orchard with the littlest one, Georgie. She could not hear what they were saying, only the rumble of Hannibal's baritone, intermingled with Georgie's falsetto.

This was Hannibal's home too, although he did not live at the big house. He lived in the cottage near the gates. Once the cottage had had wooden shingles for a roof, Ruth had told her, but now there was iron. 'I was born in the cottage,' said Ruth proudly. 'But your father was born at the big house.' Lately, Flora had taken to standing by while Hannibal chopped wood then rushing to gather the kindling into a pile, waiting only for

2

a nod of approval, or a smile. Or not wanting anything in return, secure in the knowledge that she was appreciated. That was Flora. Hannibal had brown arms, but the palms of his hands were pink.

'That is the native in him,' said Ruth.

Hannibal had The Native in him.

Ruth said that the children's father had been Hannibal's best friend. Nonie thought about that often. She had never had a best friend, but knew the way she would behave if she had. *My friend*, she would say carelessly, *my friend this, my friend that*. Hannibal never spoke of her father though, and as far as she could remember her father had never spoken of Hannibal. She had not known of his existence till Ruth had found them, and brought them to live at Greystones.

Nonie rolled over and let the grass prickle her back for a while. Patches of blue glimpsed through the green overhead. Sunlight stung her cheeks.

'This is Hannibal,' Ruth said, waving to him as he approached them on the station platform. There was a bite in the late spring air that had not been evident in Melbourne. Nonie, shivering, tried to stand in a way that might make her thin dress look longer. She huddled close to Flora. Flora was smiling in a fixed, determined sort of way. Nonie could not smile. She wanted to be sick.

Hannibal collected Ruth's small bag, nodded at the two terrified girls, and they followed him from the platform to the jinker. Recent rain had turned the railway yards into a bog. Timber was stockpiled on the sidings. They were assailed by the smell of bleeding wood.

Ruth helped them into the jinker and tucked blankets around them. Nonie was glad of the blankets, not because of the cold, she was used to that, but because they covered the shame of her too-small dress. Ruth climbed into the front seat of the jinker beside Hannibal, and they jolted into motion, leaving behind the station buildings, the timber yards, till there was nothing on either side of the dirt road but trees.

'This is our home,' Ruth said, pointing. 'We are at the foot of the mountains. There.' They looked obediently. 'Mount Donna Buang, Mount Juliet, Mount Monda and Mount St Leonard.' Their aunt's voice suggested that the view was beautiful, but Nonie saw a wilderness—menacing in its tree-filled emptiness.

The girls travelled in silence. Flora eventually leaned forward and tapped her aunt gently. 'Excuse me, missis . . . I mean . . .' Ruth turned around. 'It's my sister.' The jinker was halted and Ruth led Nonie to the side of the road where she vomited the entire contents of her stomach into plumes of bracken, for a minute or two completely oblivious of her shameful dress, so great was her discomfort. Then she was tucked back into her seat, and the journey recommenced.

'Look,' Ruth said. 'You can see St Leonard clearly now. That's our mountain. The Chum Valley is at its foot. It's where we all grew up. Hannibal and myself, and Paul. I expect he told you.' They answered her with silence. Ruth said awkwardly, 'Oh well,' and then added, 'it's your home now.'

The jinker creaked and swayed while Nonie stared at the grey-green shadow of the mountain. Her new-found aunt and Hannibal exchanged news together. Early strawberries were coming on, the recent rain had been welcome, in the city newspapers had trumpeted opinions about the war and conscription and Billy Hughes. She heard their voices distantly, like little waves lapping at the edges of a deep dark sea.

'Nonie. Here you are.' The sound of Flora's voice broke the solitude. Nonie sat up on one elbow and watched her sister approach. Flora was looking solemn. She was always concerned about something, thought Nonie, frowning. She could never leave things be.

'What's the matter?'

'Nothing.'

Only she doesn't mean it, thought Nonie. Flora sat down with her back against the tree trunk, fussily tucking her dress in so that her knickers would not show. 'It's getting hot. You have to watch out for snakes, Hannibal says.'

'I know.'

'I helped Auntie Ruth make the bread again today.'

'I know.'

'Four loaves. There was a message from Dingley that they needed extra. And one we made a plait.'

Nonie was silent. She could not pretend to know everything, and she was grudgingly interested in the plaited loaf. Flora leaned toward Nonie confidingly. 'I like it here, Nonie. Have we been here long?'

'Two months, or something.' It was nine weeks and two days exactly. Nonie knew.

'Do you think they'll let us stay?'

Nonie did not answer.

'I mean just till Dadda comes for us. When the war is over.'

'I expect so.' Nonie moved downhill into a patch of sunlight, looking for snakes, but trying not to let Flora see her doing it.

'He'll be sad when he knows about Mumma being dead,' continued Flora drearily. 'If we could write and let him know . . .'

'It doesn't matter. Don't think about it.' Nonie put her arms over her head and wished her sister away.

'Auntie Ruth will fix it anyway,' added Flora. 'Don't you think?'

'Yes.'

'Yes, she will,' echoed Flora, placated. She sat there for a few minutes then climbed to her feet and trailed off towards the house paddock. She could see the twins and Elsie there. They were playing their favourite game—Trenches. They had dug shallow holes in the ground and were casting dirt-ball hand grenades at each other. The heifer, caught in the crossfire, was bellowing. Nonie rolled further down the hill and felt alone again.

'Nonie, my dear, you must try to be happy here,' Ruth said. 'And I will try to make you happy, now that poor Lily is gone.'

Nonie wanted to say, 'I am happy here.' But it was difficult to say things, even when you wanted to. They got caught up.

'Nonie is happy,' said Hannibal. 'Just thinking.'

How did Hannibal know?

'She is so like poor Lily,' said Ruth. 'And yet, at moments she is so like Paul she makes me gasp.'

So like Paul. Dadda the soldier, the Hero with Medals.

'Why doesn't he write?' Flora asked Ruth one day.

When Ruth did not answer, Flora said, 'Because he is so busy at the Front, I expect. Fighting the Kaiser and rescuing people.'

Ruth said, with something that sounded like relief, 'Yes, I expect he is.'

The children always talked of the war, and Dadda. Everyone talked of the war. There was a map stuck up on the kitchen wall showing the Western and the Eastern Fronts, and another of Turkey. They had come from the newspaper years before when the war was new, when it was fun to put pins in where the gallant allies were. In the Greystones kitchen the maps were yellowing and brittle, greasy with fingermarks. Sometimes Ruth read out news items from the *Argus* over the meal table. This morning she had read 'Anzacs take Jericho' in her tight-lipped way, not wanting to show how glad she felt. The others showed gladness for her, without knowing what Jericho was, or where, or caring either. Do you think Dadda was there? they asked, because that was what mattered. Then they played games all day—the Cavalry in Jericho—but how did they get the horses over the walls, said Flora who knew something about walls being there, and they conferred excitedly about the possibilities. They were talking now. The twins and Elsie had been persuaded away from the heifer by the arrival of Minnie the house cow. They

6

were following Flora through the broken fence and into the orchard where Hannibal and Georgie were picking apples. Their voices bustled across the paddock toward her on the still air. Nonie tried to shut them out.

'Is Dadda a gunner?' Tom was demanding. 'Does he fire the big five-nines? Do you reckon he does, Hannibal?'

'I bet he sends crumps right down the Fritz funk-holes!' said Phip vehemently.

Nonie put her hands over her ears and rolled over again. The war made her angry. She had tried to tell Ruth earlier that day.

'Why can't it be left alone?'

'What, dear?'

'You know. The war.'

'It's not the sort of thing one can leave alone.' Ruth seemed amused. 'It rather depends on people. If all the people left it alone, well, there would be no war.'

'Good then!'

'Yes, Nonie.' Ruth smiled suddenly. 'Just as you say. Good.'

Conversation went nowhere. It was easier just to listen. To listen, yes, but not to think. Lying there warm and idle, Nonie concentrated herself on the sounds around her, sounds from a world she had never known before. Instead of the rattle and grate of trams she heard the hum of insects, a flock of white cockatoos screeling and scraping overhead. Instead of the clatter of the nightcart, there was the thud of axes from the timber mill which scarred the valley further in. Under it all was the sound of the creek, whispering along the valley floor through the dark tangle of the bush. And she remembered that as a child she had slept to the murmur and laughter of her parents' voices, hidden away in the sacred chamber of their room which she dared not desecrate by entering. Until the day it stopped.

Don't think! Don't think! implored Nonie fiercely behind closed eyes. But sometimes the thoughts, the memories just came.

'Don't cry, Mumma, it's all right. I'll find him. I'll ask the Currans, and I'll ask at the shop. Do you want a cup of tea? All right. It's all right. I'll take the twins. Flora will nurse Elsie. Don't cry, Mumma, please. I'll find him for you.'

2

What times we've had, both good and bad,
We've shared what shelter could be had,
The same crump-hole when the whizz-bangs shrieked,
The same old billet that always leaked,

THE WIPERS TIMES, 1916

uth Field was on her knees in the kitchen garden. A rivergum reached with bent arms from the house paddock over the dilapidated picket fence behind her. Minnie the house cow had brought her outraged heifer into its shade, and Ruth, while she pulled old carrots, spoke soothingly to them. She was a small woman made frail-looking in middle age by fair skin which had bloomed only briefly then faded, and by a quantity of wiry grey hair which framed her head, miniaturising her sharp features. Once her head of hair, nut-brown then, had bestowed upon her a suggestion of beauty. The farm hands had teased her in the old days. They had called her Sparrow—'sparrer' was the way it sounded. She smiled, remembering, then frowned at the indulgence. There were no farm hands any more, and no real farm, only a few struggling paddocks which Hannibal helped her to tend. But now there were the children—an unexpected gift that she had received with stout heart and trembling knees when it was thrust upon her three years ago. First came the baby and beaming Elsie, crusted with scabs and crawling with lice, then the twins. Four children, she had marvelled, for it was hard to imagine frail Lily with even one child. *'You'll have to do something about those* boys,' Queenie Cousins warned. 'Not speaking a word at their age . . . you'll have to have the doctor to them. They could be deaf as well as dumb.' But Ruth had been content to wait, confident that there was no real damage, because she could hear the twins late at night, whispering together in bed. What secrets had they, she wondered, hearing the little rustling voices through the open doorway. Over the months the twins had gained weight, lost their pinched paleness, their anxious little frowns. Then they began to speak aloud in babyish, adenoidal voices. 'Where Dodie? Where Dora?' they asked, and kept on asking. Ruth slowly realised the implications of the question. She wrote letters, made trips by train to the city. Finally she found Nonie and Flora. Paul's children. Not four of them, but six. How like him to reach across the years and cast them, penniless, motherless, tumbling into her lap. 'Onwards and upwards', Paul would have said. Well then.

Ruth eased onto her heels. She did not enjoy weeding, it was a hopeless task. The weeds always grew again, just as the bush crept back these days, up from the creek, each year pushing a little further past rotten fenceposts. First the bracken and blackberry, then the black wattle, then the sapling gums. Now the paddock boundaries, so distinct in her youth, were blurred, as though fingers of the ancient land were reaching up the valley to soothe and mend. It was as it should be, Ruth considered.

She stood up, stretched, and listened. Children's voices rang from the orchard. In the house paddock, a kookaburra began an ascending scale then stopped halfway and the unexpected silence it left was filled with the rattle of cicadas. Gang-gang cockatoos cracked ripening seed pods in the wattle trees. They were familiar sounds, but they stabbed rather than comforted Ruth. The world was changing. War changed everything. It had done so once before.

'You there, Ruth?'

'Bert? Just coming.' Ruth wiped her hands clean, collected her basket of vegetables and made her way to the front of the house. Bert Haggerty, red-faced, was hauling a crate of apples into the back of his wagon.

'Hannibal not about? I'll load this lot.'

'Let me help.' Bert had a weak heart. He allowed Ruth to take the other end of the crate. Ruth put her basket beside it. 'No carrots, I'm afraid. I've just emptied the bed. Well, there were a few, but we had a visitor last night. The fence is broken. Oh, and that's the end of the strawberries.'

Bert leaned up against his wagon and mopped his face with a handkerchief. 'That old wombat again? You shouldn't encourage it, you know.'

'I don't. I just don't discourage her. There is a difference. Anyway'—Ruth pushed hair from her face and leaned back beside Bert—'She's old, like us. I don't begrudge her a few carrots.'

'Used to hand-feed her, I recall.'

'Not her. Her mother. Or grandmother. I forget.'

There had always been a wombat at Greystones. The path of each generation had barely altered in all Ruth's years: across the front carriageway, past or through the kitchen garden, under the fence into the house paddock, and from there to the creek. Many an evening the guests from Dingley had made their way singing and shouting down the bush track to Greystones to marvel at Ruth's wombat taking supper from her hands, then to take Devonshire tea themselves, at ninepence a time, and be driven home by Paul. Poor little Lily Prendergast had come stumbling down that track, flushed with unaccustomed exercise, into Paul's life.

'Took the drag into town this morning,' said Bert. 'Collected some folk from the station. I looked in at the post office for you. Thought there might have been something.'

Ruth shifted. 'Paul never was much of a correspondent.'

'Still, it must be a worry to you.'

'No.' It was easy to admit. 'It's been a long time, now. I'm used to his absence.'

11

'But now . . .'

'I know things have changed, what with poor Lily dead, and it's even possible he doesn't know he has a three-year-old son, I suppose. I'd tell him if I could.'

Bert Haggerty, who was inordinately fond of children, shook his head. 'Well, it's a tragedy, and that's a fact. Six young ones with no mother. No father that cares for them.'

'I'm quite sure Paul would be back in an instant if he knew,' insisted Ruth, shifting again in her profound uncertainty.

'Consie sent some things down, by the way.' Bert reached around and collected a brown-paper parcel from under his seat.

'Really, she shouldn't have.'

'Now don't take away her pleasure, Ruthie. There's some woollies, and she sewed up two frocks for the two eldest, just from scraps. She says it's a joy to be sewing for children again, in between all that sewing for the Red Cross. And frocks, too. Consie always yearned after daughters, you know, though God saw fit only to give us lads.' His voice began to falter.

Ruth said, 'Any post for you? Anything from Stanley?'

Bert coughed and nodded. 'Oh, our Stan writes quite regular. Not long letters, mind. And his Auntie Queenie's always finding fault with his spelling. Yes, we had one this morning. He says he's enjoying his training and great chums with the other lads, you know Stan. Fair champing at the bit to be shipped out, I expect. He doesn't say so in as many words. He wouldn't put it like that in a letter to his mother, . . .' He shrugged away the end of the remark.

'I know,' said Ruth gently.

Bert Haggerty studied his knuckles. 'Doesn't get any easier, Ruth. The thought of losing another son, even if it is for King and Country, well it's cold comfort is all I can say.'

'I know,' said Ruth.

'Consie prays every night that he won't be sent away, well, we all do, don't we. Our Stan will be that disappointed!'

'He can live with disappointment,' said Ruth.

'My word he can. And I'll rejoice in it, I can tell you.' Bert laughed suddenly. 'How are the two girls, then. Settled in now?'

'Pretty well. Flora is up most nights with croup. Nonie is quiet. They're good girls.'

'Must be glad to be back in their own family again.'

Ruth frowned. 'They probably don't think of themselves as family—not after three years separation. Georgie doesn't know the older ones at all. But he likes them well enough. I'll never understand how Lily could have just cast them aside the way she did. God knows, she had only to write.'

Bert climbed slowly into the wagon. 'Can't figure it at all, and Consie says likewise. She was a loving little thing. It certainly was a love match, Lily and Paul. Remember, Ruthie?'

Ruth did not care to remember. She said, 'I've been wondering if it wouldn't be better to sell up and take the family into town. To a more settled way of life.'

Bert snorted at the proposition. 'You're like that old wombat, Ruth. You stick to your ground and you always will. Oh, I nearly forgot. Here's another little parcel from Jackie.' He handed it down to her. 'There's mittens and scarves. He chose the colours himself; put them together nicely. He's done that much knitting the Red Cross are going to make him a special presentation, Consie tells me.'

'Good for Jackie.'

'Yes. War's been the making of Jackie, really.' Bert Haggerty looked sheepish. 'Well, you know what they say—it's an ill wind . . .'

Ruth nodded and smiled. 'Thanks, Bert. See you next time.' She stood back to let the horse pass, scattering hens on either side. Then she sighed and wandered into the house.

Greystones had not altered on the inside for years. The high ceilings and good carpets, now sadly worn, gave the place an air of breeding. There had been money in the beginning, Ruth's mother had told her often. The house had been intended as a colonial mansion. But when the farm began to demand more attention the building slowed and the brickwork gave way at the back to a series of wooden rooms, each less well-constructed than the last. Then when the hops had finally withered and taken with them the hopes of the district, no one had had the heart or the finance left to go on with building. The tale repeated itself like clockwork in Ruth's head. She had heard it all her life, the explanation for the reduced circumstances in which they lived, although she had never felt herself deprived. Her father had died one winter after a long bout of pneumonia, and her mother had died soon after. She had been a sickly, anaemic woman who had never recovered from the unexpected birth of her son, Paul, so late in her life. Ruth had progressively taken on the roles of housemaid, then housekeeper, then sick-nurse to her mother, then nursemaid, then property manager. It had, she often reflected with satisfaction, made her a capable woman.

Ruth was comforted by the history of her home. She paused in the parlour on her way past, and inhaled memories of the life of order she no longer lived. The old grandfather clock presided here, kept watch on the leather chairs and the little tables with their trinkets—an ivory elephant from India, porcelain figurines, a few of Ruth's own watercolours in wooden frames, which gave her a twinge of guilt whenever she passed them, for she had not lifted a paintbrush in years, and on the mantelpiece a row of photographs.

Ruth contemplated the photographs as she stood there, flicked absently at a speck of dust, moved now one, now the other. There was a picture of her parents, newly married, looking as Ruth had never known them; a round daguerreotype of her grandfather, founder of Greystones; another of Harry Lambe. People always looked silly in uniforms, particularly Harry, Ruth decided, pushing the photograph a little further into shadow. In any case, she did not need a photograph; it only complicated her memory of him. There was a small square picture of herself as a young woman, with Paul, a pale little boy of four who had moved while the photograph was being taken so that his features were blurred. They were orphans by then. Paul was as good as her own child. And she, a mother at fifteen.

The last photograph was of Paul and Lily on their wedding day. Poor Lily, so slight and trusting, and Paul blurred again.

'Bert's been, has he?' Hannibal appeared, holding his work-boots in one hand. Ruth had brought up the boys to be fastidious; Paul, though, had never learned the lesson.

'Oh, you startled me. Yes, yes. Just now.'

'I meant to give him a hand.'

'It's all right, I was there. No mail. A parcel of clothes from Consie and Jackie.'

Hannibal nodded. 'Henrietta had her kittens. Five.'

'Five!'

'If you want I'll . . .'

'I can't bear them to be drowned. We'll have to find homes. Consie likes kittens.'

'Auntie Queenie doesn't.'

Ruth smiled. 'Have the children seen them?'

'Yes.'

'Nonie?'

'Didn't want to.'

'Not want to see kittens!'

'She'll come good.'

'Yes.' Ruth picked up two photographs and held them out to him. 'Look here. Doesn't Nonie look like poor Lily sometimes. When she is twenty she will be just like this, I think.'

'Probably taller.'

'Certainly stronger, too. And this one . . . Paul was about four when this was done. It's astonishing the resemblance to Georgie.' She paused, then added, 'I'll be glad if the resemblance stops there.'

Hannibal began to laugh. 'Did you see the twins and Elsie before?'

'Frightening Minnie's baby? I certainly did. If Minnie's milk dries up we'll have them to thank.'

'They were pretending she was a Zeppelin.'

'I know. They call her Minnie the Fritz. We'll have to change her name, they're certainly giving her the devil of a time over it.' Ruth frowned at Hannibal. 'Don't laugh about it! I shall have to speak to them severely.' She sighed. 'Perhaps it would be better if I took them to live in town. A more solid existence. School every day. We might get a reasonable price for the place, the timber mill has wanted the land for years.'

'Leave here?'

'Yes.' She cast her eyes around the silent parlour again, the photographs, the trinkets, the grandfather clock, and Hannibal. 'I am thinking about it. It's only fair to tell you.'

'Thank you,' said Hannibal.

3

*My friend, you would not tell with such high zest
To children ardent for some desperate glory,
The old lie: Dulce et decorum est
Pro patria mori.*

WILFRED OWEN

'It shouldn't be so hard to send a letter,' protested Flora. 'Mrs Haggerty is always writing to her Stan.'

The children were clustered under a tree-fern, eating blackberries. They had been picking them all morning down at the creek, at Ruth's request. Two billycans had been put aside for her, and now they were making themselves sick on the excess. Georgie's face was purple.

'But Stan Haggerty isn't at war yet,' said Nonie. 'He's only down the line.'

'Someone must know where Dadda is,' said Flora stubbornly.

'Why don't you know, Nonie?' asked Phip. 'Why didn't Mumma tell you?'

'Because she didn't, that's why.'

'Why not?'

'Because she couldn't. She didn't know.' Nonie stood up and sat down again, irritably. No matter what they were doing Flora always brought the subject around to Dadda. 'He just got it into his head to join up, and off he went. That's what Mumma said.'

'What about the Red Cross?' pursued Flora. 'Mrs Haggerty writes to lots of soldiers, even ones she doesn't know. She gives the letters to the Red Cross and they send them.'

'Auntie Ruth already asked about Dadda at the Red Cross', said Tom. 'And they didn't know.' This information was utterly new to Nonie. She hesitated a moment to take it in, then said triumphantly, 'There, then! Don't you think Auntie Ruth would have found him if she could?'

This point silenced them all. 'I feel sick,' announced Elsie. 'I don't like blackberries.'

Nonie looked at her youngest sister and Georgie. They were the two she knew least, really, though they had accepted her authority on arrival without question. Ruth referred to them as 'the babies', even though Elsie was six.

'Stop stuffing yourself then. You stop too, Georgie.'

'I aren't sick.'

'Stop anyhow.'

Georgie stuck out his lip then crammed his mouth with blackberries again. 'Come on,' said Nonie, getting up. 'There's heaps more ripe ones near the creek. We can cool our feet.'

They followed her further into the gully, still damp, even in these last days of summer. Where the creek bank was not choked by blackberry, it was laced with maidenhair fern. Trees towered above them.

'The trees are like giants,' said Flora. 'Aren't they like giants, Nonie?'

'Mmm.'

'White giants,' said Phip.

'With arms,' said Tom.

'I want to go 'ome, Nonie,' whimpered Georgie, lagging behind.

'It's all right. Look, I'm waiting.'

'I aren't liking giants.'

'They're not giants.'

'Tom and Phip was pretending,' added Elsie knowingly.

'No we weren't. It's true.'

They stopped at a knot of blackberry, scratching themselves to reach the darkest fruit. Georgie found a leech on his leg and

18

started shrieking. He was comforted only when Elsie had scraped it off carefully with a dead leaf and squashed it. Nonie watched her little sister's matter-of-fact accomplishment with grudging admiration. Neither she nor Flora had come to terms with leeches yet. Then they found a log fallen across the creek from bank to bank and they sat on its mossed surface and bathed their feet. The twins, tireless, climbed along the far bank, exploring.

'Well, I'm going to write to him, anyway,' declared Flora, as if the conversation had never ended. 'I'm going to tell Dadda exactly where we are, so when he gets back he'll come straight to us.'

'And he'll have medals,' said Elsie. 'I'm going to be a soldier like that.'

'Be quiet, Elsie. Well, where will you send it, Flor? What will you put on the envelope? You can't just put Paul Field—the War.'

'I can if I want to.'

Flora had a high-pitched whine in her voice that Nonie recognised. It meant she was nearly crying. Nonie was tempted to make her cry.

'You be quiet yourself, Nonie,' said Elsie. 'You leave my Flora alone.'

Nonie climbed along the log after the twins, feeling put out. She had the authority of the oldest child, but they all seemed to like Flora better. The sisters had liked Flora better, too. They had sat with her through many nights during her worst croup attacks, teaching her prayers while Nonie lay sleepless, in silence and shadow, in the next bed.

'Pray for my Dadda at war,' Flora begged between breaths. The voices of the sisters were angels' voices:
  'Hail Holy Queen, Mother of Mercy,
  Hail, our Life, our Sweetness and our Hope;
  To Thee do we cry, poor banished children of Eve,

To Thee do we send up our sighs . . .'

Poor banished children, poor banished children, taunted the prayer in Nonie's ears. While the sisters, in their halo of lamplight, stroked Flora's head, and soothed her.

'Come here, Nonie, we've found something.'

'What?'

'Come and look.'

Curiosity roused them all. They wobbled over the damp log toward the sound of the twins' voices. The twins were not far away. Ruth had warned against venturing into the bush out of sight of the flood paddocks.

'We've found a secret place,' announced Tom, crawling from under a bush to meet them. 'With a giant. Come on.'

Georgie tugged back on Nonie's hand, stiff with fear, but she dragged him after her on all fours. When they climbed to their feet they found themselves in a hollow, from the centre of which rose a gigantic tree. Georgie had to be forcibly restrained from bolting.

'It's only a tree.'

'It's a giant! It's a giant!'

'It's a giant tree.' It was by far the biggest tree Nonie had ever seen. It rose to the sky like a monstrous mast. The six children, hand-to-hand, would be unable to reach around its base. Nonie had heard Ruth speak of such trees; they were the mountain ash that had once grown in profusion up the slopes of Mount St Leonard, eagerly sought by the timber-cutters. This one had escaped the woodman's axe. Nonie felt a rush of gladness for it.

'This is a magic tree,' she said. 'It is the most magical tree in the world.'

They regarded it for some moments in awe. Elsie finally said, 'It's got a little hidey-hole, hasn't it?' and pointed. At about Flora's head height there was a knot in the trunk, and the opening at its centre made a sizeable hole. The children examined it.

'It's a secret despatch-box,' said Tom with conviction. 'If we was at the war the soldiers would put their secret messages in it.'

Flora became excited. 'If we write to Dadda and put our letters here, he will get them. Because it's magic. Nonie said. Didn't you, Nonie?'

'Yes.'

'See! And we've got to do it now, so's we can get back here before dark. Come on, Nonie. We've got to get home quick.'

Her eagerness infected them and they followed her, slipping and scrambling along the creek, back to the sunny open flood paddocks.

Nonie thought, that is not what I meant, that is not the kind of magic I was talking about.

But she went with the others, last in line.

4

This is a cheery place you will allow,
A tin of beef, a jar of rum, and Thou
Beside me, squatting in a pool of mud,
And dug-out is not Paradise enow.

THE NEW CHURCH TIMES, 1916

dear dadda gorgy is helpiNg me to rite this letre to you becus he caNNot rite yet he waNts to Now how maNy medals you have gt aNd waNts me to tel you that haN i caN Not spel it tech him to wisl aNd the cat have fiv kitiN iN the shed at scule we hav 3 flags uNiN jack aNd beljim aNd also fraNc i am lerNiN to say a pome rally roNd the baNNar for empir day wil the wor eNd sooN becas i waNt to see you agen gorgy waNts to Now if you wil briNg home al yor medals with you agaN so that he caN look at them al from elsie and gorgy

DEAR DADDA

HOW ARE YOU GETTING ALONG JOLLY WELL WE HOPE. WE HAVE BOTH LOST A TOOTH I HAVE LOST A BOTTOM TOOTH AND TOM HAS LOST A TOP ONE BY ACCADENT WITH A HAMMAR. NONIE SAYS YOU ARE A FAMUS HERO OVERSEAS. WE ARE GOING TO BE HEROS TO. IF THE WAR KEEPS GOING WHEN WE ARE ETETEEN WE WILL JOIN UP AND BE ABLE TO GO OVER WITH YOU AND BE HEROS. TOM IS GOING TO BE A MASHINE GUNNER BUT I AM GOING TO FIRE THE BIG ANTI-AIRCRAFT CANNON AND STRAFE THE RED BARON. ANTIE RUTH SAYS WE WILL ONLY KILL OUR SELFS BUT

WE WONT. WE LIVE WITH ANTIE RUTH NOW AND NOT IN TOWN
AND IT IS BETTER BECAUSE WE ONLY GO TO THE OLD SCHOOL
TWO TIMES A WEEK WHEN IT IS OUR TURN AND WE CAN RIDE
THERE ON THE TIMBER WAGGINS SOMETIMES AND NOT EVERY DAY
LIKE BEFORE. WE WISH YOU WOULD COME HOME SOON BUT IF
YOU CANNT WE WISH YOU WOULD SPARE US FIVE SHILLINGS
BECAUSE WE WANT TO BUY A DAISY AIR GUN SO WE CAN PRACTIS.
FROM PHIP AND TOM

My dearest Dadda,
It is nearly four years now since you went away and I
miss you a grete deal. I know you are very busy over in
the war rescueing soldiars but I would like you to find
some time to write to us so that we know where you are
exacly. I dont suppose you know that our mother died it
happened two years ago of namonia and Nonie and me
did not know either till auntie Ruth came. The sisters
told us something very sad has happened your mother is
dead but something wonderful also and that is your aunt
has come to take you to her house in the country which
she did and we are here now all together at your old
home and waiting for you to get here. Hanible is here
also. Also with the rest of us is Georgie who was born
after you went away so you will not know him but auntie
Ruth says he looks like you a grete deal. He was born in
our house in Port Melbourne in the morning very early
and Mumma was calling out and George Tankey with the
wooden leg heard because he was comeing by with his
rabbits and came in to Mumma and sent Nonie to the
doctor and told me to mind his barrow with Tom and
Phip and Elsie and we did. And when Nonie had got
back George Tankey had made a cup of tea for Mumma
and Georgie was rapped in my pijama coat. So Mumma
called him after George Tankey which I thought you
would like to know in case you think he was called for

the king which he was not. Mumma stayed very sick so Doctor Baker sent the sisters around to help and they looked after Nonie and me exept Nonie did not want to go but I love the sisters and will take you to meet them when you get back as they said many rosaries for you and for all the gallant boys and so did I. Please come home soon and come to us here at Greystones and dont worry about Mumma as she is in heaven now with a crown on and pearls in it the sisters told me.

love from your daughter Flora

Dear Father,

I hope you are well and that the war is not too serious where you are at present. It is rather hot here at the present time but I suppose it is winter over there. I read in the newspaper that the snow is very heavy there in some parts. I expect you have received woollen socks and mittens from the Red Cross. Mrs Haggerty and Jackie have knitted so many they have lost count. Since my mother died your sister Ruth Field is looking after us. Flora and I were at boarding school for some time before that. We have chickens, horses, two cows and a big vegetable garden and orchard. Auntie Ruth tells me that there used to be more cattle here when you were a boy as well as some sheep and the hops. It must have been very interesting for you. I suppose if the war ends soon you will be coming home. No doubt you will find us considerably taller. We all have work to do here. Elsie and Georgie feed the chickens and collect the eggs. Tom and Phip must keep the kindling box full and help pack the vegetables which are sent to town. Flora does mostly inside jobs because of her croup and I am learning to milk the cow amongst other things.

From your daughter
Antonia Adeline Field

I couldn't sleep a wink all night thinking of that stupid letter I put in Flora's magic letterbox. I just do not know what to say. I don't know why you went without saying anything. Mumma was nearly mad screaming and crying so the Currans came in. Even the grandmother who I never saw standing up before. She took Elsie in to stay next door because she said Mumma could not look after her and she had a fever. I took the twins in with Flora and me but Mumma cried all night anyway. She said you had gone to enlist but she did not know where and now there would be no money. I tried to keep the twins away and let her sleep in the mornings but sometimes they were noisy. I asked where you were to everyone but they would not say. A man said shot through and I said it to Mumma. She started screaming. I did not mean to make her though it is just I did not know what the man meant. Flora and me went on the tram to the pay office to ask because Mrs Curran said that all the pay for the soldiers wives and families would be there but they did not know your name. When Georgie was born Mumma was sick. George Tankey stayed with her while I ran to the doctor. He came three times in the week, and Mrs Curran came in every night with soup and then Mrs Curran brought the sisters. Mumma did not like them and she called Mrs Curran names. I expect it is because we are not Catholics. Flora is going to be one though. The doctor's wife made us promise to go with the sisters to boarding school. Flora promised but I did not. I tried to tell them that I had to help with the little ones. They said there are too many of you for your mother to care for and I kept on saying but I am the one who helps with all that but no one would listen. It wasn't really a boarding school. They said Mumma would come to get us when she was better but she didnt. I don't think the Currans would give her our address. I wrote some letters but she never wrote back. Once Mrs Curran came and she pretended that Mumma did know our address and that Mumma had seen my letters but I think she was lying. When Auntie Ruth came Mumma had been dead for more than a year. The sisters said all our things had got sold to pay the bills. I don't even know where her grave is only the sisters said it was a paupers grave. Auntie Ruth told me that the next-door people to Mumma had written to her to come and get Elsie and Georgie. But it was not the Currans it was new people. Tom and Phip were at the Salvation Army. Auntie Ruth got them back only no one knew about Flora and me. But Tom and Phip kept asking so she went and found Doctor Baker and then she found the Currans and then she came to us. Why don't you ever write? Is the war better than us? Mrs Haggerty says it is hard work being a hero. You can just be ordinary can't you. You have got to come home.

Nonie

5

He was brave—well, so was I—
Keen and merry, but his lip
Quivered when he said goodbye—
Purl the seam-stitch, purl and slip.

Never used to living rough,
Lots of things he'd got to learn;
Wonder if he's warm enough—
Knit 2, catch 2, knit 1, turn.

JESSIE POPE

Young Stan Haggerty was off to war at last. He came home on his final leave in the first week of autumn with a new swagger in his walk, and the beginnings of a moustache. His father met him at the station and brought him back to high tea at Dingley, where he was made much of by family and guests alike. 'Just go easy on your mother, lad,' advised Bert Haggerty in a quiet moment.

Lying in his childhood bed that night, in the small back room which he shared with his brother Jackie, Stan wondered about that remark. He'd thought of nothing but the war, and getting there, since he was fourteen. His brother Jim had marched off to war through the streets of Melbourne and the pavements had been a sea of people waving flags and handkerchiefs. There had been speeches on the steps of Parliament House, and prayers that the war would soon be over. But Stan had prayed differently: 'Don't let it end yet, God! Not till I've had my turn!' And God, it seemed, had done His bit. There would be no speeches and parades for Stan, though. It seemed, in four years that people had become less interested in the show. Just his luck, Stan thought, with a touch of bitterness. Jim got all the fanfare and fuss, had always done, while Stan was asked to 'go

27

easy'. He felt secretly that poor Jim, dead now in the sands of some Johnny Turk beach, had always been the favoured son. Because, after all, you could hardly count Jackie.

Jackie Haggerty made cooing noises in his sleep. Stan leaned across and tucked his brother's blanket in, then lay back and stared at the ceiling and thought.

The war was something you had to go to, no question of that, the old Kaiser had to be shown what was what. But there were stories he'd heard about lads taking shrapnel and choking dead from mustard gas that fair made the hairs on the back of his neck stand on end. He had not enjoyed his basic training either, though he kept that to himself. His training officer had called the lads from the country 'hayseeds' and made them drill on the hottest days till men fainted clean away on the parade ground, and then ridiculed them for days after. As well, there was that fellow Mullins, in the cot next to him but one, who had speared himself during bayonet practice and been discharged. There were rumours going around after that, and Sarge had told them stories of deserters at The Front. 'Bullet through the head,' he had gloated. 'That's the best thing for 'em. Deserters is yellow, scum yellow, boys, and no earthly good to man or beast.'

So that was it, thought Stan, listening to a possum scrabble over the roof, no turning back now.

On the second day of his leave, at a loose end, Stan kicked along the old track down to Greystones, to visit Ruth and Hannibal and to show himself off to the children. He was greeted with enthusiasm, and received the children's adoring clamour with the air of a hero. 'And he hasn't even got to the war yet', reflected Nonie in disgust.

Everything about Stan Haggerty annoyed her. He looked like a boy playing dress-ups, she thought, in a make-believe soldier's costume, so pleased with himself, so full of importance. The others gambolled like puppies at his heels. He strode up to the peppercorn tree on the hill and propped there, smugly. Nonie turned to Flora in the hope of finding an ally in her sister, but Flora's eyes were shining with admiration. Clearly Flora thought Stan cut a dashing figure in his slouch hat with its rising sun and his spotless boots.

'They're specially made,' he explained proudly. 'No rain, or mud, or even snow'll get through 'em.'

'Gee whiz!' enthused the twins.

Elsie was practical. 'They look heavy. I wouldn't like 'em.'

'Too heavy for a little tyke like you maybe,' corrected Stan with a grin. 'Not for me.'

'You must be strong,' said Flora, awed.

Stan feigned modesty. He began whistling 'Mademoiselle From Armentières' while the others competed for his attention. It embarrassed Nonie.

'Are the others as strong?' demanded Elsie.

'You mean the filthy Hun?'

'Filthy Hun!' Tom bellowed the words across the paddocks with delight. He and Phip hurled dry cowpats at each other, making sounds like mortar explosions.

'Not so strong as us,' said Stan smiling indulgently at them. 'Not half.'

'How do you know?' asked Nonie suddenly.

'Course he knows!' howled the twins.

Nonie walked away scowling. She had been usurped.

She found a niche amongst some tools behind the stable and sat there to sulk. Her aunt's voice drifted through the back wall of the stable trespassing on Nonie's hostility. Ruth was speaking to Hannibal. 'He's so young, Hannibal,' she was murmuring. 'Consie must be grief-stricken at the thought of him going.'

'They're proud of him, really. People enjoy war.'

'Don't be cynical, dear.' It was odd, thought Nonie, that Ruth addressed Hannibal the way she addressed the children. And what did it mean—cynical? 'It doesn't suit you. Besides I'm sure you're wrong. The government has twice tried to introduce conscription and been knocked back each time. That should say something of people's feelings for this war.'

'Only that they want to choose to go of their own accord.'

Ruth sighed. 'Yes, probably. But have you heard Stan?' she went on. 'Putting ideas in those young heads. Look at the twins.'

'Look at Tom.'

Nonie sat up.

'Yes, yes, well, Tom seems more impressionable than Phip. But they will always back one another up.' Ruth paused. 'Tom has inherited from Paul . . .'

'He's in them all somewhere.'

'But differently. Tom has his impulsiveness. And Elsie will do anything without a second thought.' Hannibal seemed to be laughing. 'She has no fear, or God forbid, no conscience. Then there is Georgie's stubbornness, and Flora's . . . I don't know . . . innocence, is it?'

'And Nonie?'

'Oh, Nonie is a different kettle of fish altogether.'

There was a long silence. Nonie began to pick her way to the front of the stable but when she reached the door only Hannibal was there, standing in the dimness with a handful of mewing kittens. He seemed preoccupied, so she crept away.

The others were still on the hill, clustered around Stan beneath her tree—all except Elsie, who had left the group and was now swinging on the gate leading into the house paddock. Nonie turned her back on them all. She went to look for Ruth, and found her at the clothesline, struggling with bedsheets. Nonie began to help her. The two worked in silence.

There was so much Nonie wanted to ask, if only the right words would come. She wanted to say, 'Why am I different . . . a different kettle of fish?' What she said instead was, 'Why is Hannibal the way he is?'

A pause. 'I'm not sure I understand you.'

'You know. The way he is.'

Ruth shook out Elsie's torn pinafore and frowned at the prospect of mending. 'Do you mean why does he live here?'

'Well . . .'

'His father worked here when the farm was bigger, when we had the hops. King and his wife Bella had the cottage every year during harvest. My grandfather lived in it first, while the big house was being built; my own parents lived there a short while. Hannibal was born there—he was born during the harvest.'

'Oh.'

It was not a satisfactory answer. Nonie pegged washing in silence, then glancing sideways at her aunt she realised in a rush of clarity that the answer had been given to discourage questioning.

Afterwards, she went in search of Hannibal. The sound of his axe brought her to the woodshed where he was splitting logs. Elsie was with him. What had Ruth said? 'Elsie will do anything, she has no fear—like Paul.' Nonie sat down in the shade of the house and watched them.

'Hannibal, I am being a soldier.'

'Are you?'

'Yes. And I am being a better soldier than Tom and Phip.'

The rhythm of the axe blows punctuated Hannibal's voice. 'Do you like soldiering?'

'It's a living. It's got downs and ups.' Hannibal smiled into his arm as he stopped to wipe his face. Elsie marked time. 'I can march good too. Better'n Tom and Phip.'

'Is that all that soldiers do, then?'

'No. Silly you. I know all about them. Stan told me.'

'What did he say?'

'All about chapel.'

'Chapel?'

'All falling out of the sky when the whizz-bangs come down!' She made a sound like a mortar explosion.

'Oh. Shrapnel.'

'And there are rats living in the bunches!'

'Trenches?'

'Yep.' Elsie proceeded to march a full circle around him, humming her own version of 'Mademoiselle From Armentières'. Then she stopped suddenly and made a face. She said, 'I'll murder them filthy mongrel Huns!'

Hannibal brought the axe to rest. He said, 'Don't talk like that'.

'They eat all the little Beljum babies!'

'No they don't.'

'Stan said it.'

'Don't you.' His voice was quiet. Nonie could not see his face.

'Tom and Phip said it too.'

'It doesn't make it right.'

'Stan said if we don't kill all the mongrel Huns they'll come over here and eat all our babies too.'

'It isn't right, Els.'

'Is Stan a liar?'

Hannibal did not answer. His silence infuriated Nonie. Elsie resumed marching, unabashed, while Hannibal bent to collect the split logs and carry them to the woodshed. I understand, she said to herself, but there are no words in my head to explain my understanding.

That night, as the three girls were changing for bed, Elsie said importantly, 'Hannibal told me something today that I wasn't allowed to say.'

'What?' demanded Flora at once.

Elsie clapped her hands over her mouth and shook her head, but added quickly through her fingers, 'It's what Stan Haggerty said, and so did Tom and Phip, and it's a lie!'

'Whisper it,' pressed Flora.

Elsie said quite loudly, 'The dirty mongrel Huns eat babies!'

Nonie, undressed, took over then. 'Well if Hannibal told you not to say it, then don't.' She frowned. 'Stop staring at me, Elsie!'

'But you're all lumpy,' replied Elsie. 'Look at her, Flor, isn't she lumpy?'

Flora looked with surprise. 'Yes,' she said. 'You are.'

Nonie looked too and felt hot with confusion and embarrassment, because she had not noticed it before.

'Why?' demanded Elsie with her nightdress over her head. 'I haven't got 'em.'

'Don't be stupid. It just happens.'

'You're growing up,' said Flora in awe. 'That's what.'

Nonie nodded, because here was the proof, changing her whole body. She climbed into bed at once, and pretended to be asleep. Only she did not sleep for some time, but lay in silence with her arms wrapped tightly around herself.

6   *The streets is gay wiv dafferdils—but—haggard in the sun,*
       A wounded soljer passes; an' we know ole days is done.
    For somew'ere down inside us, lad, is somethin' you put there
       The day yeh swung a dirty left, fer us, at Sari Bair.

C.J. DENNIS

Summer had strangled the farm. The creek, shrunken from its banks, sang a shriller song. At night wallabies came down from the mountain to drink, and the children lying in bed could hear the thump, thump, thump of their approach. By late March evenings were cool again, and each day began in a mantle of mist which seemed to amplify the morning scribble-song of magpies across the paddocks, while a pearl-grey sky lay sleeping on Mount St Leonard.

Ruth liked to turn out the house at the beginning of each season. It was a habit she had begun years before, when Paul was a child. Ruth was not sentimental; she sorted out her past during these seasonal turn-outs, and every season whittled away a little more. The children had made it easier. There was no time, now, for clinging to old memories when she had them; their present and their future demanded every ounce of her attention every hour, every minute of each day. So she packed old clothes into boxes, burned old papers in the kitchen stove and sat frowning over her account books at night, juggling bills, adding up diminishing finances and wondering how they were to manage for another month. It was an exhausting, exhilarating business.

'What's this?' Nonie was feeling bored. She had wandered into the boxroom at the back of the house and found Ruth busy there.

'What? Oh. It's an easel.' Ruth was engrossed. She did not welcome Nonie's intrusion.

'For painting?'

'Yes. Yes.'

'Nonie remembered the few watercolours in the parlour. 'Is it yours?'

'Yes. Oh, no it isn't.' Ruth glanced up from a trunk. 'Mine is in the far corner, there. Smaller. A little cleaner, too, I think.'

The easel Nonie was examining was crusted with paint. 'Whose is it, then? Dadda's?'

'No, your father never painted. He hadn't the patience. It belonged to your father's tutor. Mr Lambe.' Ruth began hunting through the trunk again.

'Didn't Dadda go to school?'

'There was no school in these parts until he was quite old. I taught the boys to read and write myself.'

'Boys?'

'Your father and Hannibal. Paul was a dreadful student. Not that he wasn't clever. Too clever by half, really. I was glad to hand over the reins.'

'Did Mr Lambe like Dadda?'

'Yes.' Ruth began to wish she had not been so honest with Nonie. It led to other things. 'Mr Lambe was more, well, tolerant.'

'Why?'

'I don't know. He was an Englishman. And an artist. Perhaps that is the reason. Any rate, Paul liked him.'

'Did you?'

Ruth opened a discoloured letter and glanced at it. 'Of course. He was a gentleman.'

'Where is he now?'

'Dead. In another war. He went to fight the Boers.'

35

'Why?'

'Oh, Nonie, really!' Ruth relented a little. 'You must realise that some questions just cannot be answered. Why does anyone go to war? I don't know.'

'Why should Dadda go then?'

Ruth did not reply at once. She stood up and stretched and tucked her hair back into its knot. 'I seem to be developing a headache,' she said at last, apologetically, and left the room, still clutching the crumpled letter.

'Of course I'm not going to fight, Ruthie! I'm not an actual soldier. Paul is right—it's an opportunity, don't you see?'

'I'll thank you not to bring Paul into it. The opinion of a sixteen-year-old larrikin is hardly . . .'

'Look, no self-respecting artist could pass it up. I will show through my work all the futility . . .'

'Oh stop it, Harry! You're all words! It doesn't matter what you're going as, artist or foot soldier, you're still going!'

Daly's Hall was ablaze with lanterns, adorned with rosettes, astir with blushing girls in the arms of soldier beaux.

'Come on, Ruthie. Just one dance.'

'I don't want to dance with you. I hate your uniform. I don't want you to go.'

'If you won't dance with me, I'll dance with someone else.'

'Go on then.'

'Look, Ruth, it's my last night here. The last night we can be together till I return. Then we'll burn this silly uniform in a gigantic funeral pyre, I swear it.'

'Please, Harry . . .'

'There, I've made you smile at least. I mean it. Then I'll carry you in my arms down the aisle . . .'

'Ssh. That's enough nonsense. Someone will hear.'

'I don't know what you're being sensitive about. We've given the gossips grist enough for their mill this last year.'

'Harry.'

'They're all wondering when I'll do the honourable thing and marry you.'

'I'm not listening to this.'

'Ruth! Don't walk away. I'm sorry. I am. Look, please, I won't try to make you dance. I'm serious now, just tell me you love me, at least do that.'

'I don't love you! Not dressed like that. Not when you're off to fight a despicable war a million miles away. You try to pretend you're not excited, but you are, I can see it. And you're proud. And you'll hate it, I know you will. Now go away and have your dance.'

'I love you, Ruth.'

'Go away, Harry. I'm so angry I could burst.'

'We've had all these arguments before. Just for tonight—for my sake—accept what I'm doing.'

'I won't accept it. Ever. I think you're being a fool. You'll see how right I am!'

The letter in Ruth's hand was Harry Lambe's first. And his last. It had arrived a week after the notice of his death:

Write quickly and tell me that you love me that you can forgive my foolhardiness. Oh Ruth I only want to come home . . .

Ruth arranged for Hannibal to take the children into town on his next visit. She felt, she explained, that she could not concentrate sufficiently on her sorting with them around. They were delighted to be going. For Nonie and Flora it was the first time since their arrival that they had been away from Greystones. Hannibal helped them into the jinker and took the reins. Ruth waved them away, sighed with relief, and went back to the boxroom.

There were vegetables and a basket of eggs to deliver. They drove first to Dingley, so slowly up the steep track that the children were able to run alongside the jinker, urging the old horse.

The guesthouse sprawled on a ridge, shabby in middle-age, for Dingley, like Greystones, had had its day. The bedrooms, looking west, baked hot in summer and were nearly sunless in winter. The dining and morning rooms of Dingley gazed east, across the Chum valley, over the roof of Greystones and up the shadow of Mount St Leonard.

Consie Haggerty's sister Queenie Cousins ran the guest-house. She had done so for years now, ever since the death of their flamboyant older brother Henry Cousins in the first motor accident of the district. Consie and Bert Haggerty helped out as best they could, but they were simple people not suited to the task. Queenie though, with her nurse's training, encouraged a steady, if delicate, clientele.

She greeted the jinker with customary brusqueness, taking time only to reprove Hannibal for the state of the children's clothes after their run up the dusty track.

'Haven't got the sense you were born with,' she muttered, directing him into the house with his load. 'You men are all the same. Not a thought for the women who do all the washing and cleaning and mending.' She raised her voice to call to the twins to remove their boots at the kitchen door, and Nonie, mortally offended by Hannibal's dressing-down, caught his eye and noticed him winking at her.

Then Consie Haggerty was running to meet them. 'Well, look! All of you! What a surprise! And isn't that the little frock I made Flora? Look at that, Queenie, I didn't do too badly with no measurements to go by. Jackie's in the kitchen, Hannibal. I've just made some scones for morning tea. We'll all have some, will we?' The children clamoured around her. Queenie watched with disapproval, commanding them to be quiet in case the guests should hear the noise, at which Consie smiled reassuringly, in much the same way that Hannibal had winked. 'And, fancy, you've got to go all the way into town yet. That's just where Mr Haggerty is. You'll see him, I expect. He has a box of newspapers to deliver to the Red Cross, and post to collect, and he has to fetch home a bag of chaff for our goat who's been a bit off-colour, poor love. Oopsa dais!' She lifted Georgie over the doorstep, pausing for a second to hug him to her. 'Oh my! You've got your Dadda's lovely wicked eyes!' Queenie snorted.

The kitchen was an enormous room, annexed to the main house by a covered walkway. In it Queenie's hospital training had been unleashed with a vengeance. Iron cooking pots hung along the wall beside the wood stove in order of size, like a rank of soldiers, a great black kettle sat over the heat every day of the year, and meals were prepared with zealous attention to nutrition. The only sign of sentiment was a large framed photograph of Jim Haggerty, seventeen years old, in full uniform, which sat on the stone mantelpiece above the stove with a jar of bush orchids beside it. That clearly was Consie's addition.

Jackie Haggerty sat at the kitchen table beating butter. He was a big lad, carefully shaven and dressed so neatly that his appearance was instantly peculiar. Nonie stared at him; he smiled disarmingly back.

'Hullo, girl. I'm beating the butter for Mum.'

'Hullo.'

'Hullo, Hannibal. I'm beating the butter.'

'Hullo, Jackie. How are you?'

'Oh, you know me, like a mallee bull. Beating the butter for Mum, I am.'

'Listen to you,' laughed Consie, hugging his shoulders as she went past. 'Mallee bull. Repeats everything he hears his father say! The children are having scones with us, Jackie.'

'We'll none of us have scones if he doesn't get on with that butter,' Queenie said, laying out trays for the dining room. Each tray made a neat clack as it hit the table.

'Now, Queenie, you mustn't sound like that,' scolded Consie gently. 'Jackie does a fine job. We couldn't do without him and that's a fact.' Mother and son beamed at each other behind Queenie's aproned back.

'Just yesterday, Hannibal, I couldn't find my best scissors,' Consie continued, bustling children into chairs. 'But Jackie remembered that I'd slipped them into my apron pocket when I went out to the goat, didn't he, Queenie? And you know, I can't remember doing it even now. And he went outside and found them right by her drinking trough because they'd worked a hole in my apron pocket and fallen through there. That's right, isn't it, Jackie?' Jackie nodded, flushing with pride. 'We've always said it . . . Jackie has an exceptional memory. Truly. We're very proud of his memory.'

Consie Haggerty spread comfort about her as naturally as butter on warm bread. Her sister's acid temperament could not hope to penetrate its thickness. They all sat around the great scrubbed table eating scones, hearing the muffled clatter of plates in the dining-room where the handful of guests were taking morning tea, and listened to Consie's easy, accommodating conversation.

'You know that Kester's coming home. We had a letter yesterday, Hannibal.'

Hannibal was sitting by the door with his mug of tea. He looked interested. 'When?'

'Well, you know Kissie. She forgot to put in any important details.' Consie and Hannibal laughed; Queenie slapped butter onto scones in silence. Consie said, 'It's only the third letter we've had from her in two years . . . my word she'll be in for a proper ticking-off when we do see her. And it seems the boarding house I was sending all my letters to isn't the place she's living at now. Must be at least seven letters from Ned Gannon—all the way from France—that I sent on. I hate to think of them not reaching her, for Ned's sake. That girl she shared her room with, that Ruby, well, I don't like to say it, but I never felt she was the responsible type.'

'The word for that one was "fast",' Queenie said in a deep voice to the scones.

'Now, Queenie.'

'Take it or leave it.'

'She had a job in a teashop, as you know, Hannibal, but that's finished with. I did hope there might be a mention in her letter of a young man. But there was nothing.'

A click from Queenie signalled irritation. 'You won't hear any mention of young men from that one,' she said. 'Kester is too stubborn by half. And too proud. She's missed the boat by now.'

'Oh Queenie!' protested Consie.

'I love Kissie,' remarked Jackie to Flora, who was nearest.

'Missed it years ago if you want my opinion, when she refused Esme Gannon's boy,' continued Queenie. 'Always crying for the moon. Pride is all it is. Too much of it in this valley. Between Kester Cousins and that brother of hers, and Ruthie Field . . .'

'Have another scone, Nonie,' said Consie. 'Nice and quick now, while they're hot.'

'Soon it will be my birthday,' Jackie told Elsie. 'I'm giving Kissie a piece of my cake. Aren't I, Mum?'

'Yes, my lamb.'

Elsie said, 'How old will you be?'

Jackie looked at his mother inquiringly. 'Twenty-four,' she said. 'You know that, Jackie.'

'Twenty-four,' he repeated to Elsie and widened his eyes proudly. Elsie was impressed. 'And I'm giving Kissie some of my cake when she comes,' he repeated emphatically.

'Who's Kissie?' asked Tom.

'Kester is our niece. Queenie's and mine. She's our brother Henry's girl. Won't the children love Kissie, Hannibal? You know,' Consie went on conspiratorially to the children, 'Kester was still living here with us when your Mumma first came here, and first met your father. Well, and won't she be amazed to

41

meet all of poor Lily's children!' Another snort from Queenie ended the conversation.

Nonie looked around expecting a remark, but Queenie swept from the room in the direction of the guests' dining-room, with a fresh pot of tea in her hands.

'We'd better cut along,' said Hannibal.

The town was ringed by guesthouses, beside any of which Dingley paled into commonness. Nonie glimpsed them among the trees—a splendid section of gable, a panel of verandah lace, the topmost point of an ivy-covered portico from which a Union Jack was flying. The smoke from guesthouse chimneys issued forth in delicate spirals onto the still air, to vanish in the shadow of distant mountains.

One or two of the larger guesthouses regularly bought produce from Greystones. Nonie was disappointed as they approached these that Hannibal did not drive up the carriage-ways to the front entrances, but round back paths to grubby kitchen doors and stableyards.

After the deliveries were made they drove down into the town and pulled up outside the post office.

The first person they saw there was Bert Haggerty. He tucked his bundle of letters and newspapers under one arm and came across to them to help Hannibal lift the younger children down.

'This is handy. I've just collected your post. Was going to drop it down to you on my way home.' He counted out a few articles and handed them across.

'Is there one from Dadda?' begged Flora.

Hannibal glanced at the handwriting on each letter and said that there was not.

Bert said, by way of compensation, 'But there's good news from the front'. He waved his Melbourne paper in front of their eyes. 'Red Baron was shot down yesterday over the Somme.' The children broke into whoops of enthusiasm. 'Now if that isn't a sign of good times ahead I don't know what is. Wouldn't you say so, Hannibal?'

'I certainly would.'

'My word!'

'Got a letter from your Stan?' asked Hannibal. Bert Haggerty's face became uneasy. There had been two letters, both addressed to him. The first, rather thin and crumpled, he had opened at once, standing in the shade of the post office just minutes earlier. Its contents had baffled him. It read:

Dear Dad
  Tell Mum I will be along home as soon as it is all right. Tell her I am keeping well. Sorry Dad.
                                                    Yrs Stan

The second letter was thicker and bore an official stamp. He had opened it, glanced through and hardly understood a word of what was written there. He would read it later, he thought, pull over on the road home and give it a thorough going-over before showing it to Consie. He had stuffed both the letters into his pocket, out of sight and out of mind. He said to Hannibal: 'Consie likes to open the post. I always keep it for her'.

Hannibal said, 'I hear Kester's on her way home'.

'And that reminds me!' Bert clapped his chest. 'I promised I'd look in at the cottage. Open a few windows and the rest. She didn't tell us when she was coming, isn't that like our Kissie? Any rate, best be off.' He moved away, preoccupied, but turned back the next moment. 'There's another thing . . . Cec Canning's shop got robbed last night. They were talking about it in the post office. Someone put a brick through his window. Stole some things. Seems Cec saw the culprit getting away.'

'Anyone he knew?' asked Hannibal, but with a certain stiffness, observed Nonie with interest.

'Yes. Says it's one of the chaps from the reserve.'

43

'Ah.'

Bert's voice lowered. 'What I'm getting at . . . I wouldn't recommend you go in there for the time being.'

'No.'

'Cec Canning is a good enough chap. I've passed the time of day with him. Lost his eldest two a couple of years ago, both on the same day. It's left him a bit, you know, nervy, poor fellow. Understandable.'

'Yes.'

'Any rate, police'll get onto it.'

'Daresay.'

'Here's sixpence for the children . . . buy them some sweeties.'

Hannibal pocketed the coin. Bert Haggerty turned away, frowning, leaving Hannibal thoughtful too. The entire interchange had Nonie mystified.

They walked along under the verandahed shopfronts. The twins ran backwards and forwards, having noisy dog-fights with an invisible Red Baron. Elsie gave piggyback rides to Georgie. Flora walked beside Hannibal, and Nonie walked deliberately ahead of them. The afternoon sun drove angled shadows across the wide street.

'Can we all have a sweet?' asked Flora comfortably. 'Will there be enough for Nonie and me?'

'Of course,' said Hannibal.

'Where will we get them?'

'There's messages to get first.'

'There's a shop, Hannibal.' Flora pointed across the street.

'Not there.'

'Why not?'

At that moment Georgie fell over with a bellow and Flora flew to his aid. Nonie glanced at Hannibal.

'Why not?' she repeated Flora's question.

Hannibal said, 'That's Canning's'.

She was silent for a second. 'Who was robbed?'

'Yes.'

'Not by you.'

'No.'

'I don't understand.'

The children had stopped by the band rotunda which stood opposite the Grand Hotel. Nonie looked up at the verandah of the hotel. Sun spun off its dusty iron lace and made her screw up her eyes. Hannibal moved to pass her.

'It doesn't matter.'

'I only want to know.'

'It's nothing.' But he stopped in his tracks.

She said, 'I won't ask again. I just want to know what Mr Haggerty meant'.

'About its being a man from the reserve? He meant it was a black. Like me.'

Nonie flushed and felt a rush of panic, as though this articulation of Hannibal's blackness should make her behave differently, only she did not know how. She said at last, 'If a white man robbed the shop, would Mr Canning shut all of them out . . . the farmers and everyone?'.

Her question was received with silence. When she dared to glance up she expected to meet Hannibal's inscrutable stare. But he was smiling.

7

We planned to shake the world together, you and I
Being young, and very wise;

MAY WEDDERBURN CANNAN

After buying them sweets, Hannibal left the children to look after themselves. They ran back to the band rotunda, but found it was occupied. A young woman was leaning against the wooden rail with a basket of groceries at her feet. The sleeves of her green silk dress were rolled up to the elbows. It was a most fashionable dress, entirely out of place in a country town, edged extravagantly with pale green piping and embroidered fleur-de-lys. The dress was topped by a striking green straw hat, with a deep crown and a band of crushed black silk. The woman's appearance put Nonie in mind of a word she had heard earlier that day—*fast*—a thrilling word that suggested mystery and romance. The woman was looking away from the main street, down to the river flats. She turned and smiled at the children. 'Hullo. Are you giving a concert?'

Georgie held up his paper cone and said proudly, 'We got sweeties.' And Flora, who was unconsciously generous, offered a sweet to the stranger, which she accepted. Nonie did the same, not wishing to be outdone, though she could have cheerfully kicked Flora instead.

'Is your basket too heavy?' asked Flora. 'Have you stopped to rest?'

'I stopped because it's a nice afternoon.'

'So did we,' said Nonie. 'My brothers and sisters wanted to play here, so I said they could.' She added, 'I'm the oldest.'

'I see.'

Tom, Phip and Elsie climbed over the railing, dropped onto the ground, then scrambled back up the steps.

'Is your mother in town today?'

Nonie and Flora exchanged a look. Elsie shouted cheerfully over her shoulder as she flung herself from the railing for a second time, 'We haven't got one.'

The woman said, 'I'm sorry,' then added, 'Actually, I don't have a mother either.'

Flora smiled encouragingly. 'We've got a father, though. Have you?'

'Not any more.'

'I expect we're better off than you then.'

'I finished my sweeties,' announced Georgie. 'Can I have one of yours, Nonie?'

'You can have one of mine,' said Flora.

'It's all right, he can have mine.' Nonie smiled at the stranger and passed over her paper cone with a flourish.

The woman straightened her hat. 'I'd better get home; I've rather a lot to do. Have you far to go?'

'We live up the Chum,' said Tom, clambering past her in his circuit.

'Really? What part?'

'Near the Old School,' said Nonie. 'Well, nearer to the sawmill. Our aunt has a farm . . . ' She stopped because the woman's complexion was visibly altering. She seemed momentarily white-faced then flushed.

'It's called Greystones,' finished Flora. 'Do you know our Auntie Ruth?'

The woman was staring at Nonie. 'Are you Paul's children?'

'Yes.'

'And you're living at Greystones?'

'Yes.'

'How do you know our Dadda?' said Elsie.

The woman was studying each of them in turn. Her gaze rested on Elsie for a moment; then her voice returned to normal, became cheerful and excited. 'My brother and I, and Paul and Hannibal—we all grew up together. I haven't heard a word of Paul since he married Lily Prendergast and went to live in Melbourne.'

'I know who you are,' said Nonie suddenly. 'You must be . . .'

'Kester Cousins!' But it was not Nonie who spoke; it was Hannibal.

The next few minutes passed in some chaos. Hannibal dropped an armful of fencing wire at the foot of the rotunda steps and leapt up to greet her. They grasped each other's hands and spoke rapidly, in half-sentences.

'I heard you were coming. I was up at Dingley . . .'

'Poor Auntie Consie. I've been meaning . . .'

'A letter arrived yesterday or something . . .'

'. . . carrying it in my pocket for days. If they had the telephone . . . Look at you!' Kester cried suddenly. 'It must be two years! You haven't changed . . .'

'It's a good three years, Kissie.'

'I'm an awful letter writer. The telephone makes you lazy. I'll make them have one connected at Dingley!'

Hannibal laughed at her. Nonie had never seen him so animated. She was envious of Kester's power. 'You've met Paul's family, then?'

'Now that I look at them closely, I don't know why I didn't guess.' Kester frowned suddenly. 'And Lily . . .'

Hannibal said, 'On your way home?' He indicated her basket. 'We'll walk you there if you like.'

'Good. I had to buy simply everything. I only need to stop at Gannon's for milk, then we can have a cup of tea.'

Hannibal organised the basket between the twins. He retrieved his fencing wire. 'I'll just load this up, and I'll stop off for your milk. You start without me.'

'Shouldn't we wait here?'

'What for?'

'For Paul.'

Hannibal seemed confused. Nonie said, 'He's not here.'

'Not in town?'

Flora said, 'Dadda's at the war.'

'He's a Hero,' said Phip proudly.

Kester looked astonished. Nonie watched her expression with curiosity. It switched from astonishment to fury in an instant; she stamped her foot. 'Well! And isn't that just like him! After all that we've been through, that Jonathan's been through . . .'

'Hold on, hold on,' soothed Hannibal, smiling again. 'Let me unload this. I'll catch you up.'

'All right.' Kester started down the steps, shouting. 'But I shall want you to give me the name of his unit! I'm going to write to him and tell him just what I think!' Then she turned and smiled beatifically at all the children. 'Now, you'd better tell me your names,' and set off up the street sweeping them along with her. The hugeness of her personality left Nonie breathless.

Kester's house was a small weatherboard cottage which sat placidly deteriorating in the remains of a little English garden, overlooking the main street of the town.

Kester flung open the peeling front door, unloading her groceries and her shoes in one movement. She ushered them into the sitting room which was a celebration of disorder, for Kester was an indifferent housekeeper. It was not that Kester disliked housework, but only that she did it occasionally, as the mood took her. In this she was unlike Queenie, for whom cleanliness was a source of great pleasure, and unlike Ruth, who hated housework, but did it with seething resentment every day of her life.

There was a trunk overflowing with clothes in one corner of the room. Upon this, and upon the shabby furniture and the dusty sills, the west-facing windows stippled the autumn's afternoon sun. It gave the room a faded, lived-in look—the look of past lives.

'I like your place,' said Elsie looking about approvingly.

'Why thank you,' replied Kester, amused. 'It's my Auntie Consie's and my Uncle Bert's house really—only they don't live here now. My brother Jonathan and I used to live here together. Now sit down, all of you, and I'll fetch the tea. You can occupy yourselves. Goodness knows,' she added, disappearing, 'there are enough of you to have a cricket match.'

They exchanged looks in her absence. Kester reappeared in a moment, unpinning her hat, which she flung over the back of a chair. All her movements are sudden; she is like a bird or a fish, thought Nonie, riveted.

'Now,' she said, seating herself abruptly on the edge of an armchair. 'Tell me, how did poor Lily die?'

'She was ill,' offered Flora.

'I was only little,' said Georgie.

'How long ago did it happen?'

Kester looked at Nonie, who cleared her throat. 'Um—two years ago, nearly three. About that.'

'I see.'

'We're not sure, because it happened while we were away,' explained Flora. 'Nonie and me were . . .'

'At school,' finished Nonie. 'We went there after Georgie was born. And the twins . . .'

'We wasn't at a school,' said Phip in surprise. He smiled at Kester. 'Tom and me was at the Sallies.'

After a brief silence, Elsie added, 'She used to cry a lot.'

Kester jumped to her feet and fairly ran back to the kitchen. 'The kettle will be boiling. Now, where has Hannibal got to?'

50

They could hear her clattering teacups onto a tray. She called out, suddenly, 'Does your father write often?'

'Never,' replied Nonie.

'He's busy,' added Flora. 'With the war and everything.'

Tom said with enthusiasm, 'The Red Baron's been shot down.' Both boys cheered.

Kester reappeared with the tea-tray. Her fingers made nervous tappings on its sides. Flora said, conversationally, 'How did your mother die?'

Kester seemed to find Flora intriguing. Nonie, noting this, felt a pang of resentment. 'She was ill. It was a long time ago. Both my parents died within a year of each other when I was fourteen.'

'Poor thing,' said Flora.

'Oh well, you have to get over these things, you know. And you always do.' Kester smiled at Nonie. 'Now, help yourselves to tea. Perhaps Flora will pour; I think it might be the kind of thing she would do well. Look, here's a picture of my brother Jonathan.' There was a small framed photograph trapped amongst the trinkets on the mantelpiece. Kester seized it and wiped it perfunctorily on the back of her dress. 'It was taken just before he left here to go to university.' She handed it to Nonie, then said with a burst of relief, 'There! That's the door. It must be Hannibal with the milk. I can't imagine where he's been.'

It was Hannibal, with Bert Haggerty. Bert had bought a bantam hen with feathery slippers. He set the crate down on Kester's front verandah and the children crowded around it. Nonie, loitering in the doorway, witnessed another reunion and another frantic exchange of unfinished sentences.

'Uncle Bert!'

'Don't you Uncle Bert me! I'm cross with you!'

'You look so well! How are . . .?'

'It's not good enough to receive a letter one day after not hearing . . .'

'If only the telephone were connected!'

'. . . from you for months on end . . .'

'I learned to drive when I was in Melbourne!'

'. . . as if your Auntie Consie hasn't been sick with worry!'

'You should just see me. I'm going to buy a motor as soon as I can and drive Auntie Consie and Jackie . . .'

'That's got nothing to do with it. And if your Auntie Queenie . . .'

'How's Auntie Queenie?'

Bert paused to draw breath, and smiled wryly. 'Same old Queenie.'

Georgie gave a shriek. 'There's babies!' For the little bantam had stretched one russet wing to reveal a surprising number of fluffy chickens beneath it.

'Esme Gannon tells me there's twelve,' advised Bert, turning his attention to the children for a moment. 'Hard to believe she can fit them all under her. I'm taking her back to Consie,' he said to Hannibal and Kester. 'She loves the bantams. Fox got the last few we had.'

'Goodness, you're brave,' said Kester, teasing. 'You know what Auntie Queenie will say . . . waste of good money; never lay when you want them to . . .'

Bert put a stop to her mimicry with a disapproving movement of his head. 'I've got a good idea what your Auntie Queenie will say.' He sighed with resignation. 'But sometimes things don't have to be sensible, if they bring pleasure or comfort. That's what I shall tell her, any rate, though I don't expect it will do me much good.' He added, 'Gannon's have had word of their Ned. He took some shrapnel at Arras. He's in England being looked after now, one of the lucky ones. And did you hear about the Baron?'

'Yes. I'm glad Ned Gannon's all right.'

'So are we all. I just hope he doesn't get well too soon. And that reminds me—what have you heard of our Jonathan?'

Kester shook her head. 'No word.'

'Surely someone has seen him.'

'I went everywhere, Uncle Bert.'

Flora looked up. 'Is your brother at the war too?'

'No. He is just missing.' Flora looked mystified. Kester said, 'He's gone off somewhere. I'm not a bit worried, actually. We just don't know where.'

'Did you ask at the prison?' said Hannibal quietly.

'I asked everyone. Everywhere.' Kester threw up her hands and ruffled her already disastrously untidy hair. Her face took on a look of determined indifference. At the word 'prison' all the children looked up.

'Is your brother bad?' demanded Tom.

Kester struggled with a surge of anger. 'He is not.'

'What is he in prison for, then?'

'My brother is an anti-conscriptionist.' She glared at Hannibal and her uncle, who had exchanged a forbidding glance. 'Don't you look like that! I won't have anyone thinking that my brother is a criminal!'

'They're only children, Kissie.'

'That's of no importance, Uncle Bert. Jonathan was wrongly imprisoned. I won't have anyone thinking ill of him. My brother is an anti-conscriptionist,' she repeated to the children. 'He, along with some friends—they're called Industrial Workers of the World—campaigned against the referendum that would have forced our boys to war. And there was some trouble, and he was sent to prison. But he was let out, of course, straight after the vote—well, he had to be, because it proved that he was right. We must be able to choose whether to take up arms against our fellow man . . .'

'All right, Kissie,' said Bert. 'Off your soapbox, my girl.'

'Never mind,' said Flora. 'I'm sure your brother has gone to war, and he and our Dadda are there together.'

'The thought doesn't comfort me.'

'Hush, Kissie. I expect our Jonathan knows where he is. I expect that's all that matters.' Bert put an arm around Kester's shoulders and squeezed her affably. 'Now, they're all wanting you to move back to Dingley. What do you say to that?'

Kester looked anguished. Bert said, 'Yes, well, I rather expected you wouldn't be keen, and I said as much to Consie, only they miss you, you know, her and Jackie.'

'I know.'

'And your Auntie Queenie says there's plenty of work for you up there.'

Kester rolled her eyes. 'Can you imagine it? You'd lose all your guests. They come up here to get away from the war, and Auntie Queenie and I would be worse than the Western Front.'

Bert tried, for the children's benefit, to look as though he were coughing, but Hannibal laughed outright. Nonie marvelled at Kester's irreverence. Fast, she thought admiringly.

'Stop standing about and come in for tea,' said Kester, controlling herself at last. 'It'll be stone cold soon.'

Hannibal handed over the billycan of milk. 'We can't stay,' he said. 'The light will be going soon. We want to be home in daylight.'

'Uncle Bert, will you stay?'

'My word.'

'All right. You'll come back and see me soon, Hannibal?' Kester looked urgent suddenly.

'I will. Soon.' Nonie was stabbed with jealousy again. She could not bear to think of Hannibal enjoying such familiarity with Kester. She felt trapped by being too young. They made their goodbyes and Hannibal herded the children ahead of him down the road, while Bert wandered off into the garden to cut some grass for the hen and to inspect his neglected roses. Nonie paused at the gate to hand the photograph back to Kester.

'Oh, I forgot,' said Kester. 'I wanted the name of Paul's unit. Do you know it, Nonie?'

Nonie walked away, pretending that she had not heard.

8

Singing and shouting they swept to the treacherous forest
Darkness and silence received them and smothered
their pain.

MARGERY LAWRENCE

Nonie invented a game. It was an elaborate game, involving spies and the Hun and the Industrial Workers of the World. They were the field patrol that sought out the enemy and drove them back to their own lands. There was some argument as to whether the IWW were to be considered enemies or not.

'Auntie Queenie reckons they are traitors,' insisted Tom. 'And Bolshevists. I heard Hannibal telling Auntie Ruth.'

'What did Auntie Ruth say?'

'I forget.'

Nonie twitched with impatience. She would like to know Ruth's opinion.

They were following the timber tram tracks up the Chum from the mill. Early winter rains and the relentless rolling of the timber wagons had turned the Chum road into a quagmire. The mill lay idle as it did every year during the wet months, while the ravaged bush around it slowly softened in the silence, grew damp and green again in its uneasy, shortlived peace. It was the perfect hideout, Nonie said, for the enemy.

55

Flora did not like being so far from home. 'I can't see Greystones. Auntie Ruth doesn't like us to be out of sight of the house.'

'Don't be silly, Flora. We're on a track, not in the bush.'

'We've come too far. Georgie won't be able to walk home. We'll have to carry him.'

'We always do, anyway.'

Georgie looked indignant, although it was true. He had found a large tree branch, and was dragging it along with him for a rifle. It had tripped him up twice already and he was well camouflaged with mud; soon he would be whining to be carried. Flora trailed behind, coughing disconsolately.

It had taken them the best part of the day to reach the sawmill from Greystones. They had played there a while, in and around the empty stables, kicking at mounds of mouldy sawdust, peering through windows at the great circular saws and cables, and hurling rocks into the water race. It was a scene of immutable desolation, made worse by Flora's bleating.

The timber tram tracks ran north from the mill, into the forest that hugged the sides of Mount St Leonard like a tight green shawl.

'The spies heard us coming,' said Tom, who was enjoying the game best of all. 'And they scarpered right up that track.' So they followed him till the mill was small behind them, and the ragged winter bush rose menacingly beyond.

Flora suddenly sat down on the wooden sleepers and began to cry, bringing the party to a halt. They all looked expectantly at Nonie.

'Come on Flora.'

'Can't.'

'What's the matter?'

'We shouldn't have come so far.'

'It's not.'

'It is. I'm tired. And I can't breathe.' She coughed by way of demonstration.

Sometimes Nonie did not know which she hated more—Flora, or her croup. 'We only want to go a bit further, you know.'

Tom nodded earnestly in agreement. 'Come on, Flor,' he urged and Georgie echoed him. Nonie was gratified.

'Flora's got croup, hasn't she?' observed Elsie.

'It's not too bad yet,' said Flora, smiling thinly at Nonie.

'Good then,' said Nonie. 'Come on.'

Flora had not expected that response, as Nonie well knew. She began to cry again. Phip picked his way back along the tram tracks towards her. 'Come on, Flora,' he said. 'We can walk back to the mill and wait for the others there.' It was a supreme gesture; the twins did not often choose to separate. Nonie remained undaunted.

'All right. We'll just go to the top of the gully. You'll hear us calling.' She set off at a cracking pace, dragging Georgie along with her by his tree branch. Elsie came after. Tom paused a moment, then brought up the rear while the other two slipped awkwardly down the track toward the mill.

Nonie did not really know where they were going, or why. In the final instant it had only been her desire to triumph over Flora that had made her so stubborn. It was always like that these days with games, even when she began them. She was always removed, watching, scorning the younger children, and hating herself for doing so. In grim silence she thought over excuses for turning back, without backing down.

'Nonie!'

'Ouch! Don't grab me like that.' Tom had pulled her nearly to the ground. Georgie fell on top of them.

'I seen someone!'

She stiffened at the urgency in Tom's voice. He was not playing. Georgie's face took on a look of horror. 'Spies!' he squeaked and grabbed Nonie around the neck.

'I saw someone too,' said Elsie complacently. 'I been seeing a person for ages.' They all looked at Elsie.

57

'Who did you see?'

'I been seeing a girl, sneaking, for ages.'

Georgie moaned, strengthening his grip on Nonie. She shook him off, dismayed by her own rising fear, then grabbed him back again.

'Well, where?'

Elsie pointed towards the top of the gully into an open area that had once been clear-felled and was now a blur of bracken and fern.

'That's right,' said Tom. 'That's where I saw her. A black girl. Could she be a spy, Nonie?'

'Of course not.'

'Why couldn't she be?'

'Just because.'

'I want to go 'ome!'

'It's all right. Just stop it, Georgie!'

'Take me 'ome, Elsie!'

Elsie found his clutching hand. 'You watch, Georgie,' she advised. 'And you'll see her too. Nonie's going to call out. You just watch.'

Nonie hesitated. She had been contemplating something more like a hasty retreat.

'Go on, Nonie.'

'I am.'

'No you're not.'

'I am! I'm just thinking first.' She could not think of anything. 'All right.' She rose to her feet. Georgie transferred himself, leechlike, to Elsie. The bush she faced seemed infinitely empty. Ferns glistened and dripped in the stillness.

'Hullo.'

'I think you better call louder,' remarked Elsie stolidly.

'Hullo!'

The only sound was the drumming of water, which, being constant, became silence itself.

'Is there anyone there? Hullo?'

'I'm here.' The reply was so close and so quick that it gave them all a jolt.

Nonie croaked, 'Where?'

There was no answer this time, only a movement to the right, then a face and arms, and then a whole person stood beside them, smiling. It was not a particularly warm smile. Nonie guessed that it was a smile borne of satisfaction at having caused such anxiety.

'Why were you following us?'

'Who says I was?'

The girl was clearly not younger than Nonie, although she was smaller and thinner. Her legs, bare under her woollen tunic, were like a bird's legs, with boots on.

'Did you follow us from the mill?'

'Didn't say I followed you.'

'Who are you?'

'I know who you are.'

This statement pulled Nonie up short. Georgie said, 'Are you a spy?', and the girl stared at him and shook her head.

'Do you live here?' said Elsie.

'No.'

Tom said, for no apparent reason, 'I've got a twin.'

'I know.' The girl looked at Nonie again. Her smile was an invitation that Nonie could not resist.

'How do you know? You don't!'

'I do.'

Stumped again, Nonie cast about for a remark to put her on equal footing. 'If I tell you my name, will you tell me yours?'

'I know your name. It's Nonie Field. You belong at Greystones and your father is Paul. My mum knew him.' She gazed at Nonie triumphantly.

Elsie said, 'You know everything!'

The girl shrugged carelessly, pleased with the idea. 'My name is Jessie,' she said. 'Hannibal told me about you. And my mum told me about your father. She said he had golden hair, like an angel.'

Nonie, totally humbled, surrendered to her wonderment. 'What else did she say?'

'She said he was a proper bugger.'

This disclosure was a little deflating. However it helped Nonie to collect her thoughts. 'What are you doing here?' she pursued, moving closer to the girl. Her irises were so black that the darkness spilled over into the whites of her eyes. They narrowed a little at the question.

'Nothing,' she said.

'We're playing a game,' said Elsie. 'You can play too.'

Nonie glared at Elsie. She was not convinced that inviting a black girl into their game was at all correct. Hannibal's blackness was one thing, this was another. After all, Hannibal was an adult and the rules were different.

'Don't stare at the poor wretch, girls,' the sisters had said in whispering voices like the rustling of leaves, when they passed the black man as he lay in the gutter in a puddle of sick. 'Say a little prayer to St Jude.'

Nonie did not avert her gaze quickly enough and was poked in the spine for her tardiness. 'Do as you are told, Nonie Field. A prayer is all that God asks of you.' Then the leaves rustling again in a sigh. 'The only thing worse than a black is a half-caste.'

And Flora, late at night, whispering in bed.

'What are you doing?'

'I'm saying extra prayers for the poor wretches.'

'Oh.'

'Nonie. What's a half-cart?'

'I don't know.'

'If it's worse than a blackie it must be as bad as the devil.'

'I don't know.'

'Why do we have to pray to St Jude for them, and not to God?'

I don't know. I don't know.

'I don't know.' Nonie looked apologetically at Jessie who did not notice. She had already accepted Elsie's invitation.

Tom had had a change of heart and seemed delighted with the arrangement. He was keen to impress. 'Then we better get back to the others. Hadn't we, Nonie? I have got a twin,' he repeated to Jessie as they began slithering down the tram tracks homeward. 'You come with us and you'll meet him.'

It was the perfect solution, really, all things considered. Nonie, relieved at the turn of events, began to feel in control again.

9

*I know that I shall meet my fate
Somewhere among the clouds above
Those that I fight I do not hate
Those that I guard I do not love.*

W.B. YEATS

The sound of voices retreated up the tram tracks and was swallowed into the silence. Bush silence, Flora thought, silence that was not silence but a racket of little sounds, dripping, cracking, swaying sounds. Flora was afraid of the bush, in the same way that she had been afraid of the city streets. Walking to school at Nonie's side with other girls from the Home, in their blue pinafores, she would always start at the sound of a dog's sudden enraged barking, a shout, the rumble and crash of empty hogsheads being rolled from a cart. Nonie, who did not like to draw notice to herself, would glare at Flora when she jumped, and Flora had learned to hold onto that glare, to calm herself by the steadiness of her sister's anger.

Today Nonie had taken her anger away. Flora tried to block out the bush silence by listening to her own breath, squeezing from her lungs, and the jolting sounds Phip made as he leapt from one wooden sleeper to another close behind her. The old mill lay ahead and she took comfort from the sight of it. Its very man-madeness helped to brace her spirits, brought down by the unsettling disorder of the bush, and by Nonie's cavalier departure.

Phip regretted being noble. 'Flora, is your croup going?'

'Not really.'

She stopped a moment to get a few good breaths. Phip paused with her. He said, 'I hope they don't find any spies then, without us along to help.'

'They won't.'

'Why not?'

Flora was old enough to be cynical about the children's imaginary games, but she was steadfast in her loyalty to Nonie. 'I just don't think they will; it's too cold.'

Phip digested this reason with difficulty, but without Tom was not inclined to challenge it. They began their descent again. Next moment Phip's heart lurched upwards, and he strained forward in a wild grab for Flora's arm.

Flora forgot how to breathe altogether for a few seconds. 'There's someone down there at the mill,' he whispered close to her ear as they lay tangled on the wet ground. 'Don't move!'

Flora had to move, she had to sit up; her breath whistled outwards and dragged in. 'Who?'

'It was a man.' Phip's face was flour-white. 'We got to get back to Nonie.'

'Yes.'

'Not on the tracks. He'll see us—they'll see us.' Already the one sighting had multiplied itself in Phip's memory. 'We better go in the bushes, on the side there.' The greenness that flanked the tracks seemed at once placid and safe and inviting. He began to slide towards it, keeping low to the ground. Flora followed, wanting Nonie, wanting the safety of the mill, and filled with terrible disappointment. But it was not in her nature to doubt Phip.

'Call out for them.' She would have done so herself if her chest had allowed it.

'No!' The very idea alarmed him. 'We got to be quiet. We got to be careful, Flora. It's spies. I know it.' His face was grave. Flora felt a little worm of panic wriggle in her stomach. She allowed herself a glance down toward the grey buildings and could see no sign of life, but was surprised at how threatening they appeared now—an invasion on the landscape.

The bush took them to it, kindly, like an old eiderdown, offering camouflage and solace; they did not see any nightmares lurking silently in its folds.

Tom reached the mill first, with Jessie. 'Hey,' he shouted. 'Look who we've found!'

There was no answer.

'Phip!'

Jessie said, unnecessarily, 'I can't see anyone.'

'They must be hiding.' Tom began to search for them. 'Come on! Where are you, Phip?'

Nonie arrived then with the others. She looked around and her heart began to thump. Tom said, 'I can't find them, Nonie. I've looked. They must be hiding.'

'Yes.' But she did not really believe that. The mill buildings bellowed emptiness.

'Maybe spies got 'em,' suggested Elsie.

Nonie saw Georgie's eyes bulge. 'Don't be silly. They must be around somewhere.'

'Not around here,' said Jessie.

Georgie promptly burst into tears. He clung to Nonie's legs. 'Spies! Nonie! I want to go 'ome!'

Tom looked stunned. 'Might it be spies?' he whispered. 'Might it be the Hun?'

'No!' Nonie stamped her foot and nearly knocked Georgie over. 'There are no spies here. Stop crying, Georgie!'

Jessie touched Georgie's shoulder with an unexpected gentleness. 'It's all right,' she said. 'Maybe they've gone home.'

Nonie shook her head. 'They would have waited.'

'How do you know?'

'I just do!' How could she possibly explain? She glared at Jessie, blaming her in silence for the confusion she felt welling inside her; sobs of it. 'They must have come looking for us. Flora's croup got better.'

'I want Flora!' sobbed Georgie. He struggled up into Nonie's arms and hung on her like a monkey. She closed her grip on him reluctantly, fearing that in offering him comfort she might somehow weaken herself.

She said, 'We'll look for them. We'll call out till they hear.' The frightened upturned faces bestowed upon her their immense trust. She could not bear to see them. She scrambled back along the track with Georgie clasping her neck. 'Flora! Flora!' Soon Tom's voice resounded beside hers, but to Nonie it seemed a great distance away. Even her voice was faint, muffled by the thudding of her heart. She could not think. Georgie was sniffling and moaning in her ears about spies and ghosts, and her own head was thronging with a battalion of nightmares. What if Flora had become not better but worse, much worse? What if they had been taken by something, or killed? A thousand what-ifs effervesced inside her, all bursting at the same outcome. It was her fault, her fault. Her fault.

'Why don't you go home?' suggested Jessie, cutting into Nonie's silent turmoil.

What are you doing here? thought Nonie. Go away. Go away. She said, 'But Flora and Phip . . .'

'They might be home.'

'They're not. I know they're not.' But she clutched at the idea like a straw.

'I want to go home,' said Elsie.

Tom said, 'So do I.' He could not hold back his tears. 'I want Auntie Ruth.'

At the sight of Elsie's solemn face and Tom's tears, Georgie renewed his wailing. Nonie turned her head away. 'All right,' she said briskly. 'We might as well do that.' She added to Jessie, with an air of nonchalance, 'We'll be all right. You don't have to come.'

Jessie did not reply, and when they began to walk homeward she followed along. Nonie gritted her teeth. 'We're all right without you, I said.'

'I want to come. I'll hold the baby for a while if you like.'

Georgie stopped crying long enough to say, 'I not a baby!' in a wet but indignant voice. He hung firmly on Nonie.

She said, 'Oh well, do what you like,' and made her way determinedly to the head of the party.

Hannibal was in the orchard cutting back raspberry canes that were rampant along the fenceline. He stopped his work as the dismal group straggled in.

'Been out playing?' He glanced at them, then shouldered a bundle of cut cane and flung it over into the flood paddock where later he would make a bonfire. He smiled briefly at Jessie. He knows her so well he does not even bother speaking to her, thought Nonie. Just smiles, just like that. She felt consumed with jealousy. 'Where are Flora and Phip?' he said to Nonie. She turned her head away, startled.

Georgie had exhausted his voice on the way back but he managed a resurgence of sobbing. 'Spies! Spies got 'em!' He strained out for Hannibal's arms.

'Nonie. Where are they?'

She could not answer. To open her mouth now would be to release a floodgate that must never be released. Tom was crying too much to speak. Elsie said, 'We can't find them.'

'Jessie?'

One word, burned Nonie, that is all he needs. He knows her so well.

'We were on the tram tracks at the back of the mill. They must have gone off,' said Jessie.

Hannibal took Georgie from Nonie's arms and reached out for Tom's hand, then began to walk towards the house. His wordless action put a thrill of urgency through them. They followed him. Nonie felt unsteady. She had carried Georgie, who was a strapping child, for nearly an hour without noticing his weight. He had been like an anchor and his loss set her adrift. She bit her lips. There was still Ruth to face.

Ruth, however, paid no attention to Nonie when Hannibal told her the news. She had been separating milk in the washhouse behind the kitchen and she was flushed from her work. Strands of wiry hair had escaped from the custody of their pins. She turned visibly paler as Hannibal spoke. 'You want to sit down,' he said.

'There's no time to sit.' Ruth straightened up. 'I will ride to Dingley. Then to town before it is too dark.' She began to walk away from them, through the kitchen garden toward the stable, every step resolute. Only a hand, wrestling with a knot in her apron string, seemed to suggest something else as it darted and tugged. 'There must be an hour or two of light left.'

'An hour,' said Hannibal. Nonie, glancing to the creek, was aware of the advancing chill of night.

'You must begin the search now.'

'They won't be far. Be back before you are most likely.'

Ruth managed to smile, but in a distracted way. 'Nonie,' she said suddenly.

Nonie stiffened. 'Yes?'

'Look after the children. I'll send someone down from Dingley.'

'Yes.' She wondered why her aunt had not looked at her when she spoke. It was some moments before she realised that Ruth was not able to look at anyone. Ruth did not so much as glance at Hannibal as he trotted the horse in from the house paddock and onto the carriageway. She fitted the bridle swiftly, and took his arm to help herself mount. Hannibal watched her though.

He said, 'If you'll let me fetch a saddle . . .' But she was stirring the horse into motion as he spoke and clattering to the gates.

Nonie watched numbly as the horse disappeared down the road. She felt Hannibal's hand on her arm. 'I'm going now. You heard your aunt. Look after the others and someone will be here from Dingley soon.'

She nodded, her gaze still fixed on the road along which her aunt had disappeared. The children were silent. 'Auntie Ruth was crying,' observed Elsie at last. 'Not crying. But like crying, you know?'

Nonie came to her senses then and spun around. But Hannibal was already gone. She could just see him heading round a bend in the road, in the opposite direction from Ruth. With Jessie. She hated Jessie then, in a wave of passion that nearly knocked her off her feet.

Tom's tears were long spent. They had made dirty furrows down his face. He moaned and shivered and wrapped his arms around himself tightly. 'I wish Dadda was here,' he said hoarsely. 'He'd find 'em. I know he would.'

10

They leave their trenches, going over the top,
While time ticks blank and busy on their wrists
And hope, with furtive eyes and grappling fists,
Flounders in mud. O Jesus, make it stop!

SIEGFRIED SASSOON

It was Phip's idea to climb upwards, away from the creek. 'We'll be able to see better, won't we, Flor? And when we're up high enough we'll be able to see Nonie. So we can go to her. Without . . . without anyone finding out, see.' His own fear of the figure he had seen, disappearing behind the mill buildings, was so irrational, so huge, that he could not bring himself to speak about it in anything but the most roundabout way.

Flora could not speak at all. She needed all her energy just to breathe. So when the calling began she was powerless. Phip refused to call back. He waited anxiously for the calls to cease and when they did he was relieved.

'We'll go up the gully,' he said again, quickly, placatingly. 'So's they'll see us. Or we'll see them.' But it was easier said than done. With every step they sank deep in undergrowth, while the bark and black wattle wove a tantalising barrier around them, glittering with moisture, like wicked eyes that beckoned and dissuaded. The bush shifted and swung, and pricked and pawed at them, but wherever they turned they were its prisoner.

When Phip finally stopped he knew they were lost, but he was bewildered by the knowledge. 'When we get to the top . . .'

he began to repeat his argument, to comfort himself with the logic of it.

'No.' Flora was on her knees.

'I'll help you, Flora.'

'No.'

He could see that she would have said more if she could. She was ashen. He climbed down to her and sat at her side in the silence, for the first time fully aware of her state. 'It's all right. It's all right, Flor. We'll just sit still. You'll be all right then.' But he did not want to be still. It frightened him more than anything. 'We'll get going in a while when you're better.' The light grew weak, the trees grew larger in their own shadows, and the bush sounds amplified eerily in the gathering gloom. Phip said, 'They'll find us before it gets properly dark,' and added softly, 'Tom doesn't like the dark.'

Flora did not have the strength to reply, but there was warmth in the place where their sides touched that she was glad of.

Queenie, in a starched pinafore, cut mountains of sandwiches. They were removed from time to time by Bert Haggerty or by Ruth.

'Where are they going?' Tom asked.

'You don't expect the searchers to be out there in that cold with empty stomachs, do you?'

'No.'

'Well then.'

Tom was plaintive in his oneness. He sat at the kitchen table cutting bread with Jackie and Elsie, a transparency of himself. All Consie's attempts to draw him into conversation had proved futile. He seemed absorbed by his task and more at ease with Jackie's silent acceptance and with Queenie's curt remarks than with kindness.

'It makes my heart break,' said Consie to Queenie. 'You'd think those twins had had their share.'

Consie had been bathing the children in a tin tub by the stove. She was lingering over Georgie now. He lay on her knee in a towel, like a lamb, being cosseted and sung to, drifting deliciously in the shallows of sleep. 'Look, Queenie, look at those yellow curls,' entreated Consie. 'Isn't he a cherub?'

Nobody had suggested that Nonie bathe and change. She skulked in a corner watching them through the steamy fug, feeling invisible, surprised and outraged when her eyes met Consie's.

Consie's conversation with Queenie was mostly about Kester, who had called by a week ago bringing gifts and a million plans and promises. She had a job at the post office.

'And that won't last more than six weeks, mark my words,' pronounced Queenie. 'I haven't known Kester do a solid day's work in her life. Six weeks at the most, and she'll be sick of it, and complaining.'

'But it's the perfect job for Kissie. She loves chatting. She knows everyone in the district.'

'Oh well, if it's only chatting she has to do . . .'

'Now Queenie . . .'

'Six weeks if she's lucky,' repeated Queenie. 'And then there'll be another job and another after that. She should be home with her family. It isn't right, all alone in town like that.'

'She's not a child any more,' said Consie. 'And it'll only be till Jonathan gets home. We'd love to have her at Dingley, wouldn't we Jackie, but she needs to be with more people than just us.'

'Getting herself a bad name,' grumbled Queenie, organising towels into ranks in front of the stove.

'Hush, Queenie!' Consie stood up, offering the sleeping child to Queenie for a second to admire. 'He's prettier than Paul. Paul never had enough flesh, do you remember how slight he was? You could never cuddle Paul.' She held Georgie so tightly her grip threatened to wake him. 'These curls and these lovely fat cheeks—I could eat him, Queenie, truly.'

'He would taste nasty,' said Elsie.

Consie laughed. 'He would taste of honey and cream and soft sticky cakes.' She moved to the doorway. 'He looks like Paul, but he has poor Lily's softness.'

Nonie followed Consie out of the kitchen and watched from the hall shadows as Consie's solid shape mounted the stairs to the bedrooms. She wondered if her own mother had ever carried her to bed like that, but Lily had never been strong, not in that sense. And there had always been other babies more in need of carrying. Flora, then the twins.

Flora. Phip. She kept forgetting about them for moments on end, yet they were always there, hammering inside her head. It was completely dark now and they were not home.

The grandfather clock in the parlour struck the half hour, one short gong, half past nine. Normally they would be asleep, the little ones breathing deep in the darkness of the room; Ruth's footsteps gently resonating from downstairs as she paced the floors; Nonie, awake and listening, her hands cupping her two tender plums of breasts, turning over memories in her head, putting them to rest again—the unasked, unanswered questions. Then, the final stillness of the house, the movement of the night wind around the eaves, her own slow surrender to the comforting numbness of sleep.

Consie's footsteps returned. Nonie crept into the parlour to avoid her. She listened to the footsteps retreating towards the back of the house, then relaxed and looked about herself. The fire had been left going and was smouldering in the grate; a single lamp flickered on the mantelpiece, and the normal order of the room had been disarranged by a number of bedsheets flung over the backs of chairs to dry in the warmth. It was an act of desperation by Ruth during the winter months, for the twins despite all their bravado were chronic bedwetters. Their sheets were washed every day. If there is only Tom perhaps there will be fewer sheets to wash, she thought. Her head hammered again. Flora and Phip, Flora and Phip. She felt empty.

Her eyes blinked across the hallstand, to the photographs. She had not cared to look at them before, but now she went across to them, picked out the photograph of her parents' wedding day and carried it to an armchair draped in sheets, where she sat studying its brownness. There was her mother in white silk with her grey eyes and a slightly unfamiliar smile. And there was her father. He was wearing a suit which was too big. His face was small and pale. He did not look at all suitable for such a photograph. He seemed, not bored, not unhappy, simply distracted, as though his thoughts had been captured by something more important somewhere else.

An ache dragged inside Nonie. Why did her father look like that? Why was only her mother happy? Poor Lily. They all called her that. Consie, Queenie, even Ruth. Kester Cousins had said it. Poor Lily. But how ridiculous—her mother looked so happy. She was indignant on her mother's behalf.

'Nonie?'

She had not heard the footsteps returning along the hallway. Consie's voice jolted her.

'You're here, are you?' Consie hesitated at the doorway. They are afraid of me, thought Nonie, afraid of what I might do. She wondered what it was she could do.

'Queenie's got hot milk on the stove.'

'I don't want any.'

She shrank back as Consie came closer. Consie had noticed the photograph. She lifted it out of Nonie's lap, smiling. 'Well, that was a day.'

'Was it?'

'May something-or-other, isn't that funny . . . I forget the date now. The rain came down just as we were leaving the church, and I got water spots all over the silk flowers on my new hat. Sent up from the city . . .' She dusted the photograph lightly. 'Didn't Lily look a treat. Her mother sewed the dress,

73

and she was quite poorly at the time. Passed on soon after. She was glad to see her daughter married. Come along then, lovey.' She turned away to replace the photograph.

'What else?' said Nonie with clenched fists. Her face, she was sure, betrayed no eagerness, nor her voice; only her hands, and she sat on them.

Consie looked at her in the lamplight. Her face, too, betrayed no one. 'Weddings are weddings,' she said. 'They follow the same pattern mostly.' She smiled suddenly. 'We all went to that one from around here . . . who would have thought it, everyone said. Who would have thought Paul . . . but I wasn't surprised. Love's a funny thing and poor Lily got the man of her choice, never doubt that.' A memory sparked in her eyes. 'Jackie would have been about nine, and Jim was eight, and my Stannie must have been five. We all went, and didn't I have a time of it getting a tie knotted around Stanley's neck! Fair choked him with it in the finish. Jonathan was best man. You haven't met our nephew Jonathan, of course, Kissie's brother. A very handsome lad. The two of them got the looks in our family. Kissie was flowergirl.' She rocked a little, delighted. Nonie sat perfectly still. 'She looked a proper angel. Mind you, it was all looks. She didn't like her dress one jot and she put on a turn about it before-hand—that's Kissie's way—but Jonathan talked her around. I've a photograph of her somewhere in my things. I must hunt it out one day.' She shook her head. 'Not one of Kester's best. She looks sullen in it, cross about the dress. There's a lot of stubbornness in our Kester, she gets it from her Auntie Queenie, though she wouldn't thank me for saying so.'

'Was Auntie Ruth there?'

'Of course. She was all the family Paul had.'

'And Hannibal?'

'Hannibal too. Everyone from our district came, and some folk from town. Mrs Prendergast hadn't any family to speak of, an uncle I believe, who didn't pay them much attention.' Consie shook her head. 'That's the way it is in the city, everyone living in each other's pockets you might say, and can't get away from one another quick enough. Out here, where there's space between people, there's more neighbourliness. Lily loved that, loved the Chum valley. It surprised us all when the two of them went down the line to live.'

'Why did they, then?'

'Leave the Chum?'

'Yes.'

Consie smiled. 'Well, now, I would say there's not a country boy born who doesn't want to see the city.' She stopped and looked around the room. 'That's enough reminiscing. You come back to the kitchen with me now and have some of Queenie's milk.'

'I hate hot milk!' Nonie stood up crossly and made for the door. 'I'm going to bed.' She stood at the door irresolute, waiting for Consie to speak.

Consie said, 'If you like, dear. You've had a difficult day. I'll wake you when the children are brought in.' She seemed to have no doubt that they would be. Nonie was grudgingly comforted by her assurance. Consie wished her good night and walked back to the kitchen slowly. Nonie hated her, hated the tired way she walked. She hated her for speaking of her parents' wedding as if it had been somehow so ordinary. She hated her most of all for being kind. She knew that she did not deserve kindness because the disaster that was now upon them had been her doing. They hate me, she thought with a perverse satisfaction, they will never not hate me.

She had no intention of going to bed. Georgie would be there anyhow, guzzling away at his thumb in the cot he shared with Elsie. She pulled open the front door quietly, stepped out into the dark, and made her way towards the stable.

There was a cold wind outside, which wrapped itself around her, biting her legs and arms, squeezing her chest. She shivered, then shuddered, thinking of Flora and Phip with no shelter in the bush. Still, Mrs Haggerty was sure they would be found.

75

Nonie felt a surge of anger for Mrs Haggerty and kicked out at the nearest object, a bucket of water. It fell over with a thud and a slosh. Water splashed up her legs like a cold slap of retaliation. Nonie pulled open the stable door and entered.

Her first idea was to sit out there in the darkness until someone came to coax her back, but the darkness was more profoundly black than she had anticipated. There was a lamp and some matches on a shelf by the door, she knew, so she felt for them and squatted in the open doorway fumbling awkwardly to light it. Its light cast enormous shadows up the walls, almost as alarming as the dark. Henrietta and her kittens were there, delighted by the unexpected company. She scooped up two kittens and buried her face in their warm vibrating bodies while they wriggled and squeaked.

Then something happened. Henrietta suddenly drew up into a tight hump and spat between Nonie's legs at something in the half-open doorway. At the same moment the lamp was extinguished with one swift breath. The kittens scratched their way out of Nonie's arms and scuttled sideways across the floor into the shadows. Nonie stiffened. Her head felt light.

'All right, girl,' said a voice. 'Don't go crazy now. Turn around.'

She did not know how, but she did as the speaker ordered; her eyes made out the silhouette of a man framed in the doorway.

'Are you the Field girl? Nonie?'

'Yes.' The word left her in a rush.

'There's a boy and girl in the bush.'

'Yes.'

'Your brother and sister?'

'Yes.'

'You come with me.'

Her heart was thrashing in her chest like some trapped animal. She felt unsteady. Her voice would not obey her. 'Who . . . who are . . .?'

There was a hesitation. The figure in the doorway shifted suddenly and lurched forward. An arm gripped her. She smelled sweat close to her face. 'You come now.' He was so near that she could see his tongue, his teeth, his lips. 'I can't wait any longer. I know where they are. Come on.' He turned away abruptly and began walking across the yard, into the kitchen garden, towards the house paddock. Nonie took a deep breath and plunged after him.

Phip had fallen asleep on Flora's shoulder. She was uncomfortable with him there, but she was unable and unwilling to dislodge him. Once or twice she had begun to sleep, but she had roused herself, pulled open her aching eyes and stared up through the treetops into the overcast sky. Her chest was so tired now that she had to make herself breathe; it would be easier to stop. If she slept, she knew she would no longer breathe, and it was a partly comforting thought. But Phip was there. Even now, when she could not feel her arms or her legs, she could feel him. Her open eyes ached with cold. Underneath her the ground was wet. She tried to think of her father, but that did not seem to help, so she thought of Nonie, for Nonie had always been there in the past, but even Nonie was hard to pin down in her head. Flora could not call out now, or cry. With each breath she tried to moan a sound. It was not loud, or strong, but at least it reminded her that she was still alive.

And it was strong enough to prevent her hearing the man's approach. To Flora, it seemed that he materialised from nowhere. One moment the space in front of her was merely darkness, then suddenly the darkness was the shape of a man. Her tired heart lurched inside her. She could not speak or shrink back. He reached out and took her arm.

'What are you doing here?'

She moaned out a breath. He watched her for a few seconds, then turned to Phip. He shook the child awake. 'Come on. Come on. Who are you?'

Phip blinked and swayed. He was confused and light-headed. He said, 'Hannibal?' and the man pulled back as though he had been struck. Phip shook himself. He said, 'No, you're not Hannibal.'

'No. I'm not.'

Phip looked around unsteadily and found Flora hunched on the ground beside him. He said, 'Can you take us home?'

'Where's home?'

'Greystones.'

The man grunted. 'You want Hannibal,' he said.

Phip was beginning to cry. 'Yes,' he said. 'And I want my Auntie Ruth.'

The man glanced over his shoulder uneasily. 'Get up!' He pulled Phip onto his feet. 'You too.' He grabbed Flora and realised at once how ill she was. She could not hold herself upright, she slumped onto her knees. Her eyes were dark holes.

Phip said, 'Do you know where our home is? Do you know Greystones?'

He grunted assent.

'Will you take us there, Mister?'

He hoisted Flora into his arms and signalled to Phip to follow him.

Phip struggled after him, anxious for reassurance. 'And do you know Hannibal? Do you?'

'Shut up!' hissed the man. 'Yes. I know your Hannibal. Now come on!'

Phip did not speak again for some time. He stumbled and plunged after the man who held Flora gasping in his arms. Once or twice the man paused for Phip to catch up, or reached out a free hand and hauled him over a fallen tree. Flora clung to his shoulder with all her strength, soaking in his warmth, overwhelming him with her trust. At last Phip fell headlong into a tangle of blackberry. He lay still, crying in a cracked, exhausted way. The man placed Flora down, and pulled Phip upright.

'Come on.'

'I can't walk any more.'

'I can't carry two of you.'

'I can't walk.'

Far off they heard a ringing cry. 'Flor—a! Flor—a!' The man stiffened, then shook Phip. 'Come on. It's not far now.'

'I can't.' Phip did not seem to recognise the sound. He was cut all over. The call came again. His bleeding face barely registered it.

Flora said, 'Nonie.'

'What?'

'My . . .'

'She wants you to get our sister Nonie,' said Phip slowly.

'Well I can't. Not Nonie. Not Hannibal. Now get up. You're stuck with Alec.'

He lifted Flora into his arms again. Phip staggered forward obediently. They had reached the creek now and Alec led the way, climbing and crawling along its crumbling bank. In some places it was impassable. Alec stepped into the water and splashed along, dropped Flora onto a clear space further down the bank and returned to help Phip.

'Is Alec your name?' said Phip suddenly. It had been some time since they had last spoken, though he seemed unaware of any time lapse.

'Yes.'

'My name is Philip.'

The cries were all around them now, but not close. Alec stopped suddenly and placed Flora gently on the ground, into the folds of a tree trunk. Phip collapsed at her side.

'Wait here,' he said. 'I'll get someone.'

'Nonie?' said Phip.

'Maybe. Someone. Sit tight.'

'Yes.'

He turned to go and found Flora's hand still wound tightly in his shirt sleeve. He detached it. 'Alec,' she whispered. 'Alec . . .'

11

Still wept the rain, roared guns,
Still swooped into the swamps of flesh and blood
All to the drabness of uncreation sunk,
And all thought dwindled to a moan.
Relieve!
But who with what command can now relieve
The dead men from that chaos or my soul?

EDMUND BLUNDEN

Nonie was following the mysterious man, across the paddocks towards the darkness of the creek. He moved in shadow, kept close to the trees, avoided open space. Once he stopped to wait for her. As she caught up she saw him smile. 'Not as quick as your father,' he said.

Nonie felt a pang. 'How do you know my father?'

'Everyone in these parts knew your father.'

He began to walk again. She ran to keep up. 'Where are we going?'

'Just keep moving. The girl's sick.'

Her feet sank into soft earth. They came to the creek and he suddenly pulled her down into the undergrowth. She began to protest but his hand clapped across her mouth and the weight of his body pinned her underneath him. There were voices nearby. Through the pounding of her heart she heard Hannibal's voice, and another. They were picking their way along the creek bank, stopping from time to time, listening, then moving on. A lantern flashed above her, seeing nothing. The two men passed by within touching distance, then their voices grew faint. They were heading to the house. After a moment the man's hand slid from Nonie's mouth. His face was close to hers, and the look

81

in his eyes warned her to keep silent. She tried to slow her breathing, to calm herself, but his action had terrified her.

He said, 'We don't want no one to hear us. All right?'

'But . . .'

'No one.' His voice was sharper. She nodded. 'Not even Hannibal.'

It startled her to hear him speak Hannibal's name. So he had recognised the voice too. 'How do you . . .' she began, but he silenced her by holding up a finger in warning.

'Don't worry,' he said in a low voice. 'I know him fine, girl. I'll stick a knife in him one day. Would you like me to do that?' Her look made him smile again. 'Then don't you make a sound to bring him over. Will you?' She shook her head quickly. 'This way.'

He was moving again, on all fours, down to the creek where the water, deeper now than in summer, made a rushing sound. He crossed it in a few short steps. Nonie splashed after him, not daring to hesitate in case he should disappear. The water came up to her knees, she slipped and teetered on the smooth stones of the creek bed. Then she dragged herself onto the bank and plunged into the bushes after him.

Nonie did not notice Flora and Phip at first amongst the bushes. She saw the man on his knees, and realised some moments later that he was shaking them. Phip said, 'Alec? Is Nonie here?'

'Yes, she's here.'

Nonie pushed forward and knelt beside him. 'I'm here,' she repeated.

'Is Flora there?' He seemed confused.

Alec was holding Flora's face in his hands, moving it from side to side. Flora opened her eyes and looked at him.

Nonie said numbly, 'It's me, Flor.'

Alec said to her, 'All right. You're on your own, girl. You understand?' Nonie nodded. 'And listen to me. You haven't seen anyone, right?'

'Yes.'

'You came down here and found them on your own.'

'Yes.'

He took her shoulder and squeezed it. 'Because if you say anything—anything—I'll come back. I'll kill your Hannibal. You understand?'

'Yes!'

Then he was gone. The movement of the bushes in his wake could have been made by the wind. Nonie stood stunned, unable to think. Phip had struggled to his feet, and was whimpering. 'Nonie, are you taking us home now, are you?'

'Yes,' she said, shaking herself to life, feeling for his hand. 'We have to help Flora to stand up.'

'She can't stand up.' The whimper was changing into little shaking sobs. When Nonie tried to free her hand so that she could help Flora, Phip's fingers clung tighter, his nails digging into her palm. He began to moan. She could feel the pain of his despair in her own throat. Alongside it, Flora's silence rang an even more terrible alarm. 'Listen,' she said to Phip. 'You wait here while I get Flora home, then I'll come back.' But Phip slid onto his knees, still moaning, and clutched the hem of her skirt, horrified at the idea of being left. I will have to leave Flora and take Phip first, she thought, but could not bring herself to do it. Her helplessness was an anchor weight dragging her, like Phip's hands, to the ground. She knelt down and pulled him close to her to silence him. 'Ssh! Phip, stop it!' His hands grabbed around her neck in suffocating tightness, his face flattened itself into her chest. A picture flashed like a lightning bolt in front of her. She had done this before. She and Flora had held the twins between them in bed, tightly pressed together to stop them crying. They had lain in darkness sharing the warmth of their bodies, she, Flora and the snuffling, snot-nosed twins, listening to unhappy voices in another room. They had held the twins tightly, till they were silent, till they slept.

Phip was silent now.

In the silence Nonie heard a voice. She listened, trying not to breathe. This was a voice from the present, not the past. It was Hannibal's voice. He was returning along the far side of the creek, retracing the track he had taken before. She felt relief like an explosive current, coursing through her. She heard herself scream, 'Hannibal! I've found Flora and Phip! I've found them!'

Greystones was lit up like a beacon when Hannibal and Nonie brought the children home. The kitchen was filled with people and voices. Nonie glimpsed Consie Haggerty, her face red and creased from crying, being comforted by several people whom she did not recognise. She realised that it was her own disappearance that had caused Consie's distress. Then there was a crush of people around them, a confusion of voices, asking, exclaiming, and Hannibal replying, repeating himself as each new person came up. It was all right; down by the creek; extraordinary that they had not been found earlier; Flora needed a doctor at once; yes, that place had been checked at least a dozen times; yes, they were all right; just cold; so cold. Nonie felt chilled through. Someone was leading her away now, out from the noise and turmoil up the stairs into the dimness of her bedroom. It was Queenie.

Queenie helped her take off her clothes without saying a word. Elsie and Georgie, snuggled together in their cot, barely shifted. Elsie was smiling in her sleep. Nonie lay staring at the ceiling, alone in the bed that she normally shared with Flora, and wondered if she would ever understand the events of the night, if she would ever feel ordinary again. But sleep came in its ordinary way and smoothed her face, and loosed the knots inside her.

It was a quiet household that Nonie woke into late the following morning. There were muffled voices in Ruth's room, footsteps downstairs, but lacking the urgency of the night before. The other children were nowhere to be seen. Nonie dressed herself, and went down to the kitchen. She was surprised to find Queenie still there, stirring soup on the stove. She stood in the doorway awkwardly.

'Awake at last,' said Queenie, noticing her. 'Come along then; I've been keeping your porridge warm for hours. Ruined by now, I expect.'

Nonie sat down at the kitchen table where Queenie had set her breakfast. She ate in silence. Queenie fed the stove, busied herself with pots and pans, peeled potatoes into a tin bowl.

'Where is Auntie Ruth?' asked Nonie eventually.

'Upstairs with Flora and Phip.'

'Oh.'

'Doctor came early today. Your sister's sick. It's what I've been saying all along—all this nonsense about croup—it's asthma Flora's got, and lucky to be alive.' Queenie took away Nonie's half-empty bowl. 'Haven't got time for you to idle over your food. Some of us have work to do. There's water in the basin by the door. Mind you wash your face properly.'

The water was cold. It had been sitting for some time. Nonie said nothing as she scrubbed her face and dried it, but she stopped for a second by the door and said, with difficulty, 'Thank you for breakfast.'

'Quite the hero, aren't you?' returned Queenie without turning from the stove. It was not said with good grace. She added, 'Fetch in the eggs.'

It was still outside. The air was dry and cold, threatening frost. There was a cracking, spitting bonfire in the flood paddock and Tom, Elsie and Georgie were there, running at it with sticks. Minnie and the horses stood at the fence, transfixed by the orange flames. Hannibal was feeding the fire with raspberry canes. Their voices seemed to rise and fall from a great distance. She was glad they did not see her.

The chickens were fussing in the henhouse. She stopped with the empty egg basket in her hand to admire them as they went about the business of the day. There is nothing yesterday and nothing tomorrow to them, thought Nonie enviously. She crouched amongst them and was ignored. Now, now is all that matters, the place said. That is all very well, she thought, but what do I do with now.

'Hullo, Nonie,' said Hannibal appearing at the doorway. 'I thought you weren't awake.'

She stood up and moved over to the nesting boxes. She did not want to look at him.

'Any eggs?'

'A couple.'

'That'll be last season's pullets. They'll lay right through winter if we're lucky. I've fenced off a bit of the vegetable garden where your aunt and I were clearing yesterday. I'm going to put the chickens in there. There's been a fox around.'

She did not know if he expected her to answer. She examined the warm eggs closely before she put them in her basket. Hannibal clucked at the chickens and they followed him trustingly outside. She waited a few moments and then returned along the path to the house. But Hannibal was still there, tinkering with the fence around the kitchen garden, while the chickens scratched diligently in the soft earth, chortling to each other. He stopped as she passed him. 'You were a clever girl last night.'

How could she possibly answer such a statement? She looked around in exasperation. He said, 'We searched that part of the creek ten times.'

'I know.'

'There were twenty people searching.'

'Were there?'

'And not one of us spotted them.'

She shrugged, feeling sick. What did he want her to say?

'How did you know they were there, Nonie?'

'I didn't know,' she said truthfully. 'I just went outside . . . to get out, to be alone.' She hesitated. 'I just went walking and I found them.'

Hannibal returned his attention to the fence. She started walking again. His voice followed her. 'Flora said some things last night. Nonie, was someone else there with you down at the creek?' He said it quickly. She looked around at him and saw something on his face that resembled fear. It made her inexplicably strong.

'No,' she said calmly. 'I don't know what you're talking about.' She ran back to the house.

A while later Ruth came upon Nonie dawdling at the foot of the stairs. She was carrying an empty bowl and looked dishevelled. 'Oh Nonie,' she said. 'I'm glad you're up. Fill this from the kettle, make sure it's boiling. Then bring it to me. Quickly now.' She hurried up the stairs again, pinning her hair into place as she went. Nonie did as she was told, relieved to find the kitchen empty. She carried the bowl carefully, glad of the task.

Ruth opened the door of her bedroom to her and ushered her inside. Nonie had expected darkness, instead she found the curtains hooked up around the curtain rod and the windows open wide. A fire was jumping in the grate—it was the only bedroom in the house which had its own fireplace—and the whole place smelled of gumleaves. Ruth added drops of eucalyptus oil to the new bowl of water and set it down in front of the fire to steam. Nonie looked around. Phip was sitting up on a chaise under the window eating bread and jam. He grinned at her. He looked horribly clean, except for his jammy mouth, and there was a curious criss-crossing of blackberry cuts on his face. He was wearing unfamiliar starched pyjamas buttoned up to the neck, and his damp hair was parted very straight. Nonie guessed that Queenie had had a hand in dressing him. Flora was in Ruth's bed. It was the large old bed that had belonged to Ruth's parents, with flowers carved into the bedhead. Flora looked tiny. She was propped up on a great number of pillows. There were bottles and spoons on the table by the bed, towels, jars of ointment, a half-eaten bowl of soup. Flora's face was white, but she was awake, smiling at Nonie.

'I was wondering where you were,' she said. She breathed between every word.

'Are you all right?'

'I had the doctor come.'

'I know.'

'Where's Tom?' said Phip.

'There's a bonfire in the flood paddock. They're all down there.'

Phip looked put out. Ruth said, 'You won't be up till tomorrow, so don't bother asking.' Her relaxed demeanour rather surprised Nonie, filling her with hope.

'Will I see the bonfire?' asked Flora. 'Will I get up tomorrow?'

'Not tomorrow, no. Never mind,' said Ruth. 'There'll be other bonfires.'

Flora looked content. She enjoyed being fussed over. 'Look at all my medicine,' she said to Nonie. It seemed to her a measure of how much she was cared for.

'I haven't got any,' rejoined Phip. 'But Auntie Queenie said if I don't behave she'll bring me some.' He was clearly intrigued by the prospect.

'Thank you for finding us,' said Flora suddenly, in the disarming way that always embarrassed Nonie.

Nonie flushed. 'I didn't do much,' she mumbled.

'Yes you did.'

'You did everything,' added Phip earnestly. 'The doctor said you was a hero. Like our Dadda. Do you think you'll get a medal?'

'Don't be silly.' She went over to the door. 'I'd better get going. I want to see the bonfire . . .'

Ruth came to the door with her and stepped out into the hallway. Nonie went stiff all over, but Ruth only said, 'You are the hero in this, Nonie. You did well to find them.'

'I didn't do anything.'

'Yes you did.' Ruth sounded firm. 'You did everything. We're all very proud of you.'

She did not seem proud. She seemed anxious and desperate.

12

And the flower of hopes and the flowers of dreams,
The noble, fruitful, beautiful schemes,
The tree of life with its fruit and bud,
Are trampled down in the mud and the blood.

E. NESBIT

During the night that followed, five people did not sleep.

Frost laced the plants in the kitchen garden, crocheted doilies of ice along the fence. It left a crisp carpet around the chicken run, preserving perfectly the footprints of the fox as it darted and danced, nosing its way from crevice to crack around the henhouse walls. The chickens jostled uneasily in their sleep as the fox's smell drifted in upon them. Hannibal rose at the sound and walked quietly through the kitchen garden to investigate its cause. He was in time to see the last flick of the fox's tail as it disappeared, thwarted, through the fence into the house paddock, to the creek. One of the horses, disturbed by the fox's passage, whinnied, half-waking, then returned to silence.

Hannibal looked down to the creek. Its waters hissed and crackled in the dark. He saw himself as a youth, running crookedly across the paddocks in pre-dawn gloom. He saw Paul running ahead, as he always did. It was Paul's idea. It always was.

'It'll be freezing!'

'Ssh. Don't wake the world!'

Only Paul would ever believe that you could. Frost needled their bare feet. The waters of the creek glittered. Paul was pulling off his clothes while he ran. He fell into the waterhole with a shout and rose up spluttering.

'Holy Moses! It's worse than I thought!'

'I told you.'

'It's a bloody shocker!'

Hannibal rolled in the bushes, helpless with laughter. Paul dragged himself from the water. He was white and thin like a wraith, almost glowing in the dark.

'Crikey, I'm frozen through!'

'You wouldn't listen to me, idiot!'

Paul appeared to be hunting about for his clothes, whimpering and shuddering, but when he was near enough to Hannibal he suddenly reached out and cast him, struggling, off the bank and into the water. Hannibal disappeared and rose again, bellowing.

'Bloody idiot! I'm sopping!'

Paul had forgotten his own discomfort and was laughing. Hannibal climbed out of the water, swearing at him. 'You swine! Goddamn bloody idiot!'

'Hush now!' Paul put on an expression of mock disapproval. 'What would Ruthie say?'

'She'll say plenty! These clothes won't dry by morning!'

They punched each other vigorously, each threatening to push the other down the bank once more; then Paul, rather blue by now, called it quits and made a serious attempt to collect his clothes, which were scattered across the creek bank and paddock.

Afterwards they sat together in the stable, smoking the tobacco they had stashed there. Hannibal was wrapped in a horse blanket. Outside the dark was fading. Soon it would be milking time.

'Ruth'll know as soon as she sees me that we haven't been home all night,' grumbled Hannibal. Paul shrugged. They had had a long and varied evening in town, culminating in their night swim. Paul had met his latest sweetheart outside the Mechanics

91

Institute, and gone with her for a stroll through the park. Hannibal had played cards with some lads outside the hotel. Alec had been there, skulking on the edge of the group, not saying much. His presence filled Hannibal with guilt, as always. It was unfair, he knew it was, the way Alec was not trusted, and he, Hannibal, so at ease in the company of Paul's friends. They had spoken together, exchanged news, but he was glad when Alec left the gathering. Later Paul joined them again; they had drunk stout and gone off with a bunch of the lads cheeking some of the local ladies and being generally unruly. Larrikins, Ruth would say, pursing her lips with disapproval. Larrikins indeed, Harry Lambe would agree, winking at them on the sly.

'Ruth and Harry had a fight this morning,' remarked Paul, coughing over his cigarette.

'What about?'

'The newspaper.'

'You can't fight over a newspaper.'

'Idiot. They had a fight over what was in it. South Africa.'

Hannibal shrugged. 'South Africa's miles away.' But he was interested in the fight—if fight was what it was. You couldn't always believe Paul.

'Said in the paper that our lads would be ready to go over, if they're asked.'

'So?'

'So Harry said it was the right thing, and Ruth called him a fool.' Hannibal snorted. Paul chuckled, and added, 'She even threw the paper at him.'

'Would you enlist?' asked Hannibal suddenly.

'Too right!' Paul's eyes shone. 'My God, H, wouldn't you?'

'I dunno.'

'I told Harry he'd be mad not to. He's got family in the army, back in England. Fix him up with a commission, they would, any job he fancied. He wants to, H. Should have seen his face!'

'We got nothing to do with war in South Africa.'

'Who cares!'

In the distance they heard the slam of the kitchen door, the rattle of milk cans. They both leapt guiltily to their feet, stubbing their cigarettes underfoot, falling over each other in their hurry.

'We're for it now,' said Hannibal. And they stumbled out into the grey dawn light to greet Ruth, a small brown shape in enormous galoshes, struggling with the milk cans.

Hannibal looked back across the garden to the house, half-expecting to see Ruth and the milking cans now. But it was still dark, the house was silent, and Ruth, no doubt, asleep. The old wombat was trundling along a side wall. Hannibal knew he should shoo it off, but felt disinclined. Ruth liked the wombat. He made his way back to bed.

Ruth sat at her bedroom window and watched the wombat follow its dogged path below her. It disappeared into shadow on its way to the kitchen garden which anyway had little to offer at this time of year. She thought about the vegetables in that garden that had yet to come, and felt depressed. Her life stretched out before her like a harvest calendar. She reasoned that she should be comforted by its predictability, but felt despair instead. All her life she had sought order, built walls of it around her. 'I would love to show you London,' Harry Lambe had said, and she had replied, 'I don't think I would like it much.' There was something disorderly about the thought of London. It forged a gap in her walls of order which she could not bear to contemplate. Now she would never see London because Harry was not there to show it to her. He had painted pictures of London from memory, when he first stayed at Dingley. Then, after he moved down to Greystones as tutor to Paul, he had begun to paint the bush. He had filled the house with his canvases, his brushes soaked in pots around the kitchen, his shirts, smeared and spattered with paint, flapped joyously on the line. Sometimes he stood behind Ruth while she painted and watched her so intently that she could feel colour rise up her neck till she had to plead with him to go away. He had delighted in the scandal of their love. 'Look at the way they greet us,' he had whispered in her ear as they walked through town, arms linked. His warm breath tickled her. 'An eye to our faces, then straight down to your waist, Ruth,' squeezing her. 'They're laying bets, I'll guarantee, on whether there'll be a christening before ever there's a wedding!' Then, with his mouth over her ear completely, 'What will it be then, Ruthie? A wedding or a baby, eh?' Harry had taught her to blush and to laugh; he also taught her that the future did not have to be an orderly line of predictable tomorrows, and for a while she almost believed him. Then when he died she knew that his lessons had been false ones.

When he died he took Paul away. She remembered how it was. Paul felt himself to blame, and Ruth in her grief could find no compassion for him. He hung about the house like a beaten dog for days, waiting for her forgiveness, while she briskly went about the task of tidying away Harry Lambe's life. Canvases were packed into boxes and shipped to England, to the family she had never met but whom she secretly hated, who had referred to her in letters as 'the colonial girl'. She burned Harry's painting clothes and brushes, and paint, and stowed his easel in the boxroom. His family sent her the photograph of Harry in uniform, as a kind of thanks, she supposed bitterly. She had hated the photograph when he'd had it done and refused the copy he offered her. 'Send it to your wretched family,' she'd said crossly. 'It's the way they want to see you!' Now they had sent it back.

Ruth wondered if she had ever really loved Paul. Certainly she had not loved him enough to forgive him.

She looked out across the front carriageway towards the gates and saw him, shirt untucked, hair like a haystack, swinging on the gates for all he was worth, shouting and hooting with delight. He had been a small child, but wiry and vigorous, full of fantasies. Full of the devil, really. Ruth stood up and walked around the room twice, considered bed, where Flora lay asleep breathing easily, then returned to the window with a sigh and waited for dawn.

Nonie listened to her aunt's footsteps. Forwards, backwards, circling slowly, pausing, then beginning the pattern again. She imagined her aunt's room as she had seen it that day—open, airy, comfortable in all its plainness. She pictured Flora propped up in bed being tended to. Perhaps that was what was happening now. Ruth was up there tending to Flora, talking to her, telling her things. She envied the easy way Flora accepted being cared for. Flora was like that. But not me, she thought, and wondered why. *Nonie is a different kettle of fish*, Ruth had said. Nonie churned over that remark. Her eyes ached and she closed them, but in the space behind her eyelids lay old familiar memories, waiting for her as they often were in the lonely night.

'Nonie, is that you?'
'Yes, Mumma.'
'You awake too?'
'Yes.'
'I can't find the tea caddy.'
'It's here.'
Her mother was holding onto a kitchen chair, casting about vaguely with her free hand. She seemed unsure of herself, and unsteady. Her dressing gown would not do up properly at the front, because of the baby coming. Nonie felt an ache inside at the thought of it.
'Can you fetch it, Nonie?'
Nonie stepped from the shadow of the doorway into the dim kitchen. There was a candle burning feebly on the kitchen table because there was no money for the gas. The open stove door gave off a glow. The kitchen trough was heaped with plates and a neat line of brown ants followed a course from the trough to the

windowsill. The tea caddy lay on its side on the kitchen table, its contents scattered. Nonie swept the tea leaves up carefully. Her mother watched, still standing irresolute, one hand on the kitchen chair.

'I need a cup of tea,' she said at last, in a slow thoughtful way. 'Can you make it, Nonie?'

'Yes, Mumma.'

Nonie found a cup in the trough. Lily said, after a while, 'Is it late? I meant to look at the clock.'

'Not very.' Nonie really did not know. She only knew the answer that her mother wanted to hear. She busied herself with the teapot, emptied the old leaves out through the kitchen window and carried it to the stove, watching her mother sideways, secretly. Lily had decided to sit down, but could not manage to pull the chair around. She stumbled, hesitated, then rallied and slid into a sitting position.

'I need a cup of tea,' she repeated.

'I'm making it, Mumma.'

'Are you? My Nonie making tea. You're a big girl.'

Nonie felt unreasonably happy. She lifted the kettle from the stove and burned her hands. That comes of being careless, she knew, of being too happy. She found a dishrag and tried again, pouring water into the teapot carefully, and adding fresh tea leaves after it.

'You have to warm the pot,' her mother said, but her back was turned to Nonie.

'I have,' replied Nonie, lying with confidence.

'How late do you think it is?'

'I don't know.'

'I meant to look at the clock. He said he'd be home before nine.' Nonie put the pot of tea on the table proudly, and set the cup beside it. 'Thank you, Nonie. You're a help. Have you got something on your feet?'

'It's all right. My feet are hot.'

Lily wasn't listening. Her head was resting on her hands. 'There might be a bit of milk left. Can you see?'

Nonie found the jug in the cupboard and looked under its muslin hood. She hesitated. If she gave her mother the milk there would be none for the morning. Elsie would cry and turn her head from the watery porridge. There would be the inevitable journey next door. 'Don't you give our food to that lot,' the grandmother would say, 'my son doesn't work all day to put food in the mouths of two families.' And Mrs Curran over her shoulder always said, 'Hold your tongue, Mother, I'll do as I see fit.' The billycan, quarter full, would be thrust into Nonie's hands, the door slammed, voices would be raised behind her as she ran home.

'Is there milk, Nonie?'

'A little bit.' As she withdrew it the jug knocked against the brandy bottle, which fell over noisily and began to spill onto the floor.

'What was that?'

'Nothing. It's all right.' She put the milk jug in front of her mother and turned back to confront the mess in a panic. If nothing else, the smell would give her accident away. She mopped the puddle with the dishrag and squeezed it out through the kitchen window after the tea leaves. Her mother was absorbed in pouring tea.

'Is that you, Paul?' she said once, looking up at the doorway.

'It's just me, Mumma.'

'He said he'd be home before nine.'

Nonie felt sick. The puddle of spilled brandy did not seem to be getting smaller, its smell was all over her hands. 'It isn't very late yet,' she reassured, swallowing a lump in her throat.

'That's right. It's not. A cup of tea is what I needed.'

'Yes.'

'I might have a little brandy with it. Can you see the bottle, Nonie?'

'Yes.' Tears sparked into Nonie's eyes and she battled them away. The bottle was nearly empty.

'Fetch me it.'

'I'll pour it for you.' She thought quickly, and emptied the contents of the bottle into a cup, then squeezed the dishrag on top of it. She placed the muddy liquid in front of her mother and said carelessly, 'There wasn't much left.'

Her mother drank from the cup without a flicker of surprise. 'What time is it?' she said.

'Not late.' The tears were back, scorching her, trying to escape.

'You're a good girl, my Nonie.'

'Yes, Mumma.'

They sat in silence for a while as the stove fire finally died and cold crept through the room. Lily sipped brandy and tea alternately, one hand propping up her head. She did not look at Nonie.

Then, abruptly, there was the familiar creak and thwack of the back screen door, and a voice in the hallway. Lily's head jerked upright. 'Paul? Is it you?' Her hands were patting her hair into place, pulling her dressing gown around her bulging tummy.

'It's me.' He sounded jaunty. There was the clump of his shoes being discarded onto the floor in the hall. 'Any tea on?'

Lily had hoisted herself onto her feet again. Her face had changed. It was glowing. Then she noticed Nonie and frowned. 'Why are you still up, Nonie? Off to bed. Quickly now.' She looked back towards the hallway and her frown vanished. Nonie's father was entering the kitchen, encircling her mother in his arms. Nonie melted into the shadows with her burnt hands, the smell of brandy all over her, and returned to bed.

She opened her eyes and was at Greystones again, lying in the emptiness of the bed that she usually shared with her sister. And her mother was in a pauper's grave, she remembered, and no one had ever told her where. There was movement outside. A breeze had risen and was meddling with the window panes. Nonie turned her head to the window and gazed at the night sky, at the torrent of stars, and the ice-white moon with a loose web of cloud drifting across it.

Consie Haggerty watched the moon as she stood at the kitchen door at Dingley. She had come out to make herself a cup of tea, just for something to do. She thought, if Stanley looks up tonight he will be looking at that same moon. Her fingers ached. This winter they had grown arthritic, although she continued to knit. But her Red Cross knitting mornings were becoming tedious. She would have thrown them in and carried on her knitting alone if it were not for Jackie who enjoyed the social occasions and the fuss they made of him.

She thought of the morning to come—scones and tea in someone's parlour, a warm fire and chat about this and that. How is Ned, Mrs Gannon? Fit and well now, thank the good Lord. Thank God, they all would murmur over their clicking needles. *Did you hear about Chester Poole, that young nephew of Maisie Birdwood, got his leg blown off in Ypres? Blown right off, they say.* Shame, shame, clickety, clickety, clickety click.

And what of Stan, Mrs Haggerty?

Stanley's well.

Stationed where?

Same place.

Brave lads, every one, that's the truth.

It is, it is, clickety click, clickety click.

Only it was not the truth. But the truth Consie Haggerty could not bring herself to tell. What would the ladies say if she did? 'Our Stanley didn't board his ship in Sydney. He ran away instead,' she might say. And in her mind's eye she could see the ladies' faces grow long with shock.

So she would keep it to herself for now, and tell the story only to herself. *Our Stanley won't come home, they'd come for him and lock him up if he did that. He won't even write, except just that once, for fear of being traced. And how he's making do I just can't say but I'm sick to the stomach every minute every day from worrying. And at night I never sleep. Our little Stanley's a deserter. You wouldn't be surprised if you heard it said of other lads, like Paul Field, who was never the reliable type. Yet Paul's at war, they say. And Stanley's lost.*

The kettle was making an angry rattle which finally captured Consie's attention. She closed the door, but not without a final look into the sky and a silent prayer for Stan.

Alec was watching the night sky too, and making plans. He would wait a day or two, perhaps a week, then head back into town early and grab the first train of the day. In the city you could be lost forever. Paul had done that—left, just like that, and never returned. Or he could go north, where there were farms needing hands, now that the war had taken away all the farmers' sons. He would never come back to the hills. Only thinking this filled him with unease. So he watched the sky and its storm of starlight, and reminded himself that at least this sight would not change, whatever direction he took.

13

Many the graves that lie behind the line
Scattered like shells upon a bloodstained strand,
Crosses and mounds that eloquently stand,
To mark a spot that forms some hero's shrine.

BEF TIMES, 1917

*P*hip, determined and resilient, was back at school by the end of the following week. The twins and Elsie walked to the Old School twice each week through the grey fog of early morning and back again in the gathering gloom of late afternoon, their boots crusted with mud, their clothing damp and their fingers chilled to numbness.

'They should all be at school,' announced Queenie on one of her visits as she looked critically over a pot of soup simmering on the stove in the Greystones kitchen. She added after a moment, 'Perhaps not Flora. But Nonie could benefit from mixing with a few other children, or she'll turn out too precious by half. And that boy needs a steadying hand.' She fixed a disapproving eye on Georgie, who was playing with a basket of potatoes.

Nonie was grateful that Ruth was not seriously influenced by the opinions of others, for the thought of attending school appalled her. Ruth said, 'The girls are a great help to me here.'

'They can do their work before and after school. They shouldn't be missing their lessons. They'll finish up idle as Kester. Mark my words.'

Kester, to Queenie's satisfaction and to the rest of the family's disappointment, had apparently ditched her job at the post office after an altercation with a customer. Now she was making beds at one of the big guesthouses in town, and hating it, but determined to remain independent. The events of Kester's life were relayed in instalments to Greystones. Nonie found herself looking forward to knowing what Kester's latest escapade had been. 'Our Kissie has pluck,' Bert Haggerty would say, shaking his head. Queenie's tone was rather more disparaging when she spoke of Kester, while Consie was always warm and wistful.

'The trouble is,' remarked Ruth to Hannibal as she mixed hot mash for the chickens, 'they will never let Kester be. They all spoiled her as a child—all those frilly frocks and the carry-on over her curls—and they'd still do it if they could. They'd make a proper wax doll out of her.'

Hannibal laughed. It occurred to Nonie that Hannibal did not often laugh aloud. This seemed proof of Kester's specialness, despite what Ruth said.

Ruth took Queenie's criticism to heart, however, and for a brief time prepared lessons in arithmetic and Latin grammar. Flora was a poor student, but Nonie was quick, and usually finished her own work and Flora's in a fraction of the time that Ruth expected. For want of suitable reading matter, Ruth had them read aloud each morning from the newspapers. In this way Nonie learned that the Russian royal family had been murdered by the Bolshevists, even down to the pet dog. 'There is madness in the world,' said Ruth.

'They shouldn't have killed the poor dog,' said Flora, fiercely, with tears in her eyes.

Ruth said, 'Or the children.'

'Why did they then?' asked Nonie. 'Why did the Bolshevists do it?'

'I expect because they were hungry. How can[...] Ruth folded the paper gently. 'I expect the Bols[...] children too.'

Queenie had called the anti-conscriptionists 'Bolshevists'. The thought that they were real murderers cast a new complexion on the mystery of Kester's missing brother. As to them having children, it did not seem to fit the picture at all. Nonie was surprised that Ruth should have even supposed it.

Winter rain began to fall in earnest. The kitchen garden turned to a slurry overnight, and the chickens huddled in the henhouse muttering hopelessly. Even when the rain paused for an hour or an afternoon the air stayed wet, and the mist that rolled down from the top of Mount St Leonard each evening held the hushed threat of snow. Henrietta and her kittens killed a sleepy snake in the woodshed and dragged it to the kitchen door to show off. Sometimes Ruth allowed the cats inside, and they wound themselves into complicated knots in front of the stove and slept like dead things. Every room was filled with washing laid out to dry. Banisters were draped with bedsheets amongst which the children built battlefields. The whole house smelled of carbolic.

On a still day, when the rain had held off for most of the morning, the Haggertys and Queenie arrived in the guesthouse drag. There had been plans afoot for some time, Nonie discovered, and they were being taken on an outing.

'Before the road gets too bad,' said Consie, lifting Georgie into her arms and hurrying into the house.

'Too late for that,' predicted Queenie. 'Should have gone a month ago. If you'd listened to me.' Only no one ever seems to listen to her, Nonie thought, which is probably why she is always so cross.

Ruth was dressed for an outing, in gloves and overcoat and brown felt hat. She called Jackie to load up some boxes that were standing by the kitchen door. 'Nonie, hurry now,' she said. 'Your coat, dear, and a scarf.'

Nonie looked around expecting her sister to ask the relevant question, but Flora was nowhere about. The twins and Elsie were at school, so whatever outing was planned did not, apparently, concern them. She went inside to fetch her coat, and found Consie already upstairs with Georgie, bundling him in a blanket.

'Where's Flora?' said Nonie.

Consie looked around. 'Oh, Flora won't be coming. She's in the kitchen with Queenie. Far too cold for her chest.'

Nonie buttoned herself into her coat, feeling disgruntled. Outside, Hannibal had joined the group around the drag. They loaded themselves in—Bert and Hannibal at the front, then Consie and Ruth with Georgie between them, and Nonie and Jackie at the back. Jackie smiled delightedly at her. He was wearing a ridiculous knitted hat, and a scarf which he proceeded to wind carefully around his whole face. 'Are we going into town?' she whispered to him.

'We're going to that other place,' he replied in a muffled voice. 'See them others, we are.'

Flora and Queenie came to the front door of the house to wave them away. 'Have a nice time,' called Flora, as Bert clicked the horses into motion. Nonie frowned at her diminishing figure. Then they turned onto the road and Greystones was obscured by the grey-green, dripping bush.

At first she tried to listen for hints about their destination in the adults' conversation, but Jackie chatted incoherently to her through a fuzz of wool and she had difficulty catching any of the talk that went on up the front. Eventually Georgie, bored where he was, struggled over the back to them shouting, and Nonie resigned herself to completing the journey in ignorance. Jackie produced a length of wool from one pocket and showed Georgie how to play cat's cradle. Consie called back to them from time to time, pointing out the crimson rosellas foraging in a soggy paddock, a pair of black cockatoos sweeping above. Twice Hannibal climbed down to ease the drag around a mud-filled hole. Its wheels made a sucking sound. The horses' hooves were stifled by mud, blackness crept up their shins, they snorted with the effort of the journey. They passed paddocks of wet incurious cattle, shaggy tethered goats, bedraggled orchards.

Closer to town the road carried more traffic. The horses minced nervously as they neared the station. A motor coach clattered past them. Nearby, at the seasoning works, men shouted as they loaded timber onto a waiting cart. The air was full of sound, and the smell of tar and timber and charcoal burning. Georgie was silenced by the sight of a train. He scrambled to Jackie's knee to get a better look. Nonie strained her ears. Ruth and Consie were talking about the big dam that was going to be built on the other side of town where the waterworks were. Jobs for everyone, they were saying, agreeing with one another, work for years to come.

'Will we see the waterworks?' she called.

Ruth sounded surprised. 'No, dear, the reserve is in the other direction.'

The reserve. Nonie felt triumphant for a moment, till she realised that she was no better off. What was this reserve, then? And where had she heard the word before? The drag pressed on across town, and onto another sodden track, full of potholes.

The native reserve lay to the south of the town, with the Badger Creek running through it. Mist drifted in its low-lying paddocks, even now, close to noon. The cleared land was waterlogged, its pasture ruined with bracken. Cattle gazed in silence as the drag passed through. Here and there the remains of a wooden trellis stood out, rickety and alone in a bare paddock, like a crucifix.

The drag pulled up near a row of wooden cottages, some with windows and doors boarded up, and picket fences that leaned drunkenly into overgrown gardens. A dog rushed out of a gateway barking, followed by a black woman in a faded dress and shabby boots. Nonie watched the woman approach. She was surprised to see Ruth alight from the drag and hug her.

'Ruth!'

'Mina!'

They hugged again. Bert and Jackie unloaded boxes while Hannibal hugged the woman too, and Ruth waved Nonie over to them. She approached with reluctance, envious of Georgie's comfortable excitement. He swung on the strange woman's hands. Clearly they had met before; Consie and Ruth and the woman called Mina commented on his stoutness with evident satisfaction.

'And here is Paul's oldest,' said Ruth. 'This is Nonie. Say hullo to Mrs Watts, dear.'

Nonie nodded her head awkwardly. The woman looked at her, then at Ruth. 'This is one for you.'

'She looks rather like Lily, we all think.'

'Maybe a bit.' She smiled at Nonie. 'My girl told me she met you.' Nonie frowned. 'You remember my girl?'

'Jessie?' It seemed obvious suddenly.

'She's my daughter.' Mina smiled at Nonie again, and Nonie flushed, confused, and looked away.

Then the conversation changed. How had the weather been out this way? The rains? Someone, whose son was at war, had written a long letter. There was a rumour all the boys coming home from the front would be given their own land, the government had promised.

'How is my father?' asked Hannibal, breaking in.

Mina considered her reply. 'Not too good today,' she said. 'He'll be better for seeing you.'

So Hannibal had a father, living here in this muddy, fog-drenched place. Nonie watched him walk away to a wooden cottage at the end of the row. The women were silent for a moment.

'Not long now,' said Mina quietly. They looked from one to the other.

There was a movement to one side of Nonie. She turned her head and Jessie was there, smiling her hard little smile. 'Hullo, Nonie,' she said. 'You came to visit.'

Mina said, 'There you are, Jessie Angeline. Say hullo nice to Mrs Consie and Miss Ruth.' There was an exchange of greetings again. The women commented for what seemed an eternity over Jessie's height, and her good health. 'You take Nonie for a walk,' suggested Mina at last. 'Look after her now.'

The girls eyed each other suspiciously. They watched the others file into Mina's house. Jackie and Bert were still wrestling with the boxes that had come in the back of the drag. There are clothes in the boxes, thought Nonie suddenly. Clothes and blankets and food. She remembered Ruth packing them. She looked sideways at Jessie quickly, and recognised the torn tunic as the one she had been wearing when they had met on the timber tram tracks near the mill. She had a scarf around her neck today, and she did not look healthy, despite Ruth's and Consie's exclamations. Her cheeks were hollow and her legs seemed even thinner.

'Where do you want to go?' she said to Nonie.

'I don't know.'

'I'll show you my school.'

'All right.'

'And my church.'

'All right.'

'Where are your sisters and brothers?'

'At school. Flora's at home with Auntie Queenie.'

There was a pause. Then Jessie said, 'I don't go to school any more.'

'Neither do I.' They exchanged a furtive glance.

They did not walk close by the wooden school buildings. They followed the road out of the little settlement, and Jessie pointed to things on the way—the dairy, the old kiln, the store, the church.

'Where is everyone?' asked Nonie. Jessie looked at her as though she did not understand the question. Nonie wondered if it were possible that Jessie could be unaware of the emptiness of the place. 'Do you have brothers and sisters?' she said at last.

Jessie said, 'That's what I'm showing you now.'

It was Nonie's turn not to understand. They walked along side by side in silence, their feet crunching on the gravel road. Nonie splashed deliberately through some puddles and Jessie grinned at her. Then they ran at the puddles, racing each other to be first, laughing uproariously when mud splashed up their legs, even onto their faces.

They had been following the road uphill. At the top a group of rivergums stood straight and still against the white sky with black pines growing between them, fenced about by pickets, like a misshapen crown. They came to the fence and stopped. Jessie leaned against it to get her breath. Nonie suddenly saw, with an awkward jolt of her heart, that they had arrived at a graveyard.

Jessie was in through the gate now, calling, 'Come on,' so she followed her. The sound of their footsteps was muted at once by the orange pine-needle carpet, but their breathing seemed louder. Nonie could hear her heart thumping.

'Why are we here?' she said, not wanting to look at the assembly of wooden crosses. Some were straight, some leaned, some had letters carved into the wood, while others were painted.

'I wanted to show you my brothers and sisters,' said Jessie. 'I told you. Look.' Nonie did not want to look, but she looked anyway. There was a row of crosses in a corner by the fence, with names carved into their horizontal bars. 'My dad did this,' said Jessie, crouching down. Her fingers traced the names. Jimmy Frederick, Joseph Alexander, Charles, 'he was born dead,' said Jessie, pausing over Charles, 'they named him quick. My dad and Mrs Robarts who came to help.' Her tracing finger moved on, Baby William, Annie Bella, 'this one is my sister. She got the whooping cough.'

'When?'

'Last winter.'

'How old was she?'

'Seven. Baby died a week after. Not me, though. I'm strong. Whooping cough can't get me.'

They stood in silence together with Jessie's family. Above them the pines were still, ribbons of bark drooped from the boughs of the rivergums.

Jessie said, 'Soon King is going to die. The doctor said so. He's got the cough. You know.' Nonie did not know, but she nodded. 'That's why we're still here,' added Jessie. 'They're letting us stay till he dies, see, because my mum looks after him. Then we got to go.'

'Where?'

'Another place. It's a long way away. We don't want to go. My mum says she'll never stop crying if we go.'

'Who says you have to?'

'Gov'ment.' Jessie turned away and began heading to the gate. They followed the path down the hill more quietly this time. Cold crept into Nonie's wet stockings, the end of her nose felt numb. Jessie coughed as they walked, and then spat into a clump of bracken—which surprised Nonie, it seemed such a grown-up, old-mannish thing to do. She felt a distance returning between them, but when she ventured a glance at Jessie, Jessie only grinned back.

The adults were arranging themselves into the drag when the two girls returned. Bert was fussing to Hannibal about the approaching dark. There was a mild drama over the state of the girls' clothing, until Consie insisted that it was only healthy to run about and keep warm. They all agreed that it was a stroke of luck that Queenie was not with them or they would never hear the end of it.

Nonie took her place in the back beside Jackie feeling uncomfortable in her muddiness. Mina Watts stood in the road with Jessie to wave them away. Just before Bert clicked the horses on, Jessie ran forward to Nonie and touched her knee. 'Do you know the Gov'ment?' she said quickly, half-whispering. Nonie shook her head. Jessie nodded and stepped away as the drag moved off. She did not wave.

Georgie slept on Consie's knee during the return journey and Jackie leaned his head to one side and seemed to doze. Nonie watched the shape of the trees grow dark and indistinct on either side of the road. She listened to the adults' conversation. Nothing was mentioned of the place they had been to; no mention of Jessie and Mina, or Hannibal's father dying in one of the cottages. Rain misted down coldly. There are some things that you never talk about, thought Nonie, things you never say even when you want to. There are things you never ask, even when you are old. Only, the questions stay in your head always and keep on asking inside you.

The Seed-Merchant has lost his son,
His dear, his loved, his only one.

AGNES GROZIER HERBERTSON

Nearly two weeks had passed since Flora and Phip had been lost in the bush. Nothing was said about it, neither among the adults in conversation, nor among the adults and the children. Even between themselves the children rarely mentioned the incident, only Nonie thought about it constantly. Sometimes she looked at Flora and wondered if Flora remembered what had happened. Flora gave no sign of remembering. Someone from the *Healesville Guardian* arrived on the doorstep one cold morning, looking for a heartwarming family story, and was given short shrift by Ruth. Then, when things at last seemed to be settling down, Greystones received another visitor.

The sound of an unfamiliar vehicle driving through the gates brought the children. Hannibal stood at the stable door too, a sack of chaff resting at his feet, and watched as the stranger pulled up his pony trap and alighted—a small man, middle-aged, with a shiny face and neat boots. He whistled to the twins, who looked surprised, and approached him cautiously. 'I'm after Miss Ruth Field,' he said. 'Your aunt, is she?' They nodded. 'Fetch her out then, lads. You can tell her that Cec Canning is here to speak to her.'

The name caused Nonie to pause where she stood in the shadow of the verandah, and glance across the carriageway to the stable. Hannibal had heard the name too. He shouldered the bag of chaff quietly and returned to his business. It was the name of the shopkeeper from town, the one whose store Hannibal had avoided because it had been robbed by a man from the reserve. Nonie flushed, remembering. Bert Haggerty had said that Cec Canning was 'nervy', although what he meant by that Nonie could not imagine. This man looked thoroughly ordinary, really, in his small tidy way, a man who would fit well in a storekeeper's apron.

Ruth appeared around the side of the house from the kitchen, untying her pinafore and carefully laying it over one arm. She, too, had been alerted by the sound of the approaching horse. 'How do you do,' she said. 'I am Ruth Field. I'm afraid I have not had the pleasure.'

'Cec Canning, Miss.' He removed his hat and revealed a pointed, balding head with two or three strands of hair combed carefully across it. The twins giggled at the sight of his naked head. 'I've got a shop in town. You might of heard.'

Ruth said, 'Have you been in the district long?'

'Twelve years, ma'am.'

'Ah.' Nonie guessed that Ruth did not consider twelve years to be any significant time at all.

'Don't see you in town, Miss Field.'

'Not often, no.'

A flash of irritation crossed Cec Canning's face suddenly. Nonie wondered if Ruth were trying to annoy him. Certainly she had not shown him more than the barest courtesy. 'I'll come to the point, Miss Field,' he said sharply. 'I would like to speak to you about the two children who got lost just recently. Your brother's children, aren't they?'

Ruth drew herself up, but only said, 'Yes.'

'Your brother at war, then?'

'Yes.'

'Their mother dead?'

'Yes, Mr Canning.'

The barrage of questions stopped. A shadow of softness slipped across Cec Canning's angular face.

'I'm a widower myself, Miss Field, these last eight years. Four children of my own.'

'I'm sorry.' Ruth felt for loose pins in her hair, awkwardly.

'Grown up now. Lost two at the war.'

'I'm terribly sorry.'

'They enlisted on the same day. Only a year between them in age, see. Ernest was the eldest, then came Sid. They went down on the same day, too. Pozières. Second Division. Fourth Field Artillery.'

'Mr Canning, I'm most dreadfully . . .'

'It's a battle that will be remembered, Miss Field, that's the thing. So my boys will be remembered too. I'm proud of them. Their GSO sent home a personal letter enclosing his sympathy. It was the horses, see. Both my lads were fond of animals. Sid's horse got stuck in mud, pulling a full load of ammunition. Sid wouldn't abandon the horse—that's what his GSO wrote—and Ern went to help him pull the beast out of the mud. Same shell got the two of them. They were popular lads, their GSO said. Especially Sid. Something of a humorist was Sid.'

Ruth said nothing.

'My girl Winnie is in Melbourne. Got her first aid certificate.' He spoke in short stabbing sentences, dourly, but he did not seem to want to stop. 'Young Reg, our last, is in France now. Sappers.'

Ruth looked at the ground. The twins shifted and kicked each other. Cec Canning glanced at them. 'I'll get to the point, Miss Field,' he said returning to his former tone. 'I would like to speak to you about the incident with your children in the bush.'

Ruth rallied. 'They were found safely, Mr Canning . . .'

'So I believe.'

'. . . by their sister . . .'

'I've heard otherwise.'

There was a silence then. Cec Canning took in the silence. At the other end of the verandah from Nonie, Flora coughed. Georgie grizzled to Elsie to play with him. Something inside Nonie sprang to life. She stepped forward on an impulse, out of the shadows. Ruth said, 'Perhaps we should go inside, Mr Canning.'

'Very well, Miss Field.' He looked triumphant. His eyes shifted and found Nonie's face as he followed Ruth across the verandah and in through the front door of the house. They rested there for a moment.

The other children drifted back to play, except for Flora, who remained huddled on the verandah, coughing. Nonie crept around the side of the house and through the kitchen door. From the parlour came the sound of Cec Canning's voice. He was saying a great deal, Ruth's voice only occasionally interjecting. Nonie crouched at the foot of the staircase and listened to them.

'. . . idle gossip!'

'Not in my opinion, Miss Field, if you'll forgive me, from the doctor's own mouth. One of your young ones was speaking, half-asleep . . .'

'Flora was extremely ill . . .'

'. . . and mentioned certain things. I don't need to remind you of the seriousness of the charge. This should be a police matter, Miss Field. Dangerous criminals should not be allowed to remain at large. Might I remind you that it is an offence to protect criminals?'

'If I believed for one moment . . .'

Mr Canning did not sound interested in Ruth's protests. 'That is why I should like to have a word with the children involved,' he continued, over her voice. 'Once I have enough information I will place the matter in police hands.'

'I don't think . . .'

'If the children remember nothing then we will let the matter rest.'

Ruth seemed to hesitate. Then she said stiffly, 'Very well.' There was a grunt of satisfaction from Cec Canning. Ruth's footsteps moved towards the doorway. Nonie shot off the step and flew back to the kitchen, where Ruth found her a few seconds later.

'Nonie.' Ruth did not seem to notice her breathlessness. 'I need you to come and speak to Mr Canning. Fetch Flora and Phip.'

'Excuse me, Miss Field.'

Ruth turned around to find that the storekeeper had followed her down the hall and out to the kitchen. 'Yes?' she said with forbearance.

'I would like to have a word with your man, too. Hannibal is his name, is it?'

Ruth remained silent for a ghastly second, but a rage like a roaring fire seemed to ignite her whole body so that she nearly shook with it. Nonie felt a jolt pass through her. Her heart raced. Mr Canning remained unmoved, but his eyes took on a veiled quality, hiding a moment of fear.

Ruth said quietly, 'Hannibal is not "my man". Hannibal is a member of my family, Mr Canning.'

'I would like a word,' repeated Mr Canning belligerently.

Ruth looked back to Nonie. 'Do as you are told, Nonie,' she said.

Nonie rounded up Flora and Phip and sent Elsie after Hannibal. They presented themselves in the parlour where Mr Canning was now seated. Flora hung back near the door, like a coward, thought Nonie suddenly, angrily, Flora is a stupid coward. Tom came in with his brother. Ruth introduced the children then turned away to the mantelpiece. Mr Canning surveyed them. 'Young Philip. Which lad are you?'

'Me,' said Tom brightly.

'Now then. I would like you to tell me if you remember any person, other than your sister, finding you when you were lost.'

Tom thought. 'No,' he said at last, smiling.

Nonie kicked him and he kicked back harder. The ruckus brought Ruth's attention from the mantelpiece. 'What is going on?'

'Tom is pretending to be Phip.' Nonie scowled at the twins. They grinned back. Mr Canning looked irritable. Ruth looked bewildered. The twins were not identical.

Ruth said, 'Phip, just do as you are told.'

Phip shrugged. 'I can't remember nothing.'

'Anything.'

'Anything. It was dark.'

Mr Canning frowned. 'You must have seen someone.' Phip shrugged again.

Ruth said, rather quickly, 'Off you go then, both of you.' The twins clattered off, nudging one another.

'I feel sick,' said Flora after they had gone. 'Can I go outside too?'

'First I would like you to answer Mr Canning's questions.'

'I can't remember anything either.'

'Wasn't there a man with you?' Mr Canning leaned forward in his chair. 'Come on, you can tell me, wasn't there a darkie, called Alec? Wasn't that it?'

Hannibal appeared in the doorway behind Flora. He hesitated, then stepped around her and into the room. The grandfather clock tolled the hour.

'Come on now, you do remember.'

'I don't!' Flora clutched Nonie's arm. Nonie pulled away.

'I want you to tell me the truth!'

'I am.'

'What does God think of liars?'

Flora began to cry. Ruth twitched. Nonie saw her look to Hannibal. She could not see Hannibal's face from where she stood. She wondered if Hannibal were looking back. 'Come on,

116

girlie,' pressed Mr Canning, breathing the words rather than speaking. 'You saw a black man and spoke to him.'

'I am telling the truth,' blazed Flora. 'I am. i am. Auntie Ruth, I feel sick!'

Ruth said, 'Go and lie down. You'll be all right.'

Flora turned blindly, bumped into a chair and veered to one side through the parlour door. They heard her ascending the stairs crying and coughing. Ruth said, 'Well, Mr Canning, if you have heard enough . . .'

'I would still like to speak to the eldest girl.' He seemed unperturbed by Flora's display of emotion. He turned his attention to Nonie. She looked at the floor.

'Now then.' Mr Canning addressed her gently enough. 'You've been quite the hero, haven't you? Where did you actually find your brother and sister?'

'At the creek.' Her voice surprised her by its smallness.

'Were you all alone when you found them?'

'Yes.' In front of her she saw not the parlour, but the black bush, and Alec's face close to hers; she felt the hot brush of his breath.

'There was someone else, though, I know there was, and you know too.'

Mr Canning's voice suggested a complicity that bewildered her. Nonie looked up for help, but Ruth was staring at her hands and Hannibal was behind her, still as a statue. 'I don't understand,' she said.

'Well, you must understand. Nothing simpler.' He stood up and moved closer to her. 'It's important to me and to the police, too.'

'Why?'

'Because the man you saw is a dangerous criminal.' Mr Canning spoke slowly, emphasising each word. He watched Ruth and Hannibal while he spoke. 'He is the man who broke into my shop some months back. The same man who six months ago broke the jaw of an honest white man in town, in order to steal from his pocket, and he knocked Henry Livesay out in a drunken fight last year, so that Henry had to be taken to hospital by train with serious head injuries and died three months later without ever becoming conscious!' The words exploded from his mouth. 'The police did their best to hunt him down that time, only he's craftier than a fox. They said he must have left the district. But he didn't, did he? You know, don't you? There, you have it now, young miss.'

Nonie hesitated. 'There might have been someone,' she said, and from the corner of her eye noticed Ruth shift her feet.

'I don't want "mights".' Cec Canning stepped back a little, challenging her.

'I don't know.'

'Of course you know, girl!' He lowered his voice again. 'Don't you want to help the police? And be rewarded for your help?'

Nonie's mind began to tick over in a hurry. Yes, if she told this man about Alec she would be a real hero. She would be protecting them all, and Hannibal, because if the police took him away Alec would not be able to kill Hannibal as he said he would. Why was she hesitating? There was something in Ruth's movement, and in Hannibal's silence, that held her back. Why would they never speak about that night? Only Mr Canning wanted to speak about it; so only Mr Canning could explain. Ruth did not understand, she could not possibly. Nonie gulped her fears down. 'Yes,' she said. 'There was a man there—his name was Alec.'

'Yes!' Mr Canning shouted in his excitement.

'His name was Alec,' she repeated unsteadily. 'And he said he would stick a knife in Hannibal's back if . . .'

But Mr Canning was not interested in details. He was moving through the door without a backward glance, out of the house and into his pony trap. Nonie heard him depart, urging the pony through the gates, a frenzied clattering and crunching of horse's hooves and cart wheels on the gravel. There was a lump in her throat. 'What will happen now?' she asked without moving.

'I expect that Mr Canning will call in the police and they'll search the bush for him,' replied Ruth.

'Yes. They'll probably do that.' Hannibal's voice was a remote echo.

'I expect he's gone.' said Ruth, but the statement seemed really a question and hung in the air unresolved.

Nonie looked at them. Ruth was staring at the floor and Hannibal was motionless. 'I didn't think it would come to this,' Ruth said to him, without looking up.

'Neither did I.'

'If we had said something . . . done something . . .'

'Done what?'

'I'd forgotten the way word travels, the way people are. I mean . . . the doctor! Of all people! Flora must have said the name in her sleep. She was speaking, I remember now, I should have taken more notice . . . I didn't think . . .'

'Ruth.'

'He seemed so busy, so concerned with Flora's breathing, how could he have listened and made those assumptions and not said anything?'

'Ruth.' When Ruth looked up at him he made a gesture with his hand, as if to calm her. Then he shook his head slightly, straightened up and turned to the door.

Nonie called out after him. 'Hannibal.' He stopped and looked at her, a surprised look, as though he had forgotten she was there. She said, 'He did say that. He really did. He said he'd . . .'

'I know.' Hannibal waved her away. He closed the door behind him.

Nonie said, 'I don't understand. I don't understand anything.'

'It's all right,' said Ruth. 'You haven't done anything wrong.'
She started across the room, murmuring about dinner. Nonie
rushed after her.

'Auntie Ruth!' She grabbed her aunt's arm. 'Who is he? Who
is Alec? Why does it matter like it does?'

'He's Hannibal's brother,' Ruth said. 'Alec is Hannibal's
brother.'

15

I am the enemy you killed, my friend,
I knew you in this dark; for so you frowned
Yesterday through me as you jabbed and killed
I parried; but my hands were loath and cold
Let us sleep now . . .

WILFRED OWEN

It was through a haze of misery that Nonie witnessed the arrival of the local police. They wanted to question the children again, but this time Ruth was firm. She insisted that Flora was too ill, Phip too young and Nonie too distraught. So they left Greystones with no further information and set up a rough camp at the timber mill, from where they intended to conduct their search. There were two black men in the search party.

'Why are they there?'

'They are from the reserve,' replied Ruth, not quite answering the question. She folded clean linen doggedly. Nonie trailed around the house after her.

'Will they help the police to find him?'

'Probably.'

'Why will they?'

'Because they must.'

'Will Hannibal help them?'

Ruth did not answer. Her lips tightened for a second, then she gave a wry smile. 'Hannibal will not be here if they call. He is very clever at disappearing. He is like your father that way.'

Ruth's apparent calmness filled Nonie with confusion; it burst out in a geyser of helpless rage suddenly. 'Why couldn't you tell me?' she begged her. 'If I'd known about Alec I would never . . .'

'It wasn't my business to tell you. Alec did not tell you; it wasn't your business to know. Can't you understand that?' Ruth turned her head away. 'And Hannibal and I, how could we know that Mr Canning would begin to pry? No, that's not what I mean . . . I mean . . .' she shrugged her shoulders, a gesture of despair.

'He said those things about hurting Hannibal, I didn't make it up. He said he would stick a knife . . .'

'But he didn't mean it!' Ruth said abruptly. 'I know what he said . . . I can imagine, you don't have to keep telling us . . . but he didn't mean it! It was just madness, anger . . .' Nonie's absolute stillness stopped her. She hesitated, then touched Nonie's shoulder. It was an unsettling action. 'You look flushed. Are you all right?'

'I have a headache.' She had a terrible ache in her stomach too, but she did not mention that.

'Nonie, you weren't to know. You did nothing wrong. No one expected you to lie.'

'Flora lied.'

'Flora cannot remember anything. Nor can Phip.'

Nonie knew that Ruth was wrong and she knew that Ruth knew it too. It was like a strange game that they were all playing, only somehow she had not fully grasped the rules. Ruth said, 'It is not right to protect a criminal.'

'Alec?'

'Alec is just as Mr Canning described. He did break into Mr Canning's store, and all those other things, many things. He is responsible for Henry Livesay's death.'

'But he is still Hannibal's brother,' said Nonie bitterly. They were both distracted as the kitchen door was flung open and the twins tumbled in, shouting. Dogs were out in the bush; the hunt had begun.

Once again the bush around Greystones echoed to the sound of voices. The baying of hounds rang out on the crisp winter air. 'There'll be a fog tonight,' said Hannibal to Ruth when he brought in the milk. Ruth did not reply. In the late afternoon two shots clapped out across the paddocks. Ruth jumped but kept kneading dough, only a little more vigorously than usual. Tom, Elsie and Georgie hung over the gate to the house paddock, staring excitedly down to the creek, seeing criminals behind every tree, police and dogs behind every bush. Flora sat hunched over a bowl of steaming water, coughing, and Nonie hid in the stable.

'Someone's been killed!' shouted Phip, running into the kitchen.

Ruth was feeling hot in spite of the chill of the day. 'Perhaps not,' she said. 'They might be signalling, or a gun has gone off by accident.'

Phip did not wait to listen to possibilities. He ran past her into the house calling for Flora. Ruth re-pinned her hair methodically and returned to the business of making bread.

Evening unfolded and the fog that Hannibal predicted rolled in, damp and silent, a sea of white that lapped against the trees in silent waves, blanketing everything. The police and volunteers cleared back to their base camp till first light. On the way they stopped at Greystones to buy bread and milk and tea and pass on the latest information. They had sighted Alec and fired, wounding him, but he had slipped away. Tomorrow they would close in. 'There's no accounting for it,' said the constable at the door. 'If it were me, I would have cleared out of the district months ago. These blacks always stay on their patch, that's the thing. Poor devils.'

Hannibal often stayed in the big house for meals, and afterwards played a hand of cards with Ruth, or sat and read the papers that Bert Haggerty had dropped off. Tonight he did not come in for a meal. Nonie looked through the bedroom window and saw lamplight shining fuzzily through the fog from the little cottage. Ruth had been born there, Hannibal too.

'Where was Alec born?' she said.

Ruth paused a moment turning down the cot blankets for Elsie and Georgie to climb in. 'Alec was born at the reserve,' she answered. Nonie waited to hear more, but Ruth, after tucking the children in neatly, left the room. Nonie followed her downstairs into the parlour. She stood at the door and watched her aunt stoke the fire and rearrange partly dry washing.

'Why wasn't Hannibal born at the reserve then?' she said.

Ruth shrugged slightly. 'No special reason. His father worked for my father here. It was too far to go home to the reserve during the harvest, so he stayed on, with Bella—she was Hannibal's mother—and Alec was with them of course. She died.'

'Hannibal's mother?'

'She died of consumption. We didn't expect Hannibal to live. My mother took him in. He would have died otherwise, there were so many dying at the reserve. When King and Alec went back after harvest, we kept Hannibal with us.' Ruth looked at Nonie in the firelight and remembered herself at a similar age with Hannibal balanced on her hip, serenely plump, his coal-black eyes, his absolute trust. And where was Alec in those days? Ignored mostly, she remembered with a pang, trailing after his father across the paddocks, a little, thin boy doing a man's work in the fields.

Nonie toyed with a photograph. 'Where was my father then?' she said.

Ruth busied herself with the washing again. 'Oh well, he came along a little later, a great surprise. My mother had given up hope of having another child of her own, and suddenly . . .'

'Did you give Hannibal back?'

'What?'

124

'When my father was born, did you give Hannibal back?'

'You can't just give a child back. Just like that.'

'But you kept him, just like that. So couldn't you give him back to his own family, when the new one came?'

Ruth stopped what she was doing. 'We couldn't have given him back,' she said sharply. 'He belonged to us.' She lifted a bundle of dry sheets and turned to the door.

'Auntie Ruth . . .'

'Yes?'

'It . . . it doesn't matter.' Nonie flushed. She showed Ruth the photograph she was holding. 'Is that Mr Lambe—Dadda's tutor?'

Ruth lifted the photograph from Nonie's hands and seemed to examine it. 'Yes. Yes, it is.' She placed the photograph back into shadow and walked away quickly. Nonie waited till her aunt's footsteps were faint, then she put her hand up under her dress and, bringing it out, found it stained with blood. So this is what happens, she thought, when you are bad enough God sends a punishment just like the sisters always said. This then was her punishment. The grandfather clock tocked, the fire crickled and spat. From upstairs came the sound of Flora coughing. Nonie walked quietly out of the room and through the front door.

Fog hugged the house, breathed its snowy breath around Nonie as she hesitated on the verandah, sucked her into its whiteness. She took a few cautious steps, and looking back saw the house recede from sight, then a few more steps and it was gone. She walked further and saw the stable doors loom up through the shifting whiteness. To her right, she knew, was the fence that bordered the kitchen garden. She sought it, hand outstretched, and it was there after a few paces, a comforting roughness under her palm. It guided her down to the icy wire of the house paddock fence and she felt her way along this till she came to the gate. She climbed up and sat there, surveying the nowhere of mist that swirled around her, numbed by cold outside and by grief within. They hate me, she thought, they will never not hate me. Flora knew how to be loved; she knew without asking what to do and say to make herself wanted. The sisters had loved and wanted her, but their kindness had turned to ice upon Nonie. She had tried to do the right thing by telling about Alec, to show them how she cared, to save Hannibal, to be the hero that their father was. Thinking this she was wretched with despair suddenly. Why should she have wanted to be a hero anyway, what good did it do them if her father was a hero a million miles away? She slid from the gate into the house paddock, felt ground beneath her, slimy and soft, and began to run, not wanting to breathe. Only she had to breathe, and when she did her breath came out in a moan and her stinging eyes and pounding heart demanded that she surrender. But she would not; not ever. She stopped running, breathed deep, compelling her body to be still. Her whole crashing world paused with her and froze into stillness.

The peace lasted only an instant. It shattered as she stood there, breathing, and became the slosh of feet in water-logged pasture, the thud of a body stumbling, ragged breaths. There was a flurry of leaves, then silence again. Nonie knew what the sound was. She picked her way toward it and soon the solid shape of the peppercorn tree materialised before her. Its branches drooped to the ground in a curtain, leaves patted gently along her body as she passed through. At the foot of the knobbly old trunk was another shape, shrouded in shadow, barely moving.

'Alec,' she said.

Her voice was like a clap of thunder in the silence. The shape unwound itself and sprang at her. For a second she saw Alec upright, slightly hunched, and then she was pinned beneath him on the icy earth, her hair gripped in his hands, her head pulled back. She could not make a sound. His eyes examined her at close range and slowly registered recognition. The hold on her hair relaxed, his head moved away. She could see his face now, shining with sweat, and blood. There was mud in his hair. 'What are you doing here?' he hissed.

'I . . . I just came here . . . the police . . .'

His grip strengthened. He jerked her head back and she winced. 'What about the police?'

'They're up at the mill waiting for the fog to lift.'

'I know where they are.' He dropped his hold abruptly and rolled sideways. She scrambled clear.

'I didn't know who you were,' she rushed out. 'I promise I didn't know.' There was no answer. He had curled up again, blended himself into the dark of the tree trunk, his head bowed deep in the turned-up collar of his coat. 'Alec?'

'Bugger off.' His voice sliced through the fog.

She turned away, irresolute, and turned back again. 'Let me help you,' she said. 'Please, I'll do anything.' There was no reply. She edged toward him and knelt down, searching the shadow for his face. His eyes blinked open above his collar, startling her so that she almost fell backwards. There was a knot in her chest getting bigger, making it difficult for her to speak. 'I can help,' she managed to repeat. 'I know you're hurt.' The eyes glared at her. 'I didn't know,' she bleated suddenly. 'I didn't know you were Hannibal's brother!'

For an awful moment she thought that he was laughing, then she realised that he was coughing. He spat onto the ground and drew in a long breath, throwing his head backwards to do so. 'I'm not,' he said. 'Paul is Hannibal's brother.'

She did not know what to say then. She fumbled hopelessly in the pockets of her dress. 'I . . . I've got a hanky,' she said. 'You can have it for the bleeding.' She could not find the handkerchief. She felt faint, helpless, dangerously out of control. 'Just tell me what to do!' she burst out. 'Please, please, I'll do anything!'

His hand appeared out of the hump of shadow and snatched at her arm, unbalancing her again, silencing her at once. 'Want to help?'

'Yes.'

'Get me a gun.'

'I-I don't know where . . .' The suggestion chilled her.

'At your place. Must be a gun somewhere.'

'I don't . . .' She tried to think. Yes, there was a gun. She had seen it, once, twice, in Hannibal's hands. Hannibal had used it to shoot rabbits, and when one of Minnie's calves had been born deformed. 'I don't know where it's kept.'

'The stable.'

'I don't think . . .'

His hand shook her. 'What about the cottage?'

'I don't . . .' Yes, it would be in Hannibal's cottage. She remembered now. She had seen Hannibal taking it there.

Alec read her hesitation accurately. 'Yes. That's where. You get it. Hear me?' She nodded. 'And ammunition. Make sure.'

'What if . . .'

'If you can't find it, get me a knife.'

'Don't you want food?'

'I want a gun!' he hissed, close to her face. 'No gun, then knife. You understand?'

'Yes.'

He shoved her away abruptly. She struggled to her feet, shaking, pushed blindly through the curtain of leaves, and stumbled back into the fog.

16

*But Death replied: 'I choose him'. So he went
And there was silence in the summer night;
Silence and safety, and the veils of sleep.
Then, far away, the thudding of the guns.*

SIEGFRIED SASSOON

The cottage was empty. Nonie stood outside it, staring into the fuzzed orange glow of the lamplight, until she was sure. But there was no sound, no stirring, not a suggestion of movement in the little two-roomed place. Hannibal was at the house then, as usual, reading the papers with Ruth. The lamp had been left on to show him his way home later. Nonie was glad of the lamp too. She had never entered Hannibal's cottage, not even dared to peep through its door. Now she must, and quickly, before she had time to think too much and lose her nerve. She pushed open the cottage door and stepped inside.

The first thing she felt was a wave of caressing warmth from the small iron stove that sat in the fireplace down one end of the main room. There were a table and three chairs in front of the stove, two armchairs on an old oriental rug, a chest in one corner and a dresser against the wall stacked with cups and plates. She was not surprised by the orderliness of the place, that was Hannibal, but she was amazed by something else. The walls were hung from end to end with enormous paintings. The walls in the big house were bare but here the walls were a riot of colour, an unexpected, exotic, splendid vision. She guessed

129

that they were Harry Lambe's, done while he was living at Greystones and tutoring. There was the big house, dappled in summer light; there, a view of Mount St Leonard wearing a halo of storm clouds; here, a young woman filled a basket with apples in the orchard; and there was the peppercorn tree on the hill, tossed in the wind, with the bush in a tangle of darkness beyond it. Beneath the painting of the peppercorn tree, leaning against the dresser, stood Hannibal's shotgun.

Nonie forgot the paintings at once. Her hands shook as she lifted the shotgun from its resting place. She opened dresser drawers and found, among knives and forks and string, a cardboard box of shotgun cartridges. She fumbled a handful into her pockets, while others clattered to the wooden floor and rolled rumbling into cracks or made clunking noises against the dresser's metal feet. The sound was terrifying. It called attention to her actions; it called her a thief. She grasped the shotgun firmly to her chest and rushed out through the door of the cottage.

She ran without feeling her feet, or hearing anything except her hammering heart. She collided with the kitchen garden fence, caught her breath, and pressed on again clutching the rough wood railing for comfort as much as for guidance. Suddenly a shape rose out of the fog. She had no time to turn away. 'Hannibal.'

'It's all right. It's only me.' But it was not all right and they both knew it.

She struggled to stay calm. 'I'm just going . . . just going to get . . .' She could not think of a suitable lie.

'Where is he?' Hannibal's voice startled her.

'What?'

'Where is Alec?'

'Alec?' She did not know what to do. She felt that she would burst with despair.

'Tell me.'

'I don't know.' She edged sideways, holding the shotgun low, close against her. She could not tell if he could see it. 'I left my cardigan . . . I'm just going . . .' She began to run but he had overtaken her in a few seconds, stopping her in her tracks.

'Nonie! *Where is he?*'

'I don't know what you mean.'

He said suddenly, desperately, 'You've got his blood on your clothes! You can't play games like this with real people—games of heroes and rescuings and . . .' He was speechless. It was the moment of weakness that, instinctively, she had been waiting for. In one last surge of will, Nonie sprang forward, dodging him, and went careering down to the house paddock gate under the blanket of fog.

Alec was no more than a shadow beneath the peppercorn tree. He had rolled himself up tight. Nonie fell beside him. 'Alec! I've got it! Alec!'

He unwound. A hand reached out for the shotgun and snatched it up. She emptied ammunition from her pockets into his free hand. He was breathing in a shallow gasping way, murmuring, then quite abruptly his breathing stopped for a few seconds and his face contorted with pain.

'Alec?' She was startled. 'Are you all right? I can get anything you want, bandages, or . . .'

'Bugger off, girlie,' he said, pulling himself upright and leaning unsteadily against the tree trunk.

She was bewildered. 'What will you do, though?' He did not bother to answer her and she knew before she had finished speaking what he was intending. His hands caressed the gun barrel, the stock, appreciatively. She knew that with the gun in his hands he felt strong again, he felt that escape was possible again, and he would not hesitate to shoot anyone who stood in his way. She began to back off. 'Please, I'm going now. I got it . . . I'll go away now.'

'That's right, Nonie. Go.'

They both swung about at the same moment and there stood Hannibal. Of course, she had been a fool to believe she could have dodged him so easily. She had led him to Alec, like a dog on the trail of a rabbit. Now he walked past her. Alec, fumbling for the trigger in his surprise and not finding it, simply lunged forward and thudded against Hannibal. The two men fell together, their hands locked at each other's throat, grunting and struggling. Hannibal's voice choked out, 'Alec! For God's sake, let up!', but the struggling continued.

Nonie's dazed head began to clear, she began to distinguish shapes in the murky dark under the peppercorn tree—a foot, a fist—a fist clutching a shotgun, feeling for the trigger, directing the barrel awkwardly, one-handed, into Hannibal's back. She found her feet in a new rush of terror and fell against the two bodies, pushing the shotgun out, out, away from the knot of human flesh. Alec shouted, even Hannibal's voice rose swearing, but she continued to grapple with the hand that held the shotgun, tumbling against the men's sweating bodies, till the hand yielded and the weapon fell from its grip. She grabbed it up and flung it away from her, as far as she could, and heard it thud to the ground some distance away in the sea of fog.

Alec and Hannibal were on their feet now, glaring at each other.

'Bastard!' Alec rocked unsteadily. He was covered in his own blood. It gleamed through his shirt front, dripped from his fingers. 'You bastard!'

'Please!' Nonie leapt in front of him as he lurched towards Hannibal again. 'I did what you said. I got what you wanted . . .'

'Nonie, go home.' Hannibal's voice was more angry than she had ever heard it.

'But Alec might . . .'

'Go home! Just do as I say! Haven't you done enough?'

She was stunned by his hardness. She shrank away from him into the shelter of the drooping leaves but could not turn, could not make her feet carry her down the hill away from them.

Alec was laughing, or choking, perhaps both. His body slumped against the tree trunk, slid down a little. 'Paul's little girl loves you,' he taunted. 'Doesn't want this bad blackfeller hurt Paul's whitefeller brother.'

'Alec, leave her alone. She doesn't understand.'

'What don't she understand?'

Hannibal wiped his face slowly. 'She's only a child.'

Alec tried to laugh again. He slipped further down the tree trunk, tried to hold himself upright, but could not. Hannibal moved towards him, tentatively at first then with greater confidence. Alec was on the ground now. Hannibal knelt at his side and began to pull open the buttons on Alec's bloody shirt. Alec's hand flew up to push him away but had no strength to do so. His hand closed around Hannibal's wrist instead, and stayed there. The two brothers looked into each other's face for a long time. Then Hannibal roused himself, took his hand out of Alec's grip and returned his attention to opening the buttons on Alec's shirt, slowly, determinedly, searching for the source of the bleeding.

'Too late for that,' rasped Alec. Hannibal did not answer him. He pulled off his own jacket, rolled it up and held it against the wound on Alec's chest. He looked smaller, younger in his shirtsleeves and braces. He trembled in the cold. Alec said, 'You can't save me.'

'Not on my own. But I can get Ruth. Ruth and I . . .' He sounded so unsure. Nonie ached to hear the tremor in his voice.

Alec shifted and coughed and grunted, trying to laugh at him. 'Ruth and you. You and Ruth. You still waiting for Ruth to see you?'

'Alec.'

'You fool, she don't see you. You just Paul's brother.'

'Alec.'

'Ruthie's brother.'

'I'm not! I never was!' His voice rose suddenly, helpless, exasperated. 'I can't change what they did. When our mother died they took me in. You know how it was!'

Alec's eyes moved slowly over Hannibal's face. Hannibal looked away. 'You remember our mother?'

'You know I don't.'

'That's what's wrong with you,' said Alec.

Silence settled over them like a heavy weight. Mist swirled between them and hung. Nonie could hear her own breathing and the erratic gasping breaths Alec took as he lay in the silence, his head resting on Hannibal's arm. Then Alec shifted sharply and began to cough. 'Do you want to watch me die?' he shouted out, trying to cover his pain. 'Bugger off, you, and take Paul's brat with you!'

Hannibal continued to kneel. He said at last, slowly. 'You're losing so much blood. If we can . . .'

'What do you know about it, white boy?'

'You don't have to die. We can get help.'

'I don't want help.'

'Alec.'

'They wouldn't let me go to war. Bad lungs, they said. They won't let me die that way. They'd rather I hung. You want me to hang?'

'Alec.'

'I'll die the way I want. Better than a soldier. Better than Paul Field.'

'Leave Paul out of it.'

'Why? It's him killed me. Him and you. White-haired Paul and his black brother.' He tossed his head angrily side to side, coughed and spat weakly. Hannibal wiped the blood from his brother's mouth with his free hand. Alec said, 'You hated me.'

'That's not true.'

'What is true?'

'I was afraid of you.' Alec laughed in reply, then he was silent for a long stretch of time. Hannibal's head bowed down over his brother. 'I was afraid of you,' repeated Hannibal slowly. 'Because, I suppose, I didn't understand where I fitted—with you and King, or with Ruth and Paul.' Alec stared into Hannibal's face, perfectly still, as though waiting. 'Later—when I was older—fitting in didn't matter so much, it was only that I didn't know what to say. I should have tried, but there was a distance there, you know there was.' Hannibal added after a pause, 'I don't want you to die.'

'Why not?'

'Because you're my brother.'

'You got Paul.'

'Nobody's got Paul, not even the people who want him.'

There was another silence. The tree branches above them hung frozen, glistening. The fog cradled them, rocked gently around them. Eventually Alec coughed again. 'Hannibal.' His voice cracked. 'Don't let the police get me.'

'I won't.'

'Don't tell King.'

Hannibal shook his head. Silence settled again. Nonie was tired suddenly; her eyes, aching with the cold, began to close, her legs felt weak, thoughts swam in and out of her head. Then a voice spoke her name nearby and she found herself in the fog again, shaking.

'Nonie, Nonie,' Hannibal's voice was saying. He was still bent over his brother. She could not see his face. 'Get Ruth. Do you hear me?'

'Yes.'

'Get Ruth.'

'Yes.'

She found her feet and slid and slipped down the hill away from the peppercorn tree, but a sound followed her all the way across the paddocks and back to the house, plucking at her eyes and pricking along her spine, wrenching inside her. It was a moan of utter despair. It came from Hannibal.

It did not take Ruth more than a few seconds to guess what was happening when Nonie let herself in through the kitchen door some minutes later, white-faced and gasping. She dropped her mending on the kitchen table and stood up. Her chair clattered to the floor.

'Where is he, Nonie?'

'Peppercorn . . .' She could not catch her breath. It was enough though. Ruth pulled a coat and scarf from a hook by the kitchen door. She hopped and struggled into her boots.

She said, 'Does Hannibal . . .?'

'He's there.' Nonie leaned against a cupboard, trying to slow her breathing, to hold the ache in her chest.

'Is he . . .?' Ruth hesitated. Nonie did not know what to say. They exchanged a look. Ruth pulled another coat down and threw it to her. She crossed the room and lifted a lantern from the shelf above the stove and lit it while Nonie numbly wrapped the coat around herself. It was an old coat that might have once belonged to Paul, or Hannibal or even Harry Lambe. It hung down to Nonie's ankles. Ruth thrust the lantern at her, lifted the lamp from the kitchen table where she had been mending and propelled her back outside again. A wall of cold struck them both. Ruth pulled Nonie not in the direction of the house paddock but to the front of the house. Hannibal's cottage with its orange lamplight lurched out of the fog to one side of them and disappeared again as they hurried past it and came to the front gates. Ruth pulled her along the road a little way, holding the lamp up from time to time, and dropping it down. Nonie stumbled in a pothole and hurt her foot. She said nothing.

'Here.' Ruth lifted her lamp again with relief. On the side of the road was the entrance to a little track. Fog lay across it like a veil, reflecting lamplight back into their faces. 'It's the old track up to Dingley,' said Ruth. 'It might be a bit overgrown but it will be all right. It's quicker than the road.' She pushed Nonie towards it impatiently. 'Get Queenie,' she said. 'They may be asleep; you'll have to wake them. Tell them I said we need

Queenie. Now hurry. Hold the lantern close to the ground. Whatever happens, they mustn't find out up there.' She jerked her head in the direction of the mill, and then she was gone, her yellow light bobbing in front of her as she made her way back to Greystones.

Nonie turned numbly into the track and began to run, feeling ahead of herself tentatively. Her lantern fizzed comfortingly in her hand; it made a chink-chink sound as it bumped against her. Don't think, she said, don't think and you will be all right. The track climbed upwards. The uneven ground was hard and dry. She listened to the thud of her feet and the chink of the lantern. She listened to her heart and felt the whip of wet leaves against her face, the sting of brambles. Ahead on the track a dark bulk and two eyes were caught in the lantern's hazy beam. She stopped, frozen, but the shape shifted and trundled into the bushes to one side of the track. A wombat, a wombat, she breathed the word inside herself in time with her thudding heartbeat. It held the other thoughts at bay. Suddenly she was out of the fog. It did not dwindle and thin, it simply stopped. Her lantern showed the path some distance ahead. The bush on either side of the track twinkled with moisture. She could see leaves and rocks and a sapling lying across the path. The track began to level out. There was light ahead and space. She lowered the lantern and saw Dingley, its long shape, its roofline distinct against the night sky. She felt a grateful sob forming in her throat but swallowed it down diligently. She was in the grounds now, walking on short wet grass, past the arbour that was grown over with wisteria, its bare branches twisted and knotted together like writhing snakes. She crossed the verandah, holding her breath, more frightened now than she had been before, and knocked on the door.

She had knocked softly in her sudden fear, but there was an immediate response. A commotion of fumbling and footsteps sounded from within and Bert Haggerty opened the door in his pyjamas, blinking, dishevelled, a look of dread on his face. The look changed slightly when he saw Nonie. From behind him came Consie Haggerty's voice.

'It's all right,' he called back to her. 'It's Greystones.'

It did not occur to Nonie till much later how strange it had been that he had called her Greystones. Consie's voice asked, 'Is it Stan?' 'No, no,' he reassured over his shoulder. 'It's all right, love, it's not Stan.' But how could it be all right, this unannounced visit in the middle of the night, and why would they be expecting Stan who was gone to war? These questions, too, she did not ask herself till later. Now she stared wordlessly at Bert Haggerty. He said, 'Will I get Queenie?' in a quiet, urgent voice. She nodded gratefully. He vanished into the house. She heard knocking and a muffled exchange of voices. Then Bert Haggerty was outside again, fastening a coat around himself. She followed him to the stable and watched him harness the old grey hack to the sulky. Queenie appeared, swathed in coat and hat and scarf, clutching a blanket and a large bag. 'You can put that out,' she said sharply. 'We know our way.' Nonie extinguished the lantern obediently and climbed up beside her. The sulky jolted into motion, and grated down the road into the swirling fog, the horse's flanks just visible, swinging gently between the shafts.

Ruth appeared holding her lamp as the sulky turned in through the gates of Greystones. They reined up beside the cottage and Queenie climbed down and was ushered inside Hannibal's house. No one noticed Nonie. She climbed down after them, shivering, and crept up to the door and slipped inside. The front room was dark, but still warm. The pictures on the walls were squares of shadow. There was light flickering out of the little back room now, where Hannibal slept, and the sound of low voices. Shadows climbed the walls and fell away again as people moved around the hidden room. Nonie approached the doorway.

Inside the room Alec lay on Hannibal's bed. The wooden rails at the foot of the bed obscured her view of him. She could see blankets dark with blood, though, and sticky drops of blood on the floorboards. There was the smell of brandy, of sweat. Hannibal was standing in shadow in a corner of the room by the bed, smeared all over with blood. Ruth and Queenie were moving around the bed murmuring to one another. Once, as Ruth passed close to Hannibal she put out her hand and touched his arm. Ruth's own hand, Nonie saw, was stained with blood too. She remembered that she too was bloodstained, Alec's blood on the outside of her; her own blood working its way down the inside of her stockings. She looked curiously down at herself, opening the old coat to see her clothes inside it. Warmth began to seep into her through her head, her hair, the tips of her fingers. She sank quietly onto the floor and put her head on her knees and waited.

She woke late in the morning in her own bed and sat up. Outside her window she could hear the sound of Elsie's voice, chanting a nursery song with Georgie. She climbed over to the window and looked out. The little ones were there, and Hannibal passed them pushing a wheelbarrow toward the kitchen garden, looking as he always looked.

Her clothes were gone. At the end of the bed there was an old skirt of Ruth's, a jersey of Flora's, a clean petticoat and knickers. She dressed herself in them, feeling strange. Alongside the clothes was a bundle of white rags and some safety pins. These she ignored.

She found Ruth in the kitchen peeling vegetables. There was bread and dripping on a plate. Ruth made a cup of tea and set it down in front of her. 'Quite a wind today,' she said conversationally. 'There's a tree fallen across the south fence. Hannibal thinks we'll have storms later.'

Nonie sipped her tea in silence. 'Also, Nonie, you need to use those towels till the bleeding stops.' Ruth's back was turned to Nonie while she fed the stove. Nonie stopped drinking and flushed, and waited. Ruth continued, 'Later I'll show you where to soak them.'

Flora came in with the eggs. 'Nonie,' she said with excitement, 'we're having jam roly-poly tonight. I'm helping to make it.' She made a great deal of noise rattling around in the pantry looking for pots of jam, chattering cheerfully.

Nonie went outside after her breakfast, passing the row of old coats hanging by the door. The day was clear and grey and the wind rushed at her. Tom and Phip had made a flimsy kite which would never fly out of newspaper and string, and were running in the house paddock, dragging it behind them. Over in the orchard, washing slapped wetly on the clothes line. There was Nonie's own winter dress and jersey and socks, Ruth's clothes from the night before, Hannibal's shirt and trousers and coat, and the blanket from his bed, all straining and cracking against their pegging shackles.

So that is all, thought Nonie.

And it was. Later in the day the twins reported with ghoulish delight that they had found bloodstains under the peppercorn tree, and there was much talk over the luncheon table about a chicken that had gone missing in the night. Then, in the early evening, storms came riding down the slopes of Mount St Leonard. The rain lasted a day and a night, and all the blood that remained under the peppercorn tree was washed into the earth.

17

I feel the Spring far off, far off,
The faint far scent of bud and leaf—
Oh how can Spring take heart to come
To a world in grief
Deep grief?

SARA TEASDALE

The hours of daylight began to lengthen. In the mornings the ground was wet, rather than stiff with ice. Kookaburras shouted in the trees. The wintry gloom of the bush was punctuated now with explosions of gold wattle. Hannibal took the children down to the creek one day and they brought back a bucket of yabbies, which Ruth steamed and covered with butter and salt, so they could be eaten in the fingers. It gave them all a careless, comfortable feeling, sitting about the kitchen table eating a meal like that. Even Ruth had butter running down her hands. She laughed at the children's buttery faces. Nonie felt herself laughing too. It seemed to her that she had not laughed for a long time.

Hannibal dug over a new bed for potatoes, and planted out the tubers that had been stored away from the frost. Ruth sowed peas and beans and cress and carrots. There was a shimmer of new growth on the raspberry canes and in the orchard the branches of the fruit trees were furred with buds.

Consie Haggerty took in mending over winter while Dingley was quiet. She darned great linen cloths sent up to her from the larger guesthouses and embroidered emblems onto pillowslips and sheets. When Bert Haggerty brought home a

Mark Foy's catalogue, sent down all the way from Sydney, she was overjoyed and announced at once that she would make summer frocks for the girls in white voile, just like the Mark Foy's. Ruth, while privately considering the choice of colour and material for the project ridiculous, was grateful. She packed Nonie and Flora up to Dingley on foot one day to be fitted, carrying with them a bundle of mending and a basket of eggs, and a note politely suggesting that Elsie's new dress should be made of more sturdy stuff. Hannibal had gone into town early with a long list of messages, the little ones were at school, and with only Georgie around her feet, Ruth looked forward to a day of spring sorting.

They climbed up the old track. It was hardly recognisable by day as the same route Nonie had taken only weeks earlier in the dead of night. Tender, new briars reached across their path. Higher up, heath was blooming. They stopped halfway and looked back. Greystones was a distant rooftop, a spiral of smoke, a crooked patch of cleared land. Flora said, with satisfaction, 'I like our place.'

Nonie was thinking how disappointing it looked from a distance, but she heard Flora's 'our' with envy. She could not have said it, to her it seemed a presumption to speak of Greystones as if it belonged to them. They began to walk again. Flora said, 'When Dadda comes back, do you think he will want us to go away with him?'. Nonie shrugged. 'Because we'd want to, wouldn't we,' added Flora, 'only I was thinking Auntie Ruth might mind.'

'You mean go back to our old place?' Nonie was aware of a feathering of anxiety in her stomach as pictures and sounds jostled in her memory—the whack, whack of the crooked screen door in the wind, the privy full of spiders, the smell of baby sick in the hall, draughty rooms, broken furniture, the sound of someone crying. 'It won't be there, you know,' she said quickly, with relief. 'Well, it might be, but someone else will be living in it.'

'I'm hoping he'll stay here,' confided Flora. 'With Auntie Ruth and Hannibal. Do you think he might?'

'Yes.' But she did not think that. When Nonie remembered her father, which was not often these days, she remembered a person who could not possibly fit into the routine of Greystones. And if he wanted us to go along with him, she thought with a twist of anguish, then we would have to.

Consie, like Ruth, was having a day alone, for Bert, Jackie and Queenie were also in town. She showed the girls her new catalogue proudly, and they pored over the pictures inside it. Consie had chosen pretty frocks with scalloped hems for Flora and Elsie, and a blouse for Nonie. 'It will be like the one I'm making for Kester,' she explained. 'Because of you being older now. With a skirt, like this.' She turned a few pages and found a picture. 'Rather longer, and plain. More grown-up, I think, don't you?'

Nonie flushed and felt unworthy. She admired the picture Consie showed her more than she could possibly express. As always in the face of Consie's kindness and understanding, she was dumb. Then came the business of measuring and marking down and measuring again. The girls giggled with excitement, standing on the kitchen table in turns. At the open kitchen door Consie's pet bantam chortled and cocked its head at them. Above the mantelpiece, the portrait of Jim Haggerty seemed shadowy and neglected. The jar of white heath that stood beside it was turning brown.

Flora stayed on to help with the cutting out, so Nonie left Dingley alone. She took the road this time, instead of the track, thinking she would stop at the Old School and walk home with the others. The afternoon was growing cool. Sunlight blinked forth at odd moments then sank back into banks of cloud. The only sound was the metallic ring of the bellbirds which rose straight up from the valley floor. Nonie thought of her new blouse with satisfaction. She thought especially of the way it would be gathered, loose across the chest, to make room for the changing shape of her adult body. She shifted her shoulders back a little, lifted her head, slowed her steps and felt within a stirring of her future self. She would be not plain Nonie Field, but Antonia, her real name, a name which she had never heard uttered and knew only as writing on paper. It pleased her to think of her name, just as it pleased her to feel the slight chafing of her tender breasts against her woollen singlet. She was so taken with her thoughts that she did not see a bicycle lying in her path until she had fallen headlong across it.

The indignity of the fall was lessened by her curiosity. She picked herself up quickly and turned to examine the bicycle. It was a little scratched and muddy, but had a decidedly newish shine even so. It appeared to be abandoned. This last realisation was the most intriguing of all. She pulled it upright, guiltily, and put one foot on a pedal. At the same moment there was a crashing in the bushes at the side of the road, followed by a voice.

'Hey! What do you think you're doing with my bike?'

The bicycle clattered onto the ground again. Nonie jumped away from it, flushing. An untidy, fair-haired boy emerged from the undergrowth, seized the bicycle and set it right way up again. He said, 'Can't a chap have a pee in the bush without being robbed in broad daylight?' Then, noting her embarrassment with satisfaction, he added, 'Don't think you would have got away with it either. I would have had the police after you in no time.'

'I wasn't stealing it! It . . . it was just lying there. I was standing it up.'

'That's not how it looked to me. You were going to ride it away.'

'I wasn't!'

'Were! Country people are all thieves!' He sniffed in a superior way. Nonie bristled.

'I fell over your stupid bike. Look.' There was a trickle of blood running down her shin. She pointed to it triumphantly. 'Do you think I did that on purpose?'

There was a moment's silence. The boy put his head on one side. 'Have you got a hanky?'

'No.'

'I have. Want it?' She shook her head, but when after rummaging around in his trouser pocket, he pulled out a perfectly clean, pressed white handkerchief and offered it, she took it and held it against her leg. He squatted down to get a better look. 'You don't want to get blood poisoning,' he advised. 'Kill you in a matter of hours, probably.'

'Don't be silly. It's only a graze.'

'If you were on the Western Front, that graze could be gangrenous tomorrow. They'd chop your leg off.'

'They wouldn't.'

'Would. Happens all the time.'

Nonie straightened up and held out the handkerchief to him. The boy said carelessly, 'You can keep it.'

'I don't want to.'

'Well, I don't want it back now, all bloody.'

Nonie flushed again and shoved the handkerchief awkwardly up her sleeve. She started to walk and the boy pushed his bicycle companionably along beside her. 'Actually, I don't think you're a thief,' he conceded. 'What's your name?'

She looked sideways at him. He was a little taller than she, his skin was lightly freckled. He was rather sweaty; his hair curled into wet ringlets around his ears. A tiny shiver passed through her. 'Antonia,' she said. 'What's yours?'

'My name? Timothy.'

'You're not from around here.'

'Gosh no. I'm holidaying in town. Motored up last Thursday. Rotten place, nothing to do.'

'You can't have ridden all the way here from town . . .' But she could see at once that he could have. It explained his general

145

untidiness. Mud was spattered up his socks and knee breeches—
rather good-looking clothes, for all their dirt. His hands on the
handlebars looked pinched and cold.

'Well, I did. Left town just after breakfast. I stopped a few
times along the way. This road's got potholes big enough to lose
a motorbus in.'

She laughed at the idea and he looked pleased. 'Where are
you staying?' she asked.

'Oh, my uncle's place. I stay with him whenever my father
is away.'

'Where is your father?'

Timothy hesitated, then glanced at her. 'I can't say, actually.
Top secret stuff. Last week he got a letter from you-know-who
in England. I saw a bit of it before he burned it. He always
burns his letters. Then, next thing, he's off.' Nonie did not like
to ask who 'you-know-who in England' was. She nodded gravely.
Timothy said, 'He gave me this bike before he left, to make up
for it.'

'For what?'

'For going.'

'It's a nice bike.'

'Best there is.'

Bellbirds pinged their single musical notes between them as
they walked. Nonie said, after a hesitation, 'I've never ridden a
bike.'

'Not ever?'

'No.'

He looked lofty. 'When I'm older I'll have a motor of my
own, that's even better than a bike. And an aeroplane. I intend
to be a pilot. I'm going to join the flying corps and fly sorties
into enemy territory—strafing the beastly Boche!' He added,
'You can have a go of my bike if you want.'

She touched a handlebar. 'I better not.'

'Go on.' He let go his hold and she had to grab the bicycle
with both hands to stop it from falling. She stood irresolute.

'You'll laugh.'

'I won't. Truly!' But he was already smiling as she struggled one foot across the frame and began hopping awkwardly into motion. She stopped at once.

'You're laughing.'

'I'm not.' He was grinning, though. She felt her face becoming hot.

'You can't expect me to just know how to do something I've never done before.'

'I don't.'

'Stop laughing then.'

'You can't expect me not to laugh when something looks funny.' She frowned, confused by his good-natured teasing. He said, 'Look, I'll give you a ride if you like.'

'How?'

He took the handlebars and planted one foot on either side of the frame. 'I'll hold it still and you climb on the front. Go on, it's easy.'

It did not seem a safe position, but she eased herself onto the handlebars. 'You can't see!' she accused.

'I can if I sort of look on one side,' he insisted. 'Between your shoulder and your ear.' The bicycle jolted into motion. Nonie stiffened with fright. Behind her Timothy wrestled valiantly to remain upright. 'Here we go,' he said, pleased, as they wobbled in a more or less straight line. 'And I hardly need to pedal because we're on a hill.'

The bicycle gathered speed ominously. The sensation of motion and bounce made Nonie laugh out loud, terrified and exhilarated. Timothy gave a whoop. 'I told you I could do it. This is how it's done in the moving pictures. Have you seen *Sunshine Nan*?'

'No.' She squeaked out her reply. The bicycle weaved drunkenly, going downhill more and more rapidly towards the junction with the Chum Road.

'*The Pawnshop*? When my father and I went to see that we laughed so much at Charlie Chaplin my father burst a button off his shirt! Do you like Edna Purviance best, or Mary Pickford . . .?'

Timothy's question was swallowed by a surprised exclamation. He twisted the handlebars suddenly, the wheels seemed to lock and grate sideways across the dirt. Nonie was hurled off the handlebars altogether into a wet ditch with the bicycle on top of her. Timothy pulled it off her. At any other time in her life, such an experience would have seen Nonie emerge furious and offended. Now she took Timothy's offered hand, sat up shakily and said, 'I've never been to a moving picture.'

They sat in the ditch side by side for some time after that with mud on their faces and dirt and leaves in their hair, and talked. Timothy talked mostly. He gave moment-by-moment accounts of all the best movies he had seen in the company of his more than illustrious father. He told her about the Majestic, which he had visited, and which was the biggest and best moving-picture theatre in the whole world. It seemed that Timothy's father owned the Majestic, or had built it at least. In the confusion of Timothy's stories, Nonie was not sure which. When there was a moment of silence, she said, in order to impress him, 'My father is at the war.' She was surprised at how impressed Timothy really was.

'Do you know where he's stationed?'

'Well . . .'

'Probably not. They don't let them say, you know. Commanding officer has to read every letter before it gets sent, to make sure they don't pass on any military secrets. How long has he been gone?'

'Three years or so.'

Timothy whistled. 'I'll bet he's seen some action! Has he sent you anything?'

'I don't think they're allowed,' suggested Nonie dubiously.

'I know a chap who knows a chap whose father sent him a button off a Fritz jacket. He lets you see it for a shilling.' Nonie looked suitably impressed. Timothy continued eagerly, 'Do you know sometimes the Boche planes don't drop bombs, they drop pieces of paper? And on the pieces of paper they write things in English, telling all sorts of lies and rubbish to the fellows in the trenches, so they'll lose their nerve.'

'What sort of things?'

'Things like "England has surrendered to the Kaiser," or "You can't win because the German army is too strong," that sort of stuff. I know another chap whose brother sent a couple of sheets home for them to see.'

'I don't believe you,' Nonie said.

Timothy was indignant. 'It's true! You ask your father to send you some when you write next! You'll see!'

'Why isn't your father at war?' asked Nonie.

There was a second of silence. 'It's a bit difficult to explain.'

'Top secret?'

'That's it.' He smiled cheerfully at her. 'The truth is, he hasn't got the use of both his legs, got one bitten off by a killer shark when he was younger, diving for pearls in the China Sea.'

Nonie frowned, trying to match up events. 'So that's why he goes off secretly all the time.'

'Eh?'

'When he gets those letters.'

'Oh—'

'The ones he burns. From you-know-who.' Nonie looked at Timothy sharply. He was scratching at an ant-bite inside his sock, concentrating on the action. 'You made it all up,' she said with conviction.

Timothy did not reply at once. He stood up and collected his bicycle slowly, then he looked sideways at her and shrugged. Nonie got to her feet too. 'Why did you make it all up?' she demanded, following him.

'I didn't actually. Not all of it.' He was maddeningly non-chalant.

'But I mean . . .'

'It's true about the paper bombs.'

'But your father and all that?'

'Oh that.' They had reached the Chum Road. Timothy swung his bicycle in the direction of town and put his foot on a pedal. He is going to ride away without another word, thought Nonie. She placed herself determinedly in front of the bicycle and looked him full in the face.

'You're just a liar! I expect you don't even have a father!'

He returned her look defiantly. 'What if I don't?'

Nonie faltered. 'I don't have a mother.'

He dropped his face, then pushed the bicycle around her, but he paused before riding away. Nonie did not know what to say. Timothy bent down to examine the chain and the wheel spokes. A kookaburra laughed in the trees behind them. She asked, gently, 'Who gave you the bike?'

He straightened up. 'My mother.'

'You're lucky.'

'Am I? She's always giving me things. I hate it. I hate presents. It just means she's going away and she doesn't want me around, and the next thing I'm being shoved off to stay somewhere with a beastly uncle, or a cousin, or a schoolmaster's maiden sister. If I could get away to the war, I would.'

'You couldn't. You're too young.'

'I'm fourteen and a half.' He glared at her. 'I've read about British infantrymen just thirteen years old being killed in France. It's true!'

'Even if it is, why should you want to get killed like them?'

'Just because they got killed doesn't mean that I will.'

'You might.'

'I wouldn't. I'm not completely green. I've been in the cadet corps at my school for two years already.' The argument had a cheering effect on Timothy. He looked at the sky and said: 'Girls are so soft in the head.'

'Are not!'

'Are!'

They both smiled involuntarily.

The school bell clanked in the distance. Nonie glanced around in its direction, then back to Timothy. 'I have to go.'

'All right.' Timothy leaned against the bike and looked at her for a second. 'I wish you didn't have to,' he added.

Nonie blushed. 'Goodbye.' She backed away for a few steps and he called out to her.

'Where do you live?'

'Just a bit further on. Past the schoolhouse. It's Greystones.'

He nodded. 'I'll see you again.'

'How do you mean?'

'I don't know. I will, though.'

'All right.' She watched him set the bicycle in motion and cycle off in the direction of town, then she turned away and ran as fast as she could till the old brown schoolhouse came in sight.

Children were issuing from the schoolhouse door into the muddy yard. Three sandy-haired children trotted past her on a shaggy pony and stared down at her curiously. She called out when she saw the twins and Elsie and they came over to her, dragging their satchels. Elsie looked cross.

'They put her in the stinging nettles,' explained Tom.

A boy rushed past them and pushed Phip in the back. Phip stumbled, collected himself, then tore off after the boy and caught him at the school gate. He kicked him twice, then he turned and sauntered back to the others. The boy hurled several insults before running off down the road.

'Why did they put Elsie in the stinging nettles?'

'Don't know,' Tom shrugged.

Phip rejoined them. They shouldered their satchels and walked towards the school gate. Nonie glanced along the road secretively, but there was no bicycle in sight. The road ahead was empty too. Behind them a few schoolchildren straggled, kicking at rocks. Elsie's damp, dirty hand found its way into Nonie's. She looked at her little sister then. 'Why did they put you in the stinging nettles, Els?'

The twins looked at one another but did not offer a comment. Elsie sniffed and said, 'They was laughin'. They says our Auntie Ruth is a Darkie Lover.'

That was what the boy had been shouting by the school gate, Nonie realised, only she had not understood what the taunt meant, or indeed that it had been aimed at them. Tom said, 'Well, it's her stupid fault anyhow. She shouldn't talk about Hannibal.'

'No,' murmured Nonie. 'You shouldn't, Elsie.'

'Why not?'

'Because you make it sound like he's our friend,' said Phip.

'He is,' said Elsie.

They did not speak again for some time after that. Elsie trotted along at Nonie's side. The twins hurled rocks at the trunks of trees. Nonie felt a familiar anxiety begin to grind inside her again; and a buzzing in her head.

'What's that noise?' shouted Tom suddenly, startling her. She listened, and realised the buzzing was not inside her at all. The buzzing became a rumble.

'It's a motor,' shrieked Phip. They ducked over to the side of the road. The rumble was a racket now. They strained their eyes searching for it.

'There!' Tom pointed down the road triumphantly.

But it was not a motorcar that bumped and spluttered towards them. It was a motorcycle, a red one, with a ridiculous sidecar jutting out on one side. The passenger in the sidecar had a scarf tied around his head and seemed to be clinging on for dear life. The driver was wearing goggles and a leather cap, a large coat and loose trousers. But the hair that bounced in disarray from under the cap was unmistakable.

'Kester!' shouted Nonie, jumping into the road as the machine clattered past. Kester turned her head to them and waved a gloved hand.

'Hallo . . . oo!' Her voice disappeared in the engine's roar. There was a cry of protest from the terrified passenger. 'Kester! Both hands! Drive with both hands!'

They recognised the voice at once. It belonged to Hannibal.

18

The surly blighter shoots and having shot
Moves on, while you are cursing quite a lot,
And on your tummy crawl through feet of mud,
Nor pause, till you've retaliation got.

NEW CHURCH TIMES, 1916

dear dadda,
   Kester is stayn at our place becuse she didt want to
stay in town any more an not at dinly as well she has
brung all her stuff and as well she has brung her dog
boske wich barks at the chooks and the cats and somtimes
barks at nuthing he is best at digging only he is not aloud
becuse Antie Ruth says if he digs the storberres agan she
wil ring his neck Georgie and me crid wen she sad it
becuse boske finds stiks and chase us al over the place
and can also jump the gate like he is flyn only he is also
not aloud to swing on the closeline now becuse his teeith
is so sharp they made hols in Hanibls shirt but he look
funny wen he did it and mad us lahf Kester also has a
camra but it is a long tim wen she taks a piter also Kester
has a gramerfon and we like it ther is a broode hen in
the kindlin box and we are not aloud to show boske
                              frm Elsie Dorothy May Rose Field
                                   and George Tankey Field

DEAR DADDA

KESTER COUSINS HAS COME TO SAY WITH US ON HER
MOTOR CYCLE AND SIDECAR WHICH HANNIBLE CAME IN
WITH HER. IT IS A DOUGLAS WITH TWO AND THREE
QUARTER HORSEPOWER TWO SPEEDS AND A LAMP A HORN
AND A SPECIAL TOOLBOX. MR HAGGERTY HAD TO FOLLOW
AFTER IN OUR JINKER TO BRING BACK OUR MESSAGES
BECAUSE THEY WOULDNT FIT IN THE SIDECAR AND AUNTIE
QUEENIE BROUGHT BACK ALL OF KESTERS THINGS IN HER
SULKY. KESTER HAS GOT A LITTLE DOG CALLED BOSKY
WHICH ALWAYS GETS INTO A LOT OF TROUBLE OFF AUNTIE
RUTH AND HANNIBLE BUT KESTER SAID SHE COULDN'T
LEAVE HIM BEHIND. HE SLEEPS IN OUR BED SOMETIMES BUT
AUNTIE RUTH IS NOT ALLOWED TO KNOW. KESTERS
MOTORCYCLE ALSO HAS A SPEEDO TO TELL YOU HOW FAST
YOU ARE GOING. HANNIBLE SAID THERE IS SOMETHING
WRONG WITH THE MAGNETO. KESTER IS GOING TO BE A
PHOTOGRAFER NOW BECAUSE A MAN SOLD HER A CAMERA.
SHE SAYS IT IS BETTER THAN DOING HOUSEWORK. KESTERS
MOTOR CYCLE IS RED.

from Philip Arthur Prendergast Field
and Thomas Alfred Prendergast Field

Dear Dadda,

It is a long time since I have written so I will try to
tell you of all the things that have happened. Kester has
come to live with us for a while because she did not have
any work to do in town any more but she says she has
a lot of ideas. There was a man at the guesthouse where
she was working who used to take photographes of all
the people and he told her that he was going to go to
war which he never wanted to do before. She bought his
camera off him and also his motercycle and sidecar and
he gave her his little dog too all for 100 pounds which
Kester said is a bargan. She has paid him 37 pounds 7

shillings and sixpence because it was all she had and she says she will send him more when she has earned it from taking photographes like he did. She gave us all rides in her motercycle until it ran out of petrel but Mr Haggerty said he will bring her some from town soon. She sleeps in the little room next to ours that used to belong to Auntie Ruth when she was a young girl and her little dog Bosky is supposed to sleep on the veranda only he sneaks inside and sleeps with Tom and Phip or sometimes in the cot because he is afraid of the cats. Auntie Ruth is not very happy because Bosky dug up the strawberry bed twice and she says he will put the chickens off the lay. Auntie Ruth said Kester must help us with our reading and writing and help out in the house so Kester is teaching us to write our signateures properly which she says is extremly importent. Mrs Haggerty is making me a new dress it is white and I will show it to you when you get home. Nonie is not writing a letter she said she has not got time at present so I will enclose her love with mine and hope you are well. From your daughter

Flora Lillian Field

Nonie Field
Antonia Adeline Field
Antonia Field
Nonie

19

In the line a soldier's fancy
Oft may turn to thoughts of love.
But too hard to dream of Nancy
When the whizz-bangs sing above.

WIPERS TIMES, 1916

Kester made the whole house different. 'How can one person cause so much disruption?' Ruth asked Hannibal. 'She always did,' Hannibal replied.

Suddenly there were visitors to the house. Consie and Jackie called in every other day, drank tea around the kitchen table, and knitted and chatted. Acquaintances from town took the trouble to call by with news and events. Travelling salesmen were always welcomed by Kester, who consumed patent medicines by the boxful. Once Kester walked to the Old School to meet the twins and Elsie, and soon children from the local farms and orchards began to arrive wanting to be friends with the Field children.

The bedroom she occupied was transformed into an exotic den. China animals lined the windowsills, scarves draped the bedposts and all manner of keepsakes adorned the walls. Her cupboard doors never seemed to shut. Her dressing table was littered with coloured bottles and brushes and pins, and a glass bowl full of seashells.

'My brother gave them to me,' she told Nonie and Flora as they handled the shells admiringly. 'When I was eight, after we had visited the sea for the first time.'

Kester kept a memento of nearly every event in her life. An embossed autograph album was filled with signatures and quaint rhymes and there was a basket carelessly tossed in a corner of her room heaped with bundles of letters. Kester, it seemed, had been courted by all of her brother's school chums, and a good number of the local boys. Even now, when old romances had grown cold, she could not bring herself to throw their letters out. She also kept in a hatbox at least ten years worth of the *Girls' Own Paper*, which she had subscribed to from an early age. Nonie and Flora, whose secular education had been sadly neglected, were often to be found in Kester's room now, leafing through them. They read about daring heroines called Drusilla or Blanche who invariably won the hearts of devil-may-care chaps called Young Hughie or Jarvis. It seemed to Nonie that Kester was very much like these fictional characters, except that she was disorganised and untidy, which the heroines were not. Kester chatted to them while they read, dressing, undressing, or brushing out her explosion of copper hair. Even her underclothes were special, elaborately embroidered with violets and forget-me-nots.

'It's Auntie Consie,' explained Kester. 'Such a lovely needle-woman, and me the only girl.'

Once a month, like clockwork, Kester took to her bed, and lay in a darkened room swigging liberally from a bottle of Hean's Nerve Tonic. She liked to share her misfortunes, and particularly welcomed Nonie's company on these occasions. There were many wry references to 'the curse' and looks of long-suffering complicity. Nonie, bewildered at first, slowly began to realise that the shameful secret of her own bleeding was, in fact, not a 'curse' that had befallen her especially. The reason for the bleeding was not explained to her, but her relief at knowing she was not alone assuaged her curiosity for a while.

Greystones had always been a quiet place but now sounds resonated in every corner. The gramophone played relentlessly in the parlour and Kester thought nothing of conducting a conversation from one room with someone in another. Kester argued violently and cheerfully with everyone, about anything, 'like a dog at a bone' Bert Haggerty said, keeping to her point until, for the most part, her unhappy opposition had backed down in exhaustion. She was passionate about everything.

'We don't need a lorry,' insisted Ruth as Kester thrust the classified advertisement section of the newspaper in front of Ruth for the tenth time, one day.

'Really, though, Ruth.'

'We manage perfectly well with the horse and jinker. We always have.'

'There you go! "We always have". But what about the future?'

'Kester.'

'Because the world is changing, and we have to change with it. What do you think, Hannibal?'

Hannibal was just that moment entering through the kitchen door. Nonie and Flora and Elsie were seated at the kitchen table cutting old newspapers into squares to put in the privy. Georgie had been sitting on Kester's knee making strings of paper dolls. They all sat perfectly still now and listened.

'What do I think?'

'About getting a lorry. Surely you can see the benefits.'

'Of a lorry?'

'Yes, yes, yes!' Kester hit Hannibal with her newspaper. 'Don't pretend you don't know what we're talking about. See, here's one . . . a Clement Diatto, fifteen to twenty horsepower, imagine that! four speeds and detachable sides and only £140!'

Ruth said, 'Where on earth would we find £140?'

'I like the idea of detachable sides,' commented Hannibal taking the newspaper from Kester.

'There!' Kester was triumphant.

'But we don't need a lorry,' protested Ruth.

'Not yet,' said Hannibal. 'But we ought to think about what we're going to do when Tessie's too old to pull the jinker. And fifteen horsepower, Ruth, just think what it could pull.'

'We don't need it to pull! All we ever carry is vegetables and eggs, and a bag of flour now and then!'

'All the same . . .'

'All the same nothing. You're as silly as Kester sometimes!'

Having created the argument, Kester now returned to cutting paper dolls with Georgie. She beamed at Ruth and Hannibal, who continued their heated exchange for some minutes. The children sat open-mouthed. Ruth threw up her hands in the end. 'The point is,' she announced firmly, 'that we do not have the money to buy a lorry at even half the price of this one!'

Hannibal nodded regretfully. Kester said, 'Why don't you sell one of Harry's pictures?'

Nonie knew at once that it was an unwise thing to say, even though she did not understand why. She saw Ruth's face become utterly blank, as though a wall had grown up over her features in an instant. Hannibal turned away and began washing his hands in the tin dish on the draining board. Kester said, 'Don't you think it's a good idea?'

'I have no paintings to sell,' replied Ruth. She rolled down her sleeves methodically, and buttoned the cuffs.

'Hannibal has. They might be worth a lot of money now.'

Nonie wanted to tell Kester to be silent. Ruth walked swiftly from the room.

Hannibal said, 'You shouldn't you know.'

'Oh but it isn't fair!' said Kester crossly. 'How long has he been dead, eighteen years? I want to be able to talk about him. I liked Harry.'

'Better talk about him somewhere else,' advised Hannibal.

Kester sulked on that occasion, but only briefly. Later that day she was dancing in the parlour with Elsie while the gramophone played 'If You Were the Only Girl in the World', tossing her head in the same old careless way, and erupting with laughter. Nonie, feeling dull and plain, stood in the doorway and watched her. When Elsie raced from the room to fetch Georgie, Kester flopped into a chair and beamed at Nonie.

'Come and dance.'

'No thanks.'

Kester shrugged indifferently. She crossed to the gramophone and removed the record. 'Would you like to choose the next song?'

'No.' Nonie flushed. 'I mean, whatever you like will be all right.'

Kester smiled. 'You're a funny one, aren't you, Nonie Field. Do you ever say what you mean?' Nonie was too taken aback to reply. Kester said, 'You're not like Paul. He says what he wants. And you're not like Lily either.' Kester shrugged again. 'I expect you're like Ruth.'

Nonie felt challenged. She said, quite abruptly, 'Why won't Auntie Ruth talk about Harry Lambe?'

'Oh . . .' Kester looked surprised. It gave Nonie courage.

'And why are the paintings in the cottage?'

'Have you seen them?'

'Yes.'

'They're beautiful, aren't they?'

'Yes. They should be here, in the big house.'

'I expect it hurts Ruth too much to have them here.' Nonie tried to look as though she understood. Kester added, 'She sent a lot of them back to England after he died. I think those ones in the cottage must have been given to Hannibal and he wouldn't let her send them away. I never really asked. Some things are hard to ask.'

'I know,' said Nonie. She was silent for a moment and then she said, 'Did Auntie Ruth love Harry Lambe?'

'Of course.'

Of course, thought Nonie.

'He was out from England on a sort of painting holiday when he came to stay at Dingley. He and Ruth became friendly and

161

he moved down here into the cottage to paint and to tutor Paul and Hannibal.' Kester looked through her stack of records. 'I was fairly young but I remember. It gave the local gossips a field day. Auntie Queenie said it was scandalous, him living down here and everything, and Ruth on her own really, just with Paul and Hannibal. She used to call him a Bohemian, and I'm pretty sure she didn't mean it as a compliment. They intended to be married of course, Ruth and Harry, least Auntie Consie said so. I don't know why they didn't. I don't think Harry's family liked the idea, only they shouldn't have let that matter.'

'Why did he go away to war?'

Kester shrugged. 'Oh well,' she said. 'I expect that was Paul's doing. Paul was mad keen to go . . . thought it would be such a lark. He was too young of course. But he kept at Harry. There were some awful fights. I remember thinking Ruth would never stop being angry.'

She never has, thought Nonie.

Elsie came running back into the room with Georgie in tow and Kester's terrier darting between their legs in hysterical excitement. 'Nonie, you won't say anything,' urged Kester above the clamour, as she was pulled into the middle of the room by the children.

'Of course not.' Nonie, turning to go, saw the photograph of Harry Lambe in his soldier's uniform on the mantelpiece and remembered the angry flick of Ruth's duster as it followed the path of its daily duty. Poor Harry Lambe, she thought, poor Auntie Ruth. And then she thought, poor Hannibal.

Her aunt and Hannibal were standing by the henhouse when she went outside after that. They seemed to have forgotten their argument and were absorbed in the task of patching a hole in the wire netting around the chicken run. Ruth's cat was weaving around their legs. Then there was the sound of someone calling. Nonie looked in the direction of the gate and saw Jackie approaching, walking quickly, a strange sloping walk that was

162

almost a run. He was calling, 'Ruthie! Ruthie!', and the sound of his voice, his half-formed words, were a bellow of pain.

Ruth and Hannibal dropped their tools and turned to the sound. Jackie had stopped calling now, his face was twisted and ugly, his mouth open like a baby's with a line of dribble spilling down his chin. He put his arms out to them and both Ruth and Hannibal encircled him. Nonie felt a pricking across her scalp. Then Ruth broke free and was walking toward her, stone-faced. 'Nonie,' she said. 'Get Kester at once. We have to go to Dingley. Stan Haggerty is dead.'

20

If I should die think only this of me:
That there's some corner of a foreign field
That is forever . . .

RUPERT BROOKE

*T*he kitchen at Dingley was full of strangers. Bert Haggerty was sitting at the kitchen table with his head buried in a handkerchief, two elderly ladies—the Misses Silk— were pouring tea, and a nun was folding linen in a corner, white face and white hands enveloped in the forbidding brown of her habit. Consie Haggerty was on her knees at the hearth bringing a tray of scones from the oven when they arrived. 'Ruth,' she said, climbing to her feet. 'It's a sad day for all of us.' But she smiled anyway, and hugged Ruth and kissed all of the children one after another.

'You all right, Mum?' asked Jackie.

'Yes, my lamb,' she replied, cupping Jackie's tear-stained face in her two hands for a second. 'Mum's all right, Jackie-boy.'

Kester had sobbed in the jinker all the way from Greystones, holding her head against Jackie's chest. Now she crossed to the kitchen table and sat down next to Bert Haggerty and put her arms around him and began to cry again. Nonie saw Ruth frown in Kester's direction.

'Queenie's taken some feed out to the chickens,' said Consie. She stood still for a second as though confused, then she turned back to the stove. 'I'm just doing the scones,' she said. 'The ladies are making their own tea this morning. It isn't right, but they insisted.' The Misses Silk murmured protests, smiling bleakly, and not quite meeting anyone's gaze.

The door connecting the kitchen to the main house was opened and another nun issued through it. She stopped in her tracks at the sight of them all and smiled cheerfully. Nonie felt Flora vibrate with pleasure. She shrank back beside Ruth. 'This is Sister Patrick,' said Consie, brightening. 'She came up from town with Sister Ursula.' The sisters bowed their heads to the newcomers. Sister Patrick was pink-faced. She twinkled at Georgie who held his head on one side and stood his ground. 'They brought the cablegram,' said Consie. 'Father would have come, only he had other calls to make, so he thought the sisters . . .' She turned her tray of scones onto the tabletop. Ruth fetched a pot of softened butter from the stove and stood at Consie's side, buttering scones. They spoke softly together. Nonie could not distinguish many words. There was talk of a ship, she fancied, and official letters. And 'Sydney' they kept saying, which made no sense at all. She looked up at the picture of Jim Haggerty over the stove. Now there might be a picture of Stan there too, she thought, with the same eyes and a different mouth. Stan Haggerty's mouth stuck out more and there were creases down one side of it because he grinned crookedly. It was funny how she remembered that grin all of a sudden. She remembered, too, that she had disliked Stan Haggerty, the way he brayed, the way he whistled 'Mademoiselle from Armentières'. And now he was dead.

She was startled from her thoughts by Kester who appeared at her side, sniffing. 'You'll help me, won't you Nonie?' Her voice was subdued. It was disconcerting.

'How?'

'The housework.' Clearly a conversation had been taking place between Kester and Ruth.

'Yes,' Nonie said quickly, noticing Ruth looking meaningfully in her direction. She followed Kester toward the door, relieved to be escaping.

Outside, Kester altered visibly. Her shoulders straightened and she almost sprang along the little walkway to the main house giving one or two determined, final-sounding sniffs. She feels like me, thought Nonie. 'What about those sisters?' said Kester in a horrified whisper to her as they entered the house. 'I know they're supposed to be very good and everything—and Uncle Bert thinks they're simply wonderful, because he's a Catholic— but really they send shivers up and down my spine.'

Nonie looked at Kester with amazement. She would never have dared say such a thing, even the thought seemed sinful. She offered tentatively, 'Flora's going to be a Catholic when she's grown up.'

'Ugh!' said Kester, then looked apologetic at once. 'Sorry, I forgot. You and Flora went to,' she hesitated for a moment to assess the words she was about to utter, which was something she rarely did, '. . . to boarding school run by Catholic sisters, didn't you?'

'It wasn't really . . .'

'Did you like it?'

'Flora did.' Nonie's eyes met Kester's for a moment. Kester's face was blotched from crying and her eyes were puffy. Nonie looked away.

The bedrooms at Dingley were sensible and austere, their wallpaper faded and stained in places. There were two adjoining rooms where the Misses Silk slept. Kester and Nonie stripped the beds and remade them with fresh hard linen from a press in the hall. Kester made beds with characteristic carelessness. Nonie could see why she might have had difficulty keeping her job at the guesthouse in town. The only other guest at Dingley beside the Misses Silk was a retired professor, an amateur naturalist, who had taken himself out as soon as the news of

Stan Haggerty's death had arrived. His room smelled stale from cigar smoke. Kester flung open his windows to the spring air.

'He must be a favourite,' she remarked, pulling back the bedcovers. 'Auntie Queenie hates cigars. She used to make my father smoke outside. Come to think of it, I haven't seen her today.'

'I think she's feeding the chickens.' Nonie tucked the bedsheets in and thought of Auntie Queenie feeding Consie's pet bantams, for which she reputedly had little patience.

'Escaping the sisters more like,' said Kester knowingly. 'She won't come in till they're gone. Auntie Queenie hates Catholics.' She smoothed the blanket over the bed and left three or four more wrinkles in it than had been there before.

Kester said things so easily. 'Why?' breathed Nonie.

'It's just her.' Kester shrugged. She was back at the window pulling the curtains open further. Nonie watched her from behind. There was nothing in her movements now that suggested grief. But that is the way Kester is, thought Nonie. It is just her.

'I don't think she's ever forgiven Auntie Consie for marrying a Catholic. She likes Uncle Bert well enough, but goodness knows she never had a civil word to say to my mother.'

'Was your mother a Catholic, too?'

Kester gave an amused smile. 'Not quite,' she replied.

Nonie did not understand this. She felt frustrated and angry suddenly. There are always secrets, she thought. She followed Kester into the large common room. The wallpaper here was yellowed from smoke, lifting a little at the corners. There was an open fireplace with a china shepherd and shepherdess on the mantelpiece above it and a lacquer box containing dominoes. There were leather chairs, a bookcase, and a pianola against a rather damp outside wall. Kester lifted the lid as she passed it and ran her fingers down the keys. They jangled tunelessly. 'My father loved the piano,' she said. 'My mother could play. We spent evenings singing here. All the guests would join in. Paul used to ride up from Greystones.' She paused. 'Auntie Consie and Uncle Bert would be here sometimes too. Jackie used to pretend he could play, he loved watching the roll go round. I can just see Stannie in his pyjamas . . .' She let the pianola lid drop with a crack. Nonie scanned the room for something to look at so that she would not have to watch Kester's shoulders shaking, something that would ease the tight drag in her own chest.

'Such a terrible way to go,' said Kester shakily, between sobs. 'It's all been so awful, because of what he did. Poor Stannie!' She burst into fresh sobbing. 'It isn't fair!' She added, almost choking on the words, 'And I can't help thinking . . . it might be . . . it might be like this for . . . for my brother!'

The door opened and Ruth came in, her mouth set in a hard little line. Kester immediately dived into her pockets for a handkerchief and turned away to dry her face. 'They're saying the rosary,' Ruth informed them. 'Hannibal is outside chopping wood. You might go outside and keep an eye on the children, Kester. Keep them quiet.'

'All right.'

'I'll get on with dusting. Nonie, see if you can find Queenie. Consie's fretting about her. She went outside a while ago with some scraps for the chickens.'

Nonie hated the idea. 'What shall I say?' she asked dubiously.

'You don't need to speak to her. Just see that she's there, so Consie can stop worrying. She has enough to worry about.'

Kester said, 'Is there a body, Ruth? Did they tell you? After not having Jim's body home to bury and everything, I hope at least . . .'

'There's no body,' said Ruth quietly.

'Poor Auntie Consie,' sobbed Kester.

'Pull yourself together, Kester, really!' said Ruth in exasperation. 'You're no good to anyone like this.'

'I can't help it.'

'Try to help it. Think about Consie.'

168

Nonie was glad of Ruth's firmness. It steadied her, although it had no noticeable effect on Kester.

'If I think of Auntie Consie it makes me worse,' protested Kester. 'I don't know how she can bear it, losing two boys like this. And poor Stannie, all alone.'

Nonie headed for the door abruptly. She could not bear to be pulled into the pit of Kester's misery. She held her breath for a moment, but no one came after her. She began to breathe again.

Outside there were wattlebirds rasping, the whack of the axe, the sound of children's voices. Nonie walked quietly around the lawns looking for Queenie. On the west side of the house, where the land sloped down to Miner's Gully, Bert Haggerty's pet nanny goat was tethered beside a patch of blackberry. It bleated when it saw her. Nonie patted it and it rubbed its horn stumps against her thigh and fluttered its tail.

She wandered back to the east side of the garden. The arbour was a picture of blooming wisteria. Mauve tassels curved upwards, outwards, and lay languidly along spiralling stems. There were bees humming in the blossoms. As she approached, Nonie could hear chickens. She saw a speckled head, then another, and flashes of tail feathers, as the chickens bobbed in and out amongst the drooping blossoms. They are eating the bees, she thought, then she stopped. No they're not, she thought, they are in the arbour with Auntie Queenie.

She could not see Queenie, but she sensed her presence. She stood perfectly still for a few moments while the young bantams chuckled and crooned within the blossoms. Then she eased forward quietly and peeped around the wall of wisteria and in through the entrance.

Queenie was sitting on the ground with her legs stretched out in front of her. She was wearing a heavy brown skirt that was rucked up untidily, exposing her legs, which was shocking to Nonie. They were thick, shapeless legs covered in wrinkled lisle stockings. She was wearing old grey slippers and her feet were turned in. Her apron was untied at the back and her hair, which she always wore pinned back severely, was loose. Strands of it hung down her back. A pin dangled from behind her ear, threatening to drop. She was like an old woman and a child all at once. It made Nonie's heart thump to look at her. An upturned pot was near one foot, and bread scraps and wheat were scattered around it on the hard earth floor of the arbour. Six or seven chickens were scratching around the scraps. Queenie seemed oblivious of them. In her aproned lap sat the russet-coloured mother hen, Consie's pet, and it was pecking wheat politely from Queenie's outstretched hand, stopping every so often and cocking its head to one side to look into Queenie's face. It was purring like a cat.

'She's in the arbour,' reported Nonie in reply to Consie Haggerty's questioning look a short time later. The rosary was over. Ruth was making more tea at the kitchen stove, and Kester was handing around scones. Sister Ursula was sitting in a corner with Flora, while Georgie and Elsie were on the floor beside her playing with the wooden beads that hung down the side of her skirt. The twins were under the kitchen table, Jackie was knitting army socks in his chair by the stove, and the younger nun, Sister Patrick, was working her way through a bottle of brandy with Bert Haggerty. She had a high flush on her lovely Irish face. Consie looked as though she would say something more to Nonie as she stood in the doorway, but Hannibal came through it with an armful of wood, so she merely nodded and smiled.

Later that day as they drove back to Greystones through a light rain, Nonie remembered that she still did not know how Stan Haggerty had died. She knew she would never ask. She wondered if she would ever be considered 'grown-up' enough to be told.

21

Pack up your troubles
In your old kit bag and
Smile, smile, smile . . .

GEORGE ASAF

Nonie sat up late into the night while rain drummed steadily at the bedroom window. Flora was staying at Dingley and without her the bed was empty and cold. Elsie and Georgie breathed noisily in their cot. Halfway down the cot, in a furrow made by their legs, Kester's dog was sleeping too. He lay on his back, twitching.

Nonie thought about Stan Haggerty. The twins had been more upset than anyone, she remembered. At bedtime they had clung to Kester. 'Why wasn't our Dadda there to save him?' Tom had wanted to know, urgently. But there was no answer to a question like that. They were sleeping soundly now. 'They'll be all right,' she had overheard Ruth saying. 'In the morning it will be as though nothing happened. Children are like that.'

Nonie thought, no they are not like that. Auntie Ruth is wrong. It is only because it is easier to pretend to forget than to think of the right questions to ask.

The sound of the rain died away then renewed itself. She looked into the watery darkness and experienced an instant of shock. A white face, drenched and drawn, was looking in at her. It took her a few more seconds to realise that the face could not see her. It was, however, searching the darkness for something. It took her another few seconds to realise exactly who the face belonged to. In that time Bosky had awoken completely, sensing in his sleep the arrival of an intruder. He leapt vertically out of the cot, barking furiously. Nonie threw herself after him and caught him up in her arms, pressing her hand around his muzzle. 'Be quiet! For goodness sake, Bosky!' She managed to wedge him under one arm and lift the window awkwardly with the other. Rain pelted in. She leaned her head out into it and came face to face with Timothy.

'At last!' he said.

'What are you doing here?'

'I told you I'd see you again.'

He was standing precariously on the sloping verandah roof, clutching the window ledge to keep his balance. Bosky worked his way free and sprang at him. Timothy lost his hold and his footing at once and slid down the roof with the startled dog on top of him. He managed to collect himself for a moment at the roof edge and hook Bosky swiftly to him, before the two of them disappeared into the darkness. There was a small thud as they landed, then silence.

That no one awoke seemed a miracle. Nonie held her breath for a moment, listening for stirrings within the house, but the rain was her ally, its rattle and hiss covered everything. She tiptoed through the house to the kitchen, pulled a coat and hat from the hook by the kitchen door and ran outside to Timothy.

He was hunched by the side of the verandah holding Bosky in his arms, with his bicycle leaning on the wall beside him. Bosky had come around to the idea that Timothy was not an intruder, but a saviour of little dogs who fall off roofs. He was licking Timothy vigorously and squirming with excitement.

'I didn't know you had a dog,' said Timothy.

'Ssh! You'll wake everyone. Come here, quickly!'

She pulled him to the stable, dragged open its doors and ushered him inside. The sound of the rain was muffled at once.

'I can't see anything.'

'I'm looking for the lantern. Just a minute.' There was a small clatter.

'It smells nice in here.'

There was another clatter and a whimper as Bosky leaped out of Timothy's arms and tangled himself in a roll of wire. Then there was a low warning growl and a hissing sound. Timothy's voice sounded alarmed. 'Are you there? Did you hear that?'

'I expect it's the cats. There!' The lantern gave a muted roar and light sprang up the stable walls, chasing back the darkness, startling them both. They tried not to look at each other. Bosky had crawled out of the roll of wire and was leaning up against Timothy's feet, while Henrietta and her grown kittens paced around the walls with lashing tails.

Timothy said, 'It looks like there might be a war.'

'Not if Bosky behaves himself.'

Timothy looked down at Bosky. 'You'd better, old chap.' The dog wagged its stump of tail feebly back at him. Timothy grinned at Nonie. 'Are you surprised?'

'Yes!'

'I'm glad I found you. It was the devil of a job getting up on that verandah roof in the rain. I knew I'd fall.'

'Did you hurt yourself?'

'Not much.'

They were silent again for a moment. Timothy shivered. His fair hair was plastered to his head, his clothes dripped into a puddle at his feet. He looked like a scarecrow. 'I've run away, in case you're wondering,' he said, and sneezed twice.

Nonie could not think of anything to say for a while. She hung the lantern on a piece of wire from the roof where it swung, making shadows dip and rise on every wall. Then she found a rug for him on the front seat of the jinker. He accepted it gratefully, wrapped himself up and sank down onto the floor.

'Are you hungry?'

'I'll say I am.'

173

She nodded. 'I'll see what I can find. You'd better stay here.'

He did not look as though he wanted to come with her. He suddenly seemed exhausted. His eyes were sunk into dark circles. Nonie made her way through the rain back to the kitchen. She moved cautiously, listening, feeling her way around cupboards. She found bread and dripping, a jug of milk covered with a cloth, and half a jar of apple jelly which she bundled under her coat and hurried back to the stable. Timothy's eyes were closed when she arrived, but they opened as she laid the food down in front of him, shooing Bosky away from it. He sat up and ate and drank hungrily. She said, 'Have you really run away?'

'Don't you believe me?'

'Well . . .'

'It's not the sort of thing a chap would be bothered telling lies about.'

'How did you do it?'

'On my bike.'

'No, I mean . . .'

'You mean when? Day before yesterday. It was a lot easier than I thought it would be, actually. On account of being school holidays, so I was pretty well on my own.'

'On your own?'

'At school. See, my mother didn't think I needed to come home for the hols because I had my holiday a few weeks ago, when she brought me here. Anyway, she was off somewhere.' He looked around the stable, as though uninterested in the story he was telling. 'Do you want some of this food? It'll be gone in a minute.'

'So you just ran away?'

'Told my housemaster I was going for a ride for an hour or so down to the barracks. I got a good start before they would have begun to miss me.'

'But why?'

He frowned at her over the lip of the milk jug. 'What do you mean? Haven't you ever wanted to run away?'

She hesitated and nodded.

'Why didn't you?'

'I don't know.' But right at that moment she did know why she had never run away from the sisters who had hated her. It was because of Flora, of course, because Flora was all that she'd had.

Timothy stood up and cast the rug away. The meal had clearly revived him. 'I always planned to.'

'What will you do now?'

'Simple. I'm going to join up. I would have done it straight away, only I promised you I'd see you again, and I don't like to break a promise.' He sounded dreadfully pompous, but looked so earnest that Nonie did not know how to respond.

'They won't take you.'

'Well, I'll manage on my own till they do.' Timothy began to pace around her so that she had to keep turning to see him. Bosky circled Timothy in little excited leaps, while the cats continued to growl warnings from the shadows. 'I'll work in a circus, or something.'

'What could you do there?'

'I don't know! Anything. Feed the elephants or something. Have you ever been close up to an elephant?'

'I've never seen one.' Nonie felt giddy watching him.

'Well, I could do that, or . . .' He stopped. 'Or, really, I'd like to learn to fly aeroplanes. They'd have to take me then. Good airmen are hard to come by.'

Nonie could not laugh. Timothy was so enthralled with his dreams, they were real to him already. She felt, instead of irritation, an ache inside. 'What about your mother?' she said.

Timothy merely tossed his head. 'Oh her. Well, I expect she'll be glad I'm gone, if you want to know.' He began to pace again, only this time he was looking at Nonie sideways. 'See, there's this man called Ivan who's rather taken up with Mother.

He's a Russki, frightfully rich, so he can't go back to Russia because it's like the French Revolution all over again over there, you know, all the poor people bayoneting the rich people—which probably seems quite a good idea if you're poor, and not so good if you're someone like Ivan.'

'Stop it!' Nonie shut her eyes. 'I can't keep up with you. I don't understand what you're talking about!'

He was silent for a moment and perfectly still. 'What I'm saying,' he said at last, 'is that I'm rather in the way, if you know what I mean.' A smile spread across his mud-spattered face. He bent down and scratched Bosky's ears. 'Anyway,' he added, 'I'm sick to death of waiting to be old enough to do anything. I'm going to jolly well do it all now!' He looked up at her and grinned. 'What about you?'

'Me?'

'Come with me.'

'Come with you?'

'That's what I said. Only I'll take it back if all you can do is repeat everything after me like a softhead. That sort of thing would get right on a chap's wick!' He stood up again, brightly, and snatched both her hands into his. 'Come on, Antonia. What do you say?'

'What?'

'You heard me.'

'What did you call me?'

'Antonia. It's your name, isn't it?' He stared at her curiously. 'Hey! You didn't tell me a false name that day I met you?'

'No!' Nonie's heart was racing. Her hands, enclosed in Timothy's, burned as though they were on fire. Her face burned, too.

'Well, then?'

What could she say?

'Come on, Antonia!'

'I can't.'

He released her hands with a smile and stepped back. 'Doesn't matter,' he said.

'You don't understand.'

'Yes, I do.' He turned his back on her and tucked in his shirt and pulled hay off his jersey.

He is going away, she thought, just like the other time, just like that. 'You don't understand!' she said sharply. 'I can't go because of my auntie, and my sister and the little ones.'

'I understand,' he repeated, heading for the doors.

She stamped her foot. 'You don't! Sometimes you have to stay because you . . . because of other people, who just need you . . . oh, what's the use?' She glowered at his wet back. 'You'll never understand, how could you, you haven't got a mother or a father or anyone at all who loves you, so it's easy for you!'

The words had a far greater effect on Timothy than she could have imagined possible. He swung around to her and she saw that his face was almost black with rage and there were tears making wild crooked tracks through the mud on his cheeks. 'I have! You've no right to say that! All right, I haven't got a father any more. He's dead, and he didn't even die in any special way. He just died because he was old . . . he was so old when I was born he could have been my grandfather! But my mother's not old and it isn't fair if she has to stay at home with me and can't go about with people and she loves me all right . . . she just, she just . . . It's just that she has things she has to do before she gets too old.' Suddenly his rage died. He stood in front of Nonie and simply cried, and did not seem to care that she was watching him. Then, just as suddenly he turned back to the doors and began to pull them open. The sound of the rain greeted him like cruel applause.

'Don't go yet,' called Nonie, helplessly.

'I have to.' His voice was quieter. 'I've got a lot of things to do, you know. I can't waste time visiting people.' He turned back to her. 'Oh, by the way, I've got something for you.' He frowned and felt about in his trouser pocket. Then he withdrew something small and held it out to her. 'Do you remember I told you how I knew a chap who had a Fritz button?'

'You said he let people see it if they paid a shilling.'

'That's right.' Timothy gave a wry smile. 'I paid to see it four times.' The smile faded. 'Well, I told my mother about it too, how super it was that this chap had been sent it from the Western Front. When she came to see me, to tell me that I wouldn't be coming home for the holidays, she gave it to me as a present.'

Nonie was silent. She stared at the tiny button in his outstretched hand.

'See, she went and found that chap and she bought it from him. Paid two guineas.' He lifted her hand and tipped the button into it. 'You can keep it. Your brothers and sisters might like it. I don't care for it any more.'

Nonie stared into Timothy's face and for a few seconds he stared back. Then he gave a cheerful grin and turned into the rain. Nonie found her feet in a rush and propelled herself after him with Bosky leaping against her as she ran. She caught up with him at the side of the house where he was pulling his bicycle upright. 'Wait! Wait!' she hissed, catching hold of his arm. He pressed on doggedly. 'You mustn't go! You mustn't!' She struggled to keep up with him and to make him hear her through the sound of the rain. Water streamed over her eyes and into her mouth. 'Timothy! You can't go until you understand!' He stopped and looked at her again. She said quickly, 'I was wrong. What I said before. About your mother. It's only because she doesn't understand, see? But I do, I understand perfectly, and . . .' she gulped down a mouthful of rainwater that might have been a mouthful of tears '. . . I'm sure she does love you. I was wrong when I said she didn't. So it's all right, you see.' Timothy's face was utterly blank. Nonie felt hot with embarrassment. She wiped water off her face and pulled her coat from around her. 'You'd better take this.' She flung it over his shoulders. 'It's an awful long way back to town.'

'What did you call me?'

'What?'

'Just now. You said my name.'

'I only said Timothy.'

'I liked you saying it.'

Nonie felt breathless. Timothy was wheeling his bicycle through the gates now. He was smiling again and making plans out loud, oblivious of the rain.

'I expect I will write to you. Will that be all right?'

'Yes.'

'You can write back if you like.'

'All right.'

'I was just thinking.' He paused to mount his bicycle, steadying himself with one muddy boot on the road. 'It would be a jolly piece of luck if I were to run into your father over there. I'll tell him how you are.'

Rain was running down the neck of her nightdress, dripping from the tips of her fingers. She stood up to her ankles in a puddle of water and was able only to nod in reply.

Timothy suddenly leaned forward and kissed her squarely on the mouth. 'That's how they do it in the moving pictures,' he said. Then he was in motion, cycling away as fast as he could.

22

If you can grin at last when handing over,
And finish well what you had well begun,
And think a muddy ditch a bed of clover,
You'll be a soldier one day, then, my son.

BEF TIMES, 1917

They began to see less and less of Hannibal around Greystones. 'Where's he going?' demanded Elsie, watching the jinker rattle through the gates. 'To the reserve,' replied Kester briefly. 'You know that King is dying.' They all knew. Even though they had never met him, Hannibal's father's dying had a place in their daily business. King was rarely spoken of, except in passing. 'Hannibal, I've put aside some soup,' Ruth might say. 'Enough for four.' Hannibal would nod. Then the billycan of soup would be gone from the draining board, and Hannibal would be gone to the reserve, with enough soup for himself, and King, and Mina and Jessie. Often he stayed away overnight. On those occasions, Ruth woke Nonie in the early mornings to help with the milking.

The winter's mud dried on the road. The mill workers came by and filled the potholes with sawdust and stones. They began to hear the buzz of the circular saw again and the groan and crack of a tree being felled somewhere up the valley. Elsie and the twins came home from school on the back of the timber wagons sometimes, covered in bark and shavings.

Up at Dingley the house was silent. Now, Consie and Jackie were most often at Greystones. Consie sewed at the kitchen table. Jackie knitted, or sat outside with the twins playing jacks, or followed Hannibal around the paddocks. Bert Haggerty had aged in the weeks since Stan's death. His face had lost its red shine, and his mouth was downturned. There was a hesitation in his voice. He had become forgetful. Consie spoke tenderly to him and found him little jobs. He ran errands into town or tinkered with Kester's motorcycle. When he could find nothing to do he simply stood, his arms limp at his sides. Then it would be Kester who would take his hands and lead him on a walk somewhere, to look at the buds in the orchard or the new chickens, talking to him gently. 'I always wanted a daughter,' said Consie to Ruth. 'But the Lord gave me Kester instead, and there's not a daughter I could have loved more. And He gave me my Jackie-boy too. There was a time when I used to wonder why He gave me a child not quite right, but now I know. He saw to it that I would have one son the war couldn't take away. I've a lot to be grateful for when you think about it, Ruth.'

Queenie Cousins was not one to tolerate idleness. After Consie and Bert decided they would not be taking in customers again, and while they thought about what to do next, Queenie took herself off to town and found work there. She had no difficulty. Her nurse's training put her much in demand at all the guesthouses, where wounded servicemen were arriving in increasing numbers. There was fear, too, that the terrible influenza that was sweeping Europe would find its way south.

'Well, of course it won't,' declared Kester. 'We're just too far away from Europe.'

Queenie hissed with contempt, making Kester flush. 'Well it won't, Auntie Queenie,' she repeated. 'Just look at the weather over there, for one. All that snow and fog.'

'And I suppose it never gets damp and cold here?'

Consie exchanged a look with Ruth. They were fitting Elsie's new frock at the kitchen table. Elsie was standing on the tabletop turning in circles while Ruth and Consie pinned the hem. Nonie was holding the tin of pins and saw the look. It seemed to say, 'Here they go!'

'Of course it gets cold, I'm not saying that. Only it's not as bad as over there.'

'Well, excuse me, I didn't realise I was in the presence of an expert.'

'Now now, Queenie,' said Consie mildly.

'Hush, Kester,' said Ruth.

'And how on earth could germs travel all that distance?' pursued Kester, ignoring reason.

'I'll tell you how, my girl. They'll travel in the dirty clothing of returned soldiers, that's how, and in their fingernails and in their lungs. But I wouldn't know, of course, not being a medical genius like you.'

'Ow! A pin is stickin' me!' exclaimed Elsie. 'My leg is bleedin'!'

Ruth and Consie returned their attention to Elsie apologetically. Queenie said, 'See that you don't bleed all over that new frock. It'd be a wicked shame to have to wash it before it's even had a wear.'

Kester was bored with her life again, and it was making her irritable. For the most part she avoided confrontations with Queenie, with whom she could never see eye to eye. She took advantage of Elsie's distraction to leave the room now, and the hem-pinning continued for a while in peace. Consie said at last, sighing, 'Kissie needs a husband.'

Nonie saw Ruth frown at Consie in warning, but it was too late. Queenie was off again. 'A husband? There's not a man alive who'd take on a wilful headstrong girl like Kester. She had a chance with Ned Gannon and she knocked him back, like the fool that she is, all because she was holding her heart in her hand out to . . .'

'Queenie!' commanded Ruth.

'It's hard work Kester needs, and plenty of it,' continued Queenie. 'Only our Kester is too much of a duchess to stick it with any job. I hold her father responsible for that, for both of them. There's no good come of her brother either, you can depend on it. All those high notions he picked up at the university. Joined the Bolshies, and probably in Russia now for all we know, and good luck to him.'

'Please Queenie!' begged Consie tearfully. 'At least not in front of the children!'

Queenie quietened down in deference to her sister's tears.

'It's all right, Auntie Queenie,' said Elsie placatingly. 'I've stopped bleeding.'

Kester decided to resurrect her plans to become a photographer. Her first attempts at taking pictures had been appalling failures, and since shortly after her arrival at Greystones the camera had lain idle in a corner of her room. Now, inspired by boredom, she took it up again, determined to master it. She sent away for books and information, new plates, and coloured bottles of chemicals. For several days she roamed around Greystones, both in the house and outside, with her tripod under one arm and her camera under the other, setting up her equipment in various spots and studying light and depth of field, and calculating exposure times in a notebook. She was utterly absorbed and a good deal more cheerful.

'It is not a fitting occupation for a respectable woman,' declared Queenie.

But Consie tidied out a box of photographs from Dingley and brought them down to show Kester for encouragement. These were a great delight to the children and they were examined and passed around the kitchen table many times. 'Kester's father loved having photographs taken,' Consie explained. 'So I expect it's in the blood. There was a photographer chap called Archie Singles used to come up to Dingley quite regularly, with all his bits and pieces in the back of his van. Queenie would remember him, although Kester is too young.'

'I remember feeding sugar to his horse,' said Kester absently, peering at a photograph of a picnic party by a waterfall.

'Oh, yes, of course you'd remember his lovely old horse. Archie Singles learned his trade in the Crimea,' continued Consie. 'I remember him telling Henry all about it one day, how they would develop their plates in the back of a van with fighting going on all around them.' She looked up. 'Now you'd remember him, Ruth. Archie Singles.' Ruth, not interested in the photographs, was peeling potatoes into a tin bowl. She shook her head. 'Of course you would. I remember Harry having such a barney with him. Old Arch saying taking photographs was just like painting a perfect picture and Harry as cross as can be at the very idea.'

Nonie, exchanging pictures with the younger children, held her breath. She glanced up and met Kester's alarmed face for a second. Ruth pursed her lips and shrugged. 'I don't remember,' she said.

'Fancy that,' remarked Consie, smiling gently. She uncovered another photograph and exclaimed over it. 'Now, here's the one I said I'd look out for you, Nonie. Do you remember? It was taken on your mother's wedding day. Look here, Kissie, it's you in that lovely dress you hated so much.' Nonie took the photograph from Consie, and the children clustered behind her to look.

'I never hated that dress,' said Kester. She did not look, though. She began to pick up photographs that were strewn across the table top and to tidy them into piles. It was not like Kester to be neat, thought Nonie. In fact, Kester's tidying was like Ruth's potato peeling—a way of seeming not to care. She considered the two of them for a moment.

'When I think of all the work I put into that dress!' Consie went on. 'Kester was so ungrateful! First she wouldn't put it on at all. Then, when she did she wouldn't tie the ribbon at the back, and wouldn't have her hair done! Do you remember, Kester?'

'Vaguely, I suppose,' said Kester, with her back to them. 'Really, Auntie, it isn't fair of you to bring all that up now. I was only a child.'

'You were fifteen. And then you wouldn't stand up for the photograph.' Consie chuckled. 'But Jonathan talked you around, didn't he? He always had a winning way.'

Nonie looked at the photograph and saw a younger Kester, plump, sullen, in a rather lacy dress. One hand, held at her side, was clenched in a fist.

Kester said, 'I don't know what you mean by "talked me around", Auntie Consie. I think he threatened to throw me into Evans' pig wallow.'

'That Jonathan!' smiled Consie, fondly.

'He meant it, too.'

A short while later, Queenie came in from the kitchen garden to announce that Bert had arrived back from town with the mail. He appeared in the doorway behind her almost at once, with a bundle of parcels and letters in his arms which he flung onto the kitchen table. He was breathless. 'There was a note waiting for me at the post office,' he said. 'Hannibal must have ridden into town this morning to drop it off.' Nonie was aware of silence again. All eyes turned to Bert Haggerty. 'The note says that King passed away in the early hours.' The piece of paper rustled in his trembling hands. 'There'll be a funeral tomorrow.' He looked up from the note into Consie's face, then Ruth's.

Ruth said, 'Flora, take the children outside.' They followed Flora out of the kitchen with surprised looks, but in silence. Nonie sat still, clutching the photograph of Kester, wondering why she had not been sent away too. She waited for someone to speak. Queenie broke the silence.

'How long?'

Ruth appeared to be calculating something in her head. 'Eight, no perhaps nine, eight or nine weeks.' Her voice was sharp. They are not speaking about Hannibal's father, Nonie thought.

'It would be better if it had been longer,' said Queenie. 'Hannibal will have to be careful.'

Ruth stood up. 'He'll need help. Queenie, you and I had best go there at once. There'll be the laying out. We must all be there for the funeral tomorrow.'

'That's right,' agreed Consie. 'All of us. And the children.'

'Yes, yes, all of the children, Kester, Jackie, all of us. If there is a crowd it will be harder . . .'

'That's the way,' said Queenie, folding her apron into a perfect square and laying it on the tabletop. 'Come along then, Ruth. No time to waste.'

'I'll get those frocks finished,' said Consie. 'It's only respect-ful they should be dressed in their best. We'll be all right. Kissie and Nonie will do the milking.'

Kester nodded but did not look up from the tabletop. Queenie and Ruth left the room in search of coats and hats, murmuring together. Bert Haggerty moved over to Consie and placed a hand on her shoulder. He smiled bleakly at Nonie.

'After tomorrow it'll all be done, then,' he said with an encouraging nod.

'Now then, Kissie, we'd best get on with our jobs. You're not going to sit about all gloomy now,' said Consie rousing herself.

'No.' Kester looked at Nonie for a second, then back to her aunt. 'I was just thinking—who will dig the grave?'

Nonie sat on, baffled by Kester's question, and frightened by the strangeness that had greeted the news of King's death.

'Leave your Auntie Queenie to sort that out,' advised Bert, helping Consie out of her chair. 'There's no call for bothering the young ones with that sort of talk.'

Consie sighed as she followed her husband to the door. 'Too much misery, too much death, poor Hannibal, and now this,' she murmured.

Kester nudged Nonie. Nonie stood up and followed Kester outside.

She was hoping to have Kester explain the mystery into which she had been included, but Kester was not feeling talkative. If I want to know the answers I will have to ask, Nonie thought suddenly, fiercely, and then she realised that she did not know any questions.

Kester was not much help with the milking. She had snatched up the post as she left the kitchen and she idled in the shed doorway glancing through it while Nonie fetched in Minnie, who was waiting at the house paddock gate. Kester condescended to give Minnie some hay when she had been safely closed into her headstall, and Nonie went to the wash-house to collect the milking buckets. When she returned she found that Kester had pulled a stool into the doorway and was reading a letter. Nonie felt a stab of resentment. She settled herself down on another stool and washed the cow's udder.

'Kester?' she said after a moment. 'Will you pass me the tin of petroleum jelly?'

Kester looked up, making a face, and pushed the tin towards Nonie with her foot. 'Horrid stuff,' she said. 'I hate getting it on me.'

Nonie settled a milking bucket between her knees and began working the greased teats in her hands. The process occupied her completely for some time. It was Kester who broke the silence.

'What a lot of letters. I must have at least six addressed to me. I'll see if your name is on any.'

'It won't be.'

Kester did not hear her. 'There's one from my friend Ruby. We used to work together at the Excelsior Teashop. We were great chums.' She read for a while, then exclaimed. 'Oh look here, she says she's getting married! Her chap is coming home. Ruby says they're going to open an ironmongery. Fancy that!'

There was another silence. Nonie, pausing for a moment to hook the cow's tail up over a nail in the side of the stall, stole a glance at the doorway. Kester was not reading. She was leaning back against the doorframe and gazing into the yard.

'Kester?'

'Mmm?'

'Will you be going to Ruby's wedding?'

'Oh, I don't know.' She shrugged indifferently and placed her friend's letter underneath the pile. Minnie stamped and shifted a little and Nonie patted her warm side. There was no sound for a while, except for the hiss the milk made. Nonie breathed its comforting smell. Then she heard Kester shift restlessly on her stool.

'Kester?'

'Mmm?'

'What are you thinking about?'

She heard Kester laugh lightly. 'Well, I suppose I should be thinking about King, and Hannibal, and the funeral tomorrow. Dear God, how I hate funerals. Auntie Queenie will be so proper!' There was a pause. 'Only I wasn't thinking about any of that, if you want to know.'

There was a further silence. 'What were you thinking about?' Nonie squeezed Minnie's teats gently. Milk hissed out blue and frothed up white in the bucket.

'Nothing important.'

'Please tell me.'

'Oh. Silly things. I was thinking about Paul . . . about your father . . . Paul.' There was a clatter as Kester's stool was knocked over. Nonie looked around Minnie's side and saw that Kester was standing now, facing the yard. She held the bundle of letters at her side. 'Do you know, Nonie, I'm twenty-nine. Well, so close to thirty now I might as well start calling myself thirty. Does that sound old to you?'

'Well . . .' Nonie was glad that Kester did not wait for her to finish.

'I don't feel old. I just feel so young and so stupid. Do you know what I was thinking—I expect you won't like me saying this—I was thinking how much I hate Paul sometimes!'

'So do I,' said Nonie.

Kester did not hear her. 'Not that I have any reason to. But it's just, oh damn!' She stamped her foot. Nonie, without looking around, could picture her doing it, and thought how childish Kester was. 'Paul always did whatever he wanted, Nonie. Always. It wasn't any good arguing with him if his mind was made up. So no one bothered arguing and he just went along doing whatever he fancied. It isn't fair!' She stamped her foot again. 'Now me, take me, for example. Whenever I have a plan, I have to fight the whole world to get something done. Is it because I'm a woman, Nonie, do you think? Or because I'm not Paul?'

'I don't know.'

'He used to say "Onwards and upwards!", laughing the way he did. Do you remember the way he laughed? And how he sang? And teased—he was a shocking tease—do you remember? Well, he used to say that, "Onwards and upwards". And he went onwards all right, upwards too probably, and we just sort of shuffled sideways while he was doing it. Oh, I hate him for it! If I had done something with my life it would be different, only I haven't. I just stood about waiting for Paul to tell me what to do.'

She stopped abruptly. Nonie, shocked, became aware that the milk had reached the top of the bucket. Minnie bellowed impatiently. Her tail flicked off its nail again and slapped across Nonie's hunched shoulders. Nonie deftly shifted the bucket away from danger and put another in its place. There was a further period of silence while Kester examined envelopes without interest.

Nonie said, tentatively, 'Kester, what would you do, if you could do anything?'

Kester shrugged. 'I don't know. I'm not good for anything. I didn't get much in the way of education like some girls do nowadays.' She laughed. 'My father used to worry that I'd pick up lice from school, so he kept me away. I learned reading and writing from Auntie Queenie, and sewing from Auntie Consie, and my mother taught me to play the piano. They sent Jonathan away to be educated properly. I used to look in his schoolbooks when he was home. He seemed so clever.'

The milk was flowing more slowly. Nonie leaned her head on Minnie's warm side and listened to Kester.

'Auntie Queenie wanted me to get my nurse's certificate. Just like her. But I wouldn't. I couldn't bear to be like her. Anyway, I'd rather be a doctor than a hospital sister if it came to that. I'd rather be the real boss, than just plain bossy, if you know what I mean. I don't know why I'm talking like this, it's silly. Nearly finished?'

'Nearly.'

'Oh, look, here's a letter from Ned Gannon.' Kester's voice brightened. 'He's in England. He got a terrific injury in France, you know. Goodness, it's four or five pages. I'll save it.'

'What would you do, though, Kester?'

'What? Oh, you mean if I could do anything? Anything really?'

'Yes.'

'Oh, I'd . . . I don't know. Once, I would have . . .' She hesitated before continuing. 'But there's no point wanting that any more.'

Wanting what? Wanting what? thought Nonie.

'If I could do anything, now, I would find my brother Jonathan. What would you do?'

'I don't know,' replied Nonie truthfully.

'Oh yes, I know. You'd bring your father home.' Kester laughed. 'It's what you all want. The little ones, and Flora, always writing letters and stuffing them in that hole in the tree near the creek. Did you know?'

'Yes.' Nonie felt herself flush.

'Such sweet letters. They make me laugh. I wonder what Paul would make of them.'

The bucket was half full and Minnie's udder was dry. Nonie shifted it from her knees and sat on, stung by Kester's flippancy. Kester was quiet as she read through another letter, then when she spoke her voice was different.

'Nonie. This letter. It's addressed to me. I don't know what to make of it.' There was a catch in her voice. 'It's an official letter, naming me next of kin to a . . . a Jack Cousins. They say he's missing in action.' Nonie turned her head and looked at Kester. Kester's hand was on her throat. She looked at Nonie with startled eyes, then back at the letter. 'Missing. Presumed killed. It must be a mistake. Well, it must be! Jonathan wouldn't be at war—not without telling me—he's a conchie.' Her hand left her throat and ran itself through her hair. 'And of course this isn't his name. He's never called himself Jack. This is a Jack Field Cousins . . . isn't that odd, "Field" . . . and my brother is Jonathan Henry Talbot Cousins.' She looked relieved suddenly. 'Oh, no, it's a terrible mistake, that's all. It was addressed to the post office. I shall speak to them. How awful for Jack's real family.' She crumpled the letter into a pocket of her skirt and came over to Nonie. 'Finished then? I'll help you carry a bucket.' Nonie stood up and Kester grabbed her arm suddenly. 'Listen,' she whispered, 'don't say anything about this letter, will you? Promise?'

'Yes.'

'There's enough to worry about. Just keep it to yourself. It's a secret Nonie. Promise!'

'Yes.' Secrets, secrets, thought Nonie, the grown-up world is full of lies and secrets.

'Oh, look!' said Kester, brightly, pulling an envelope out of her bundle as she bent to collect the half-full bucket. 'There is a letter for you after all. It must be you, but there's no surname.

Antonia.' She handed the envelope over to Nonie. 'Aren't you going to tell me who it's from?'

Nonie turned the envelope over in her hands. 'It's—it's just a girl I used to know in Melbourne.'

'That's nice!'

Nonie nodded. She made to follow Kester out of the shed with her bucket, but hesitated in the doorway and waited till Kester had disappeared behind the house. Then she pulled the letter out in the dying afternoon light and gazed at the slanted printing again. Her heart thumped. It was a letter from Timothy.

23

I am not sad; only I long for lustre.
I am tired of the greys and browns and the leafless ash.
I would have hours that move like a glitter of dancers
Far from the angry guns that boom and flash

SIEGFRIED SASSOON

Dear Antonia

Still in Mufti as I have thought it best to lie low for a bit. I had my picture in the paper—M was quicker than I thought to hear about me being Absent Without Etc. Bet some trouble was stirred up. M would have gone in to school with bayonets fixed I should think when she heard.

I have been on a good few trains of late. Some guards are very friendly and not the type to squeal but you have to be careful which of course I am.

It's jolly good news that Bulgaria has surrendered and the allies are making a brilliant push through Belgium we have certainly got old Fritz running scared.

I heard them talking about it in a store where I went to buy some cram they said it was bound to happen sooner or later but I think it was because of the yankees.

My money is getting tight but I'm told there will be fruit picking up north by christmas if I can wait that long. After that I will be enlisting because I expect they will have given up the search by then and I am hoping to have grown a beard at least the beginnings. If you want to know I wish I had taken your dog with me as it would be cheering to have someone to talk to at nights. But I am all right anyway. I don't know if this letter will get to you as I forgot to ask you your surname but if it does I hope it finds you as it leaves me—as they say—in the pink.

Cheer-o. Tim.

The reserve lay in the early morning shadow of the mountains. Bert Haggerty's long drag pulled in through its gates and laboured along the uneven road. It had been a quiet trip from Greystones. The twins and Georgie were uncomfortable in new shirts with cruelly starched collars that were already grey from being twisted. The girls were stiff in their frocks. Nonie secretly stroked the stuff of her new skirt with satisfaction, and felt guilty at the pleasure her clothes gave her. We are going to King's funeral, she thought from time to time, then she would look down at herself and smile.

There were a number of people gathered outside the little weatherboard church. Hannibal was there, standing apart from the group, waiting for the drag to arrive. He came over to them and helped Ruth down and spoke softly to her. Nonie watched Ruth reach up and touch his face. Mina Watts and Jessie were there. Nonie's eyes met Jessie's for a second, then Jessie looked away. She climbed out of the drag after Kester, and standing on solid ground, she felt the pleasure her clothes had given her slip away. She thought, we are here for King's funeral, and her spirits began to sink.

There were some other black-skinned people there, a pasty-faced minister, and a small white woman in a black dress. 'That's the Superintendent's wife,' whispered Kester, poking Nonie from behind. 'If she wants to talk, try to have a long conversation. Tell her all about yourself. That's what we're supposed to do.'

Why? thought Nonie, but she only nodded in reply. Queenie appeared behind them and, quite uncharacteristically, linked arms with both Kester and Nonie and propelled them forward. 'Over on your left,' she murmured to Kester. 'Is that the Mayor?' Kester half-turned her head, then turned back to Queenie and nodded. She looked terrified. Nonie stole a look over her shoulder and saw Ruth in earnest conversation with the man in question. Another man in a straw boater—quite an inappropriate hat for a funeral—stood beside the Mayor.

'That's Artie Taft,' said Kester, with a slightly quaking voice. 'He's a newspaperman, Auntie Queenie!'

'Well, it's only to be expected,' said Queenie, leaving hold of them abruptly. 'King Jimmy was a fine man and very much respected, the last full-blood of his tribe. Remember that.'

Kester nodded and gave Nonie a meaningful look. Queenie strode away. Nonie reminded herself, if I want to know anything I will have to ask, and said rapidly, 'Kester, why do we have to remember all that about King?'

Kester said. 'Well, because it's true. They don't know any-thing. They're here because of King. If they ask you anything, just talk about King . . . oh well, you didn't know him really, so just talk about Hannibal . . . no, not him . . . talk about Paul, and where you lived in Melbourne, you know, unimportant things. Just don't mention Alec.'

At the sound of that name, Nonie started. She looked at her feet at once so that Kester would not see her face. Kester, however, did not appear to notice the shock she had given Nonie. She was called away by Consie Haggerty to speak to the Superintendent's wife and she left Nonie's side smiling.

Alec, Alec, this is all about Alec, thought Nonie, sweat pricking coldly in her scalp. She thought, well, Alec is Hannibal's brother so he is King's son too, but that in itself did not offer an explanation. Then she thought, that is why they think I know what is going on, because I was there in Hannibal's cottage that night, only I don't know. And now, she thought, it is too late to ask.

The church service passed her in a blur. Nonie, standing quite still, recalled over and over the details of the night when she had come across Alec under the peppercorn tree. Sunlight wavered through the church windows, but offered no warmth. The unpolished wooden casket lying in the aisle, fragrant with newness, was bleak. The minister repeated words like 'noble' and 'humble' and even 'savage' once or twice, and reminded them all that King Jimmy had been baptised into the Christian faith and that there would be a place for him in the Kingdom. Then they sang 'Shall We Gather at the River', and Nonie was startled from her numbness by seeing Ruth, who was some distance away, lean her head forward and begin to weep. Her aunt made no sound, but there were tears rolling down her face and her shoulders shook. Nonie looked around for Hannibal. He was standing at the back of the church beside Mina and Jessie, along with several other people from the reserve. She remembered the way her aunt had touched Hannibal's face when they had arrived, full of tenderness and sympathy. She wondered why Hannibal was not there to offer some of that comfort to her aunt, and then knew in the same instant that such a display was not possible. Today, especially, her aunt and Hannibal had different places. Hannibal's place was with the black people, while Ruth must stand with the white folk of the town—the Mayor, and the Superintendent's wife, the newspaperman, all of them. She noticed Hannibal pass a hand across his brow and realised that he was looking at Ruth too. Then she remembered the child who had called 'Darkie Lover' mockingly from the school gate, and she felt chilled through.

Hannibal and three other men carried the casket from the church up to the little graveyard on the hill inside the ring of black pines. The other mourners followed. Sunlight dappled the quiet paddocks. Nonie walked behind Consie Haggerty and the Superintendent's wife, holding Georgie and Elsie by the hands.

Ahead, Jessie walked holding her mother's hand, and Flora held hands with Ruth. They seemed a great number of people gathered to pass through the narrow wooden gate into the graveyard. The Superintendent's wife said to Consie, 'Perhaps the children might do better to wait outside the fence?' But Consie shook her head and replied, 'It wouldn't be right. They should pay their respects too,' and she stopped and ushered Nonie and the little ones ahead of her, smiling.

The crowd of people made a crush around the graveside. 'It's deep,' whispered Elsie, leaning forward for a look. Nonie squeezed her little sister's hand to make her quiet. The grave had been dug alongside the row of wooden crosses that marked the resting places of all Jessie's brothers and sisters. A mound of earth lay against the fence to one side, waiting to be used to fill in the grave again. It was covered by an old tarpaulin. Nonie remembered that Kester had asked who would dig the grave. It was a funny thing to ask, she thought. Very likely Hannibal had dug it, and what did it matter anyway? At the side of the grave there were three great bunches of flowers that Consie had made from the wisteria and jasmine that was blooming at Dingley. They were tied with black ribbons and cast a heavy scent. The Mayor appeared to be allergic to the smell and sneezed repeatedly into a white handkerchief.

The pasty-faced minister squeezed his way to the front of the group, read out from his dog-eared prayer book, and the casket was lowered. There was silence briefly, then everyone was moving and murmuring again, heading out through the gate. Queenie Cousins stopped by Nonie and said, 'We've been invited to morning tea in the Superintendent's house. You wait back a bit with Jessie and follow along later.'

Nonie nodded. She watched the mourners leave in twos and threes and make their way down the path away from the graveyard. Hannibal and two other men remained to fill in the grave. She saw Jessie motioning to her from the gate. She went over. Jessie was wearing an old skirt that had been passed down from Nonie to Flora, and a new-looking jersey that might have come from Consie. She looked thin. 'We have to keep a look out,' she said. 'You stand over there,' she pointed a little way down the hill. 'I'll stand on this side.'

'Yes,' said Nonie, bewildered.

'Give Hannibal a wave if you see anyone.'

'All right.'

Nonie made her way to the place she had been shown. She wondered if she were meant to be watching for Alec. Perhaps they think he will come here to see his father's grave, she thought. It seemed the most likely explanation. She was relieved to have thought of it. She gazed diligently down the hillside and across the paddocks for the first sign of movement. She stood there for a long time and saw no one. Then she heard Jessie calling her. When she turned and looked up towards the graveyard again she saw Jessie standing at the gate and Hannibal and the other men disappearing down the hill carrying their shovels. The job was done, then. She went up to Jessie.

'I didn't see anyone.'

'Neither did I. It'll be all right now.'

Jessie walked in through the gate and over to the new grave with the bunches of fragrant flowers draped across it. Nonie followed her. They looked at the row of crosses. 'We made a cross,' said Jessie. 'Mum and me. Hannibal helped. It isn't as good as these other ones that my father made. We'll put it up tomorrow.'

Nonie said, 'Where is your father?'

The question seemed to surprise Jessie. She looked at Nonie and frowned. Then she pointed to the fresh grave.

'Was King your father?'

Jessie looked at Nonie again. 'King Jimmy Watts was my grandfather,' she said slowly. 'My father's name was Alec.' She added, 'He died at your place. You were there, Hannibal said. You found him.'

Nonie stared at the names on the little crosses: Jimmy Frederick, Joseph Alexander, Charles, Baby William, Annie Bella. She said, 'I didn't know he died.'

'They couldn't stop the bleeding.'

Nonie nodded, remembering.

'Auntie Queenie and Hannibal brought him home in the sulky and my Mum helped them to bury him. We had to do it straight away before the police found out. I held the lantern. It was terrible foggy.'

'Yes, I remember.' There was a faint moan of wind in the pine trees. Nonie looked up and saw clouds moving past the black tops of the trees. For a moment she thought she would lose her balance and fall down. She looked down again. 'They didn't tell me,' she said.

'They don't know my father is here—the police, I mean,' explained Jessie. 'When King Jimmy died, Hannibal had to come and dig out the grave again. My mother cried all day. We hid my father's body in the dirt by the fence, and now they've put it back again. If the police found out they would take Hannibal away and Auntie Queenie and your aunt too, because they helped.'

Nonie said tentatively, 'That day we met you up at the mill?'

'My dad was hiding out there,' replied Jessie calmly. 'I went over to stay there, so I could see if he was all right.'

'He found Flora and Phip. I pretended I did, but it wasn't me.'

'I know,' said Jessie, shrugging. 'Hannibal told me.'

So they all knew, thought Nonie. They all knew everything. They thought that I understood, but I didn't.

'Come on,' said Jessie. 'We have to go to the big house and have a cup of tea.'

'Jessie.'

'What?'

'What is going to happen now?'

Jessie paused. When she spoke again she sounded completely beaten. She spoke softly. 'Now my mum and I have to go to that other place. King Jimmy is dead now and the Gov'ment says we can't stay. They're going to cut this land up and give it to the soldiers when they come home from the war, that's what my mum said. They say it's better at the other place. But it's not our place. Here is our place.' She looked again at the array of graves.

Nonie said awkwardly after a moment, 'I—I'm sorry that your father died.' Jessie shrugged and turned her head. 'My mother is dead,' offered Nonie after some thought. 'She died of pneumonia.'

'Did she?' Jessie looked at Nonie curiously. 'Hannibal told my mother that your mother died of the drink.' She turned away. 'Come on,' she said.

Nonie did not follow her. She watched Jessie descend the hill without her, and when she was finally alone Nonie began to cry. She did not cry for Jessie and Mina, or for the little brothers and sister buried in the graveyard, and she did not cry for Alec, or for King Jimmy whom she had never met. She cried only for the child she once had been, who was abandoned by a mother who did not want her, and by a father who did not care. She stood under the solemn pines and cried until she was empty.

Ruth smoothed out the newspaper. This was the best part of the day, she thought, when the children were safely in bed, and the house was her own again. Kester's camera was in pieces on the kitchen table and Kester was examining each piece in minute detail and making notes. Hannibal, home again, rocked on the back legs of his chair in front of the stove, with Ruth's cat on his knee. The room was warm, and more quiet than it had been in weeks. The kettle, which had a slow leak, made regular hissing sounds. Ruth was reading out items from the newspaper from time to time, but otherwise the room was silent.

'I should think,' mused Ruth after a while, 'that it is really only a matter of time. The Germans are losing their allies, and the British are doing so well now in the Middle East. And the way President Wilson is talking about conditions . . .'

'I'm tired of hearing about the war,' said Kester peevishly, stretching. 'Isn't there something else?'

'Not much.'

'All the papers will have to close down when the war really is over,' said Kester. 'They won't know how to print ordinary things.'

Hannibal snorted and reached forward to poke the stove embers. Ruth looked up. 'Nonie,' she said. 'I didn't hear you come in.'

Nonie stepped out of the shadowed doorway. 'I wanted some water.'

'Can't you sleep?'

Kester looked up at Nonie and smiled. Nonie said, 'I'm just thirsty.' She crossed to the trough on her bare feet.

Ruth turned a page idly. 'Here's something, Kester. There's a boy gone missing in Melbourne, fourteen years old, his mother is offering an enormous reward for any information about him. It's a familiar name—Hadlow-Waller. Where have I heard it?'

Kester turned her attention from her camera to Ruth. 'That's the soap millionaire. Hadlow's Beauty Products. Lally Hadlow-Waller is the wife of that American soap millionaire. Well, the widow, he's dead now of course. She came back to Australia with all his money. Oh, I know all about her!'

'Oh yes,' said Ruth. 'Hadlow's Beauty Soap, I've seen it in catalogues.'

Kester was full of intrigue. 'Goodness yes. It's everywhere. My friend Ruby told me her cousin used to clean for Lally Hadlow-Waller. And do you know, in the whole of her house there was not one cake of Hadlow's. I stopped buying it when

I heard that. I mean to say! She had lots of stories about Lally Hadlow-Waller. Apparently Lally is a great one for parties, plays tennis all day, always going to dine with the Governor.'

'Really, Kester, you shouldn't gossip.'

Kester pouted. 'I'm only telling you who she is. That's not gossip. Fancy that about the missing boy. I didn't even know she had a son. What's his name?'

Nonie finished her drink and replaced the cup on the draining board. Ruth looked around. 'Are you going back to bed?'

'Yes.'

'I expect you'll sleep at once. It's been an eventful day.'

'Yes.'

Nonie walked through the kitchen slowly. Ruth turned her attention back to the paper. 'His name? Oh yes, here it is.' Nonie hesitated in the shadow of the door and held her breath, hardly daring to listen. 'It's Theodore. Theodore Osgood Sherman Hadlow-Waller. Quite a name for a young boy. "Known to his family as Oggie".'

'Oggie! Not seriously!'

'That's what it says.'

Nonie breathed. She turned her back on the warmth of the kitchen and headed to her bed again, disappointed and relieved. Kester giggled. 'If it were my name I'd probably want to call myself Joe.'

Ruth nodded. 'He probably does. Or some such name like that.'

24

We've done with mud and shell and stench
Hope ne'er again to see a trench
No more to hear the crumps come in
The whizz-bang's shriek, the minnie's din
The long last years have been well worth
If once again we've 'Peace On Earth'.

BETTER TIMES, 1918

Kester organised the Field family into sitting for a photographic portrait. It took a great deal of persuasion. Ruth insisted that she did not need a family portrait, but the children were delighted with the idea, and she finally relented.

Kester took most of that November afternoon setting up chairs in the parlour, and nearly all the rest of the afternoon arranging people on them. The parlour curtains were flung over the tops of their rods to allow as much light as possible into the room, and, as the afternoon progressed, lamps were brought in to take over where the light failed. Ruth sat on a dining chair in the centre of the group, nursing Georgie in order to keep him still. Georgie objected to being held, and growled about not being a baby and wanting to sit with the twins. The twins sat cross-legged at Ruth's feet. They wanted Kester's dog to be in the photograph too and one or other was always missing as he went to fetch Bosky. Bosky refused to co-operate, and the fetching and refetching continued without pause. Flora was ill again and had spent the week in bed with a temperature and an infected throat. She was assigned to a dining chair too, placed sideways to the untidy group, so that she had to turn her head to see the camera. She was thin in her new dress, and the jaunty ribbon Kester tied into her hair on one side rather dwarfed her face. Elsie was placed to one side of Ruth's chair with her hand on the chair's arm. She too, was positioned on an angle, more from necessity than artistic choice, as she had fallen out of a tree the day before and grazed her face. Hannibal reluctantly took up a position behind Nonie, in the gap made between her and Flora.

'It isn't a proper family photograph with me in it,' he objected.

Ruth turned in her chair and glared at him. 'Of course it is,' she said. Then turning back to Kester she said, 'For goodness sake, I can hear Minnie at the gate. She's never been milked so late. Get on with it, Kester.'

'I'm going as fast as I can!' Kester was on her knees measuring the distance from the twins' feet to the camera with a wooden ruler.

'You can't possibly expect to make a living from photography at this rate!'

'I'll get quicker with practice. Ouch, Bosky, go away!'

Kester climbed to her feet, looked at the window despairingly, and positioned herself behind the camera. 'I'm just about ready. Are we all settled?'

'Get on with it!'

She frowned. 'I'm worried about the light.'

Hannibal said, 'There won't be any soon.'

'That's what I mean. We might have to put it off till tomorrow.'

Ruth said, through gritted teeth, 'Take it now, or not at all. Be quiet, Georgie. Watch Kester!'

'Don't want to.'

'Here, Bosky! Here, boy!'

'Leave that wretched dog alone, Tom.'

Kester looked up. 'Straighten your back, Nonie. Flora, there's a crease in your dress.'

'For pity's sake, Kester,' implored Hannibal.

'All right, all right. I'll count to three. Quite still now.'

Ruth began to speak and then closed her mouth.

'One. Two. I hope you're all ready—three!'

The shutter clacked and froze a moment in their lives forever. Georgie was scowling, and the twins had blurred slightly as they turned at the same moment to see that the dog was looking at the camera. Elsie was caught with her mouth open and Flora with her eyes cast wearily down. Nonie and Hannibal were looking directly before them and Ruth was captured forever with her head to one side and a faraway concentrated look in her eyes, because at that very second she was hearing the bells that were being rung out from all the churches in town, proclaiming the Armistice.

'Listen!' she said, raising her hand, as they began to move. 'Listen!'

They were louder now. Peal upon peal rolled toward them on the evening air, the sound plunged in the valleys and tumbled back upon itself when it struck the wall of the hills.

'What is it?' asked Elsie.

'It's bells,' said Phip.

'What for?'

'The war is over,' said Ruth. She let Georgie down, stood up, and left the room.

'Let her go,' said Hannibal quietly when Nonie turned to follow.

'What does she mean?' asked Elsie, surprised.

Kester shrieked suddenly. 'It's over! The war is over!' She flung her arms around Hannibal and hugged him. And then, whether they understood it or not, they were all of them shouting and jumping and hugging one another.

The war which had been inside people's lives for so long, rubbing up against everyday occurrences, everyday thoughts, which had formed the way people lived and spoke and behaved, was suddenly gone. Into the void it left, there now flooded a view to the future, where before there had been only the day-to-day. The newspapers announced with cheerful irony that at least some of the troops would be home, four years late, by Christmas.

The first plans for the new order came from Dingley. Consie and Bert Haggerty announced that they were selling up the old guesthouse and its surrounding land. The money from the sale would be divided, rightfully, between the Haggertys, Queenie and Kester, with a fourth portion to be put aside for Jonathan Cousins. Consie and Bert and Jackie intended moving back to their cottage in town. Shortly afterwards Queenie revealed that one of the large guesthouses in town was closing its doors and reopening as a repatriation hospital for returned soldiers, and that she had been invited to take up a position as senior matron. Without further ado the guesthouse was packed up, its furniture moved, sold or disposed of, and the Haggertys and Queenie were installed in their new old home. Along with Bert Haggerty's pet goat, and several other bits and pieces, the pianola was moved down to Greystones. Consie insisted that it was Kester's really and it was welcomed by the children although Ruth put her hand to her head in despair more than once after its arrival. The house, she thought, was growing smaller. Meanwhile, Dingley was left without so much as a backward glance, empty and silent on its ridge.

At the Old School there was a picnic day to celebrate the Armistice. They all went along and watched Elsie and the twins sing 'Rally Round the Banner', and 'God Save the King', and form a patriotic tableau with a spotty girl dressed up as Britannia surrounded by Union Jacks. Nonie, in her best clothes, exchanged shy looks with other children her own age. Ruth surprised her by appearing to know everyone. It occurred to her for the first time that Ruth's lack of sociability was self-imposed, and that there were many people in the district who knew them and knew about them. She did not dislike the idea. She listened to snatches of conversation as she moved around the groups of people and heard tales of husbands, sons and brothers who were still in Europe and whose return was eagerly awaited.

That night Flora pinched her awake.

'What's the matter?'

'I can't sleep.'

Nonie pulled herself up on one elbow. 'Why?'

'My throat hurts, and my legs are aching. And I'm thinking about things, Nonie.'

'What things?'

'Dadda.'

Nonie sat up and tucked her knees under her chin. 'What about him?' she said cautiously.

'If all the troops are coming home soon, then he'll be coming home too.'

'Well . . .'

'What if he wants us to go away with him?' There was a pause. Nonie did not speak. Flora continued, 'I know I said I wanted to a long time ago. But I don't want to leave Auntie Ruth. Do you?'

'I don't know.'

'I want to stay with Auntie Ruth, Nonie. I'm frightened.'

'It's all right, Flor. It'll be all right.'

'Will it?'

Nonie thought, if I want to know things I have to ask, and if I want to say things, I have to say them. She said, 'We won't go away from Auntie Ruth, Flor.'

'But how do you know he won't want us to?'

'We just won't go. That's all.'

Flora was silent as she thought her sister's answer through. 'Cross your heart?' she said at last. Nonie crossed her heart and Flora watched her solemnly. 'Nonie, will he mind?'

'It doesn't matter.'

Flora was silent again. Nonie thought back to the day when she and Kester had been in the stable together, talking about what they wished they could do. 'Flora,' she ventured at last, 'do you remember Dadda laughing and singing?'

'No,' said Flora.

'Do you remember him teasing?'

'Teasing?'

'In sort of a funny way.'

'No,' said Flora. 'Why?'

'It's just something Kester said.'

'Do you remember him doing that?'

'No,' said Nonie smiling to herself. 'Not ever.'

Kester's old friend Ned Gannon was one of the first soldiers to return to the district. He had been halfway home on a hospital ship when the Armistice was announced, along with hundreds of other young men who had been deemed too badly wounded to return to the trenches. He arrived at Greystones unannounced, riding on the back of a timber wagon. He was a tall, broad-shouldered young man with straight sandy hair and a grinning mouth, a missing arm, and a missing eye covered with a patch. But he alighted from the wagon while it was still moving, with all the grace of the sportsman that he once had been, waved a thanks to the driver, and as he came through the gates he bellowed a coo—ee that was loud enough to break glass.

'Where's Kissie?' he shouted to the first person who arrived in answer to his call, Elsie. She pointed toward the orchard. There were people issuing from the house, the stable, the paddocks by now. Ned Gannon winked a greeting at them, slung his kit bag onto the verandah and leapt one-handed over the kitchen garden fence, taking the shortest possible passage to the orchard, where he found Kester, lifted her off the ground with his good arm and danced around the apple trees with her, laughing and singing. By the time everyone had collected and been greeted and greeted again, Kester had already organised that Ned was to stay with them for a few days.

'I was hoping you'd be asking,' said Ned. 'Which is why I brought me kit.'

'Your mother.' protested Ruth faintly.

'Oh, Mam'll be tickled pink, Ruthie, don't mind about that. I've been back barely three days and she's already complaining that I'm eating her out of house and home. I ask you! And me a returned soldier!' Then he lifted Ruth off the ground and kissed her on each cheek. 'That's the French way of kissing,' he explained affably. 'You'll notice I've picked up a great number of sophistications since I've been on the Continent. Not that I hold with foreign customs to any degree, but I do say—and I bet you'll agree with me, Hannibal—that when it comes to the ladies, two kisses are better than one!'

Ned Gannon spent three weeks with them. He stayed in the cottage with Hannibal at night, and during the day he made himself useful. He split logs for the wood pile wearing an old shirt of Hannibal's with the empty left sleeve pinned up to his shoulder, he brought in Minnie to be milked, and even tried to milk her with one hand, and he did a hundred odd jobs around the house as a way of paying for his keep. The children were enchanted by him. He entertained them with fanciful stories of life on the Western Front, and unpinned his shirtsleeve so that they could see his stump. He did not, however, unbandage his eye, for all the children's pleading, and he did not tell them of the stinking mud of No Man's Land, where he had lain for half a day waiting for a stretcher-bearer, or of the lice that had crawled through his scalp and his clothing, or of the mate who had fallen dead across his body and saved him from being picked off by sniper fire.

Kester's motorcycle was uncovered and dismantled again. Ned was extremely competent with motor vehicles, and for the first time in a long while the motorcycle ran perfectly. After that there were innumerable trips to and from town, Kester at the handlebars and Ned hallooing from the sidecar. They brought back messages for Ruth, and the mail, and news of other friends who were on their way home. They also brought back one or two of Ned Gannon's brothers and sisters, clinging on behind Kester or crammed into the sidecar with Ned.

Ruth was tolerant of the influx of visitors, but she did not participate in their picnics in the orchard, or their noisy sing-songs around the pianola. With Ned there to help Hannibal with the daily tasks, she spent more time in the house, sorting through papers and boxes, and adding up accounts. Nonie came upon her aunt frowning over the post at the dining table one afternoon. The room was dark but there was a shaft of early summer light pushing through the doorway which led from the kitchen. Shouts of laughter from the yard invaded the silence.

'What on earth is going on out there?' said Ruth, looking up for a moment and seeing Nonie.

'They're playing cricket.'

'Is Ned batting?'

'No, he can't quite get the hang of the bat with one hand. He's bowling all right, though.'

Ruth nodded, smiling, and looked back at the papers in her hands, then she looked up again. 'Did you know they have a buyer for Dingley?'

'Have they?'

'Kester came back with the news this morning after she collected the post. The sale is going ahead quickly. Local folk—I don't know them personally—they intend to put in an orchard and market garden. And poultry.'

'So it won't be a guesthouse any more?' Nonie wandered closer to the table.

'No. Guesthouse days are over for Dingley.' Ruth leaned back and re-pinned her hair. 'It's the way of things, I suppose. Changes happening everywhere.'

'I suppose.'

'It won't make things easier for us. People won't be buying our little offering of fruit and vegetables, or our few dozen eggs if these folk are there.' Nonie nodded, not sure if a response was required of her. She drifted towards the doorway in her indecision. Ruth said, 'Do you miss the city, Nonie?'

Even the mention of the city brought Nonie out in goosebumps. She said nothing. 'Because I was thinking,' added Ruth, 'that we should move away too. Not to the city of course, but into town. Actually I have been considering it for months. At least the others could go to school every day.'

'Would I be able to go back to school, too?'

Ruth looked surprised. 'I didn't think you would want to.'

'It would be all right.' If Nonie was surprising her aunt, she was surprising herself more.

'Well, yes, if you wanted. There might not be many girls there your age. You know that Jessie has a job now.'

At the mention of Jessie's name, Nonie looked up quickly, her heart thudding with relief. She had been unable to even think of Jessie in the last weeks without feeling helpless and guilty. 'I thought Jessie was going away,' she said.

'Away?'

'She told me they would be taken to another place because King was dead.'

'We couldn't possibly allow that. Queenie has taken her on at the Returned Soldiers' and Sailors' Hospital. Jessie and Mina are both living with Consie and Bert for the time being.'

Nonie wondered why she had not realised that something would be done for Jessie and Mina, the way something had been done for Alec. She said, 'Would Hannibal mind?'

'Mind what?'

'If we went to live in town.'

Ruth suddenly flushed. 'I assume he would be happy with the idea . . . of course I need to speak to him about it.' She hesitated and seemed embarrassed. Nonie felt a warmth coursing through her, she had placed a thought in her aunt's mind.

It was easy to do really. Now her aunt was thinking about Hannibal, not as another child in the large Field family, but as an adult. She turned to the door, then paused and turned back with confidence.

'I just want to say, Auntie Ruth . . . Flora and I both want to tell you, that if Dadda comes back now that the war is over, we won't be going away with him.'

Ruth looked at her. 'Well, of course not,' she said.

When Ned Gannon finally returned to his mother's home, Kester became glum. It was a subject of great amusement to her family. 'Why Kissie, anyone would think you were sweet on Ned Gannon,' said Consie mischievously. 'The way you're missing him.'

'I'm not sweet on him, and I'm not missing him,' retorted Kester, tossing her head.

'Ned was always one for the girls,' commented Bert Haggerty, winking at Nonie. 'I'm surprised he didn't bring back an English lass, or a French one.'

'I expect he left a string of broken hearts behind him,' said Ruth, entering into the teasing for once.

Hannibal said, 'Ned told me all the English girls were thin and bony.'

'Well, it's not something you'd ever say of Kissie,' said Bert. 'Always first up for pudding, wasn't she, Mother?' Consie nodded assent.

This was too much for Kester, who flounced from the room indignantly. Nonie found herself laughing. She noticed Ruth looking at her and wondered what her aunt was thinking.

Ruth was marvelling at how Nonie had changed in a year, from the morose child she had brought home on the train, white-faced and tight-lipped, to this smiling young woman who said little, but noticed everything. How has the change happened, she thought, when the year has brought us nothing but tragedy and sadness? But perhaps good can come even out of the worst sorrow. Then, quite carefully and deliberately, she pictured Harry Lambe in her mind for the first time in nineteen years, and she saw that his soft pink and white English face was smiling at her.

'You're a long way away, Ruth,' said Consie, noticing her.

'Yes I was, I suppose,' replied Ruth, smiling. 'I was just thinking about Harry.'

'You could have knocked me down with a feather!' said Consie to Bert later, as they drove back to town. 'The way she said it, so casual, as if it hadn't been nearly twenty years since she uttered his name!'

Bert replied, 'It's peacetime, is what it is. Making us all change.'

'If you ask me,' said Consie, shifting closer and tucking her hand into the crook of her husband's arm, 'it's the change that has been brought about since those children came that has done it. I know we never thought Paul would ever do anything worthwhile in his life. Probably he hasn't, either. But it's through Paul that Ruth got those children, and that's been worthwhile.'

'Ah,' Bert nodded. 'Well, there you are, like I always say—it's an ill wind . . .'

25

Shall they return to the beatings of great bells
In wild train-loads?
A few, a few, too few for drums and yells,
May creep back, silent, to still village wells
Up half-known roads.

WILFRED OWEN

December passed, and Christmas, and the year was new again. Kester was anxious to spend her share of the money from the sale of Dingley. She made trips into town and considered shops where she might set up a photographic studio. Her family implored her to be cautious.

'You've only one little camera,' reasoned Bert Haggerty, who could not understand the fuss about photographs at all. 'You don't need a whole shop to keep it in.'

But Kester was determined. She needed a shop to set up as a studio, with a room at the back where she could develop her own plates. As for the camera, she intended to dispose of it as soon as possible, and furnish herself with the very latest photographic equipment money could buy.

Once Nonie said to her, 'I didn't know you wanted to be a photographer really. I thought you wanted to be a doctor.' Kester looked amazed and stated that she had never in all her life entertained such a ghastly and preposterous idea. Nonie considered reminding Kester about what she had said on that day in the stable, but then decided to give up and leave her alone to carry on with the photography plans.

At Greystones Kester met with less opposition. Ruth had her own concerns about money and could not be bothered with Kester's notions. The strawberries had cropped poorly and the runner beans were infested with mites and showing no promise. The small quantity of money that had been left to her by her parents had dwindled to nothing, she noticed with consternation. On top of this, Flora had developed rheumatic fever and was needing constant care. Kester's trips to town were useful, at least, because they allowed Ruth to communicate with the doctor and to receive lengthy instructions from Queenie, who was herself busy treating returned soldiers. Ruth encouraged Nonie to accompany Kester. Kester was not reliable with shopping lists, and was too often distracted visiting friends. They always stopped by the railway station if a train was due, to see if any soldiers were disembarking that day. The stationmaster had decked the building with ribbons and a paper banner which read: 'WELL DONE, BOYS—HEALESVILLE WELCOMES YOU HOME.' The sign, put in place in January, was tattered and tawdry by March, and generally ignored by the handful of soldiers who stepped off the train every other week. Kester knew a number of the returned soldiers, by face if not by name. Most recently they had seen Cec Canning's youngest boy, Reggie, looking older than his twenty years, helped off the train by his sister Winnie.

'Are we visiting the Gannons today?' Nonie asked, climbing out of the sidecar near the station gate one hot morning, to stretch her legs. It had been a dusty drive from Greystones. Her arms were coated with yellow dirt and her throat was dry.

Kester giggled at her. 'You've got two white patches around your eyes where your goggles were!' She removed her own cap and goggles and they giggled at each other. 'We might call by,' she added indifferently.

Nonie did not believe Kester's indifference. They never made a trip into town without visiting the Gannons. Ned was working in his father's dairy and waiting to be called back to the city. The army had promised to fit him with a glass eye and an artificial arm. His name was on a waiting list. Nonie thought about Ned Gannon for a while, then she said, 'Kester, did you ever find out about that soldier with the same name?'

'Oh, that Jack Field Cousins? Nobody knew of him at the post office. They said I should go into the city and check the rolls at Victoria Barracks. And I will, too, or I might ask Ned to do it for me when he goes in. Poor fellow, Jack I mean, I suppose he's got a family somewhere, wondering . . . Oh look, here's the train!' Kester stood on tiptoe and shaded her eyes. Nonie turned to watch too.

The train from the city came to rest, grinding and hissing, alongside the station platform. A small group disembarked and were met by a man who ushered them to his motor coach. 'They're off to the guesthouse where I used to work,' remarked Kester, who recognised the man. She made a face. 'I'm glad I won't be making up their beds every day.' She turned her attention back to the platform in time to see two soldiers climb down from a carriage and be greeted by a woman and a rowdy collection of children. The woman hugged one of the men and shook hands vigorously with the other.

'Do you know them?' asked Nonie.

'Hard to say at this distance.' Kester screwed up her eyes. 'Oh, yes, it's that woman from Narbethong—Flint, or something—I remember her coming in for her mail. It must be her husband come home, perhaps that other chap is a relation.'

There seemed to be no one else. The stationmaster began to unload parcels from the guard's van. Kester fixed her goggles back into place. 'Come on,' she said. 'We might as well call in at Gannon's, since you suggest it, Ned's mother nearly always has nutloaf for morning tea.'

The motorcycle, rather hot after its run from Greystones, refused to start. Kester kicked down on the starter lever several times to no avail, then she got off and kicked the front wheel. 'We'll have to walk all the way to Gannon's,' she said crossly. 'And get Ned to come back and fetch it, I suppose.'

Nonie began removing her layers of protective clothing. She noticed that one of the soldiers was standing some distance away watching them as the Flint family climbed into their sulky. Nonie nudged Kester, who was on her knees examining the starter lever. 'That soldier is staring at us,' she said.

Kester got up. 'Well, if he were a halfway decent sort he'd offer to help,' she said in a disgruntled voice, and looked around.

'Hullo, Kester,' said the soldier, approaching them and removing his hat. 'I thought it was you.'

The soldier was Jonathan Cousins.

Jonathan's homecoming was a noisy business. After hugging him as if she would never let go, and then bursting into tears, Kester walked him proudly into town and up to the Haggerty's cottage, leaving Nonie to trail behind carrying all their belongings. Bert Haggerty and Jackie were working in the garden when they arrived. The sound of their voices brought Consie and Mina out of the house. After that there was so much noise that several people came from nearby to see what was causing the commotion. 'It's like the prodigal son come home again!' said Bert Haggerty over and over. They led him into the house all talking at once, with Consie wiping her eyes on the hem of her apron.

Nonie was relieved to be ignored. She sat in a corner of the morning room and watched Jonathan Cousins. He had Kester's dark eyes, but they were lined at the corners, and his mouth turned downwards whenever he allowed himself to stop smiling. Surrounded by his family he smiled incessantly at first, as they swirled around him fussing and exclaiming, but Nonie fancied that left alone he would simply sit, and his face would be empty. He did not resemble the serene, smooth-faced youth in the photograph she had seen, or even the brother of whom Kester had so often spoken, who had given her seashells on one occasion and threatened to throw her in Evans' pig wallow on another. Nonetheless, she liked Jonathan Cousins' face. She wondered when he would notice her.

'How could you have gone off like that and not told a soul!' cried Consie, holding his hand to her cheek while Kester plumped cushions around him and Jackie patted his knee. Jonathan flushed and stumbled, and turned his face upwards to his aunt. When she let go his hand he held it up to her again, and she took it, smiling, and kissed it.

He said, 'I'm sorry, Auntie Consie. It was because of everything that had happened.'

'But that business never meant anything to us, not to make us give you up,' said Bert Haggerty, leaning forward. 'All that anti-conscriptionist palaver . . . if you want to know the truth I agreed with you, it was only your Auntie Queenie going on, and you know what your Auntie Queenie is like.'

Jonathan nodded wryly. 'It wasn't just that. It was awful when they put me in prison, but they only kept me six weeks, then they let me out one morning, at dawn, without a word of warning and I thought, well, I could hotfoot it down to Kester's for a cup of tea and some sympathy, or I could just take myself off for a bit.' He shrugged. 'So I took myself off, got myself some new lodgings down near the markets, and a day job humping boxes of cabbages.'

Mina came in to the room with a pot of tea, and Jackie went out to the kitchen to help her bring the cups. Kester said urgently, 'But what made you go, Jonny, after all those times I heard you speak down by the river, telling people they were fools to send their sons to war?'

'Oh Kester, it doesn't matter.' Jonathan rolled his head back on his chair and closed his eyes. For a moment there was silence in the room. He opened his eyes again. 'It was the blasted white feathers that did it in the end.' He smiled. 'Such a stupid reason, but I suppose one reason is as good as any other. They kept appearing under the door of my room—it was probably my landlady who was doing it—morning and night. Whenever I opened my door they were there, she must have been plucking chooks clean to keep up the supply. I ignored it at first, then I began to wish I didn't have to go home after work because I knew they'd be there, then I began to get angry about it, and angrier, and angrier, then one day I woke up and thought—if I could just get my hands on the blighter that's sending me all these damnable feathers, I would fair choke him to death.' He smiled around the room abruptly. 'Funny sort of thing for a conchie to think, wasn't it? After I thought it, well, I just took myself down to the town hall and signed the papers.'

No one said anything. Jonathan cupped his hands in his lap and seemed to examine them. Nonie looked at his hands and noticed that they were scarred all over, and that his fingernails were chewed down to their nubs. 'So it was you, that letter with the false name,' said Kester gently.

'Eh?'

'You enlisted as Jack Field Cousins. You named me as next of kin.'

Jonathan shook his head. 'Not me. Actually, I named Auntie Queenie as next of kin. I thought it might give her some satisfaction to be first to hear that I was dead.'

'Now Jonathan, that's a wicked thing to say,' scolded Consie, shocked. 'Your Auntie Queenie has been worried half out of her mind, as we all have!'

Jonathan looked repentant. 'But it wouldn't have been hard to find me,' he said. 'You only had to look at the records.'

'It's the one place I never thought of looking,' said Kester. 'It's the one thing I was certain you would not do, Jonathan!' She laid her head against her brother's leg and Nonie could not tell if she were laughing softly, or crying.

Jonathan said, 'Mind you, if I'd been thinking straight I would have given a false name. They recognised me right away from the newspapers and, my oath, they were pleased to have me. I got two weeks basic training and I was put aboard the next ship out, before I even knew how to hold a rifle. On board I was treated like a leper—would have shot through in Cape Town, only they never gave me shore leave. My CO was

219

determined to get me to the front line in one piece, so that I could be blown into a hundred bloody pieces, he figured.' Jonathan gave a short laugh and closed his eyes again. 'Actually,' he said after a moment. 'I can't work out, for the life of me, why I wasn't blown up.' Nonie noticed that Jonathan's eyes were open again and that he was looking straight at her. She blushed and lowered her head. Mina and Consie handed around cups of tea. Jonathan nudged Kester. 'You haven't introduced me to your friend yet, Kester. Typically ill-mannered of you.'

Kester sat upright and gasped. Nonie, eager to be introduced, saw a look of consternation pass between Kester and Consie and Bert. 'This is . . . she's Nonie,' said Kester all at once. 'She's . . .'

'She's Lily's daughter,' said Jonathan, leaning forward in his chair and holding out his hand. Nonie took the offered hand. It was hard and warm.

'That's right!' exclaimed Kester. 'How did you guess?'

'It took a little while,' admitted Jonathan. 'But really she's very like Lily. How do you do?'

'Hullo.'

Consie began to speak quickly. 'Oh, yes, very like Lily, we all think. More so than the others. There are six children, Jonathan, Lily and Paul had six children, and Nonie is the oldest. They all live out at Greystones with Ruth.' She hesitated, then looked at Kester.

Kester said, 'Lily is dead, Jonny.'

Jonathan only nodded. He removed his hand from Nonie's and picked up his cup of tea in a slow, thoughtful way. 'I'm sorry about my hands,' he said after a few seconds. 'I'm sorry if it felt unpleasant shaking my hand just now, Nonie. They got cut about. I had this job unravelling the wire, you see. Of course they gave you gloves, but some mornings the gloves were frozen stiff and there wasn't time to wait for them to soften.'

'It's all right,' said Nonie, trying to smile.

Jonathan nodded, then he said. 'I thought she must have died. I first thought it—I don't know—ages ago. Then just now, before you told me, I thought it again.'

The silence that followed was as solid as a wall. Jonathan continued to examine his hands. Jackie, leaning toward him to offer him some fruitcake, tapped him tenderly on the arm. Jonathan looked up into Jackie's face and smiled. 'Good to see you, old man,' he said gently. 'How's your little brother Stan?'

The silence became fluid then, worse even than that first silence. Pain flowed between them as cruel as acid. Jonathan, sensing the change, looked inquiringly at Kester, but at that moment Queenie's voice rang out. She stood in the doorway in her grey nurse's uniform with Jessie behind her. Her mouth was set in a firm, straight line. 'All the way up the street they've been calling out to me, "He's home! He's home!" I don't know why you didn't bring a brass band with you!'

'Hullo, Auntie Queenie,' said Jonathan, smiling.

Jonathan's smile, every bit as endearing as his sister's, had no noticeable effect on Queenie Cousins. Nonie shrank back with a beating heart as Queenie entered the room. Queenie looked him over quickly, then cast an accusing eye at everyone else. 'And you've let him into the house—just like that—sitting on the best chairs with goodness only knows what vermin breeding inside that shirt! Jessie! Get the kettle going at once!' Jessie hurried through the room and out to the kitchen, throwing a grin in Nonie's direction. 'Come on then, my lad, we'll have those clothes off you. They're for burning.'

Jonathan began to laugh as Queenie tried to unbutton him. 'You can't burn them! They're army issue! The army might want them back!' He struggled against her, laughing.

'My! Haven't we done a turnabout!' Queenie's face was still grim. 'Don't just sit there, girl,' she said briskly to Kester. 'Get his boots off.' To Jonathan she continued, 'There was a time, I recall, when you wouldn't have had an ounce of regard for anything that belonged to the army. Well, you tell them for me, if they want this dirty, lousy uniform back they can take the matter up with your Auntie Queenie!'

'It's not lousy,' protested Jonathan as his jacket was forcibly removed. 'Parts of it are nearly new.'

'I'm sure you know best!' retorted Queenie, wrestling with his shirt. 'But I can tell you I've seen inside enough soldiers' uniforms by now.'

Consie, alarmed by the immodesty of the situation, caught Nonie's arm and whispered, 'Go and help Jessie, dear, we won't get a moment's peace till poor Jonathan's been broiled!' Nonie reluctantly did as she was told. She was astonished at the turn of events. She had expected some sort of rage from Auntie Queenie, but nothing like this. Kester and Jackie were unwrapping Jonathan's puttees and giggling hysterically, and Consie and Bert were shaking their heads at each other and smiling. Queenie continued to hold forth: 'Lice, and fungus between the toes like something that should be in a museum, and rat bites—yes, rat bites—all gone to scars, and ears full of pus . . .'

'Auntie Queenie, I'll be sick!' cried Kester, still laughing.

'. . . and worms, and what I've seen coughed up from their lungs, the smell of it . . .'

'Now, now, Queenie.' Consie's voice had a soothing note.

'I don't know, I just don't know what the good Lord can have been about, letting young boys suffer so!' Nonie realised with a shock as she closed the door behind her that Queenie was weeping. She heard Jonathan's voice, muffled now, comforting her. She turned and faced Jessie who had tied a pinafore around herself, and whose grey starched dress was far longer than Nonie's. Jessie had grown up. Nonie smiled at her wanly and wanted, more than anything in the world, to go home to Greystones.

In the afternoon Hannibal arrived because Ruth had grown anxious when Kester and Nonie did not return. By this time Jonathan had learned about Stan Haggerty's death, and Alec's death, and a great deal more about how the Field children had come to be at Greystones. As well, there had been a steady stream of visitors to the house, as news got about that Jonathan Cousins was home. Nonie would like to have listened in to Kester's quiet conversations, but she was not included. Jonathan did not speak to her again, although occasionally when she brought in a fresh pot of tea from the kitchen, or collected plates, she felt his eyes on her. It seemed possible that he wanted to speak to her, she thought, only he did not know what to say. In the kitchen she was kept busy washing dishes. She felt shy with Jessie. Once she ventured to ask her if she liked her job, and Jessie had replied loftily that she enjoyed it very much, but had not said more. Jessie had filled out and looked more healthy than she had ever looked. Nonie, beside her, felt wretched. She was glad when she heard the shout of greeting from Jonathan, and Hannibal's voice coming along the hall.

It was arranged, after another pot of tea, that Hannibal should return to Greystones with Nonie, and take Jackie for a few days, to make room for Jonathan, and to allow Kester to stay on too. Jackie, who missed the younger children, was delighted. While they waited for Consie to pack a bag for him, Nonie slipped outside into the shadow of the front verandah and listened to Kester and Jonathan and Hannibal talking together as they stood around the jinker. They would collect the post before they left town, Hannibal was saying, because Ruth was expecting an important letter. The other things that Kester had been instructed to bring home with her would have to wait till another day. They laughed together, and teased Kester, who pouted as she always did. Kester told Jonathan about Ned Gannon's terrible injuries.

'But he saw London,' she added. 'When he was well enough to get about a bit. He saw the Tower, so that's something I suppose.'

'Saw a good few English girls, too, I expect.' Jonathan smiled and looked at his sister. 'Or is Ned still foolish enough to be

223

waiting for you?' Kester looked away. 'I saw the Tower too,' remarked Jonathan, becoming animated suddenly. 'And the British Museum, and the National Gallery. I had a fortnight's leave one time—oh, eight months ago now,—and I met a girl who took me all over the place. She was an English girl. Drove a field ambulance. She was on leave too. She said she'd write to me after the war.'

'You should write to her first,' said Kester. 'What's her name?'

'Cecily.'

'Is she thin and bony?'

'That's a strange thing to ask me.'

Kester and Hannibal laughed and explained.

Jonathan shrugged. 'I've probably been more of a fool than Ned,' he said after a moment. 'Yes. I will write to her.' He turned his head to the verandah. Nonie felt his eyes on her and she tried to look as though she could not hear them. Jonathan said, 'So where's Paul?'

There was a brief moment when no one spoke, then Hannibal replied, 'They say he went to war.'

'Who says it?'

'The children. Ruth made inquiries.'

'It's not the kind of thing you can imagine Paul doing.'

'Now don't start being unkind!' objected Kester, serious suddenly. 'He might have gone!'

'And not left his name on the rolls, and no money being sent home to his wife and family? Kester, I don't know why you should be defending him after all this time,' Jonathan said. Nonie thought, at the mention of her father how quickly all happiness had died between them all. Jonathan's voice was bitter. 'He'd never have stuck it, anyway. He could never stick anything.'

'If you're talking about Lily,' Kester retorted peevishly. 'Then you can stop now. Everyone always talks about her as if she was some kind of saint, it makes me sick. And they make Paul out to be the very devil.'

'After they moved away from here we never heard another word. None of us ever knew where they were!'

'Lily could have written just as easily as Paul, but she didn't. You can't blame him completely.'

'Kester, you are still a damned fool,' said Jonathan.

'All right, all right,' Hannibal climbed up into the jinker. 'Leave it alone now.'

Consie came out of the house with Jackie and hurried Nonie in front of her. Queenie followed, calling instructions to Hannibal which were to be taken back to Ruth. Bert Haggerty handed a basket of scones wrapped in an old dinner napkin up onto Jackie's knee. Mina and Jessie stood in the doorway to wave. Goodbyes were passed back and forth. Jonathan took Nonie's arm in his warm, scarred hands and helped her into the jinker. 'Goodbye,' he said, then after a hesitation he continued. 'I wanted to ask you—how did your mother die, Nonie?'

The group of people around the jinker fell silent. Consie said gently, 'I believe she died of pneumonia.'

Nonie caught Jessie's eye. She said, 'No, she didn't, that's just what they say.' She faced Jonathan with a steady gaze. 'My mother died of the drink.'

Consie, looking visibly upset, began to wave them off in a rush. Hannibal clicked the horse on but Jonathan ran after them, calling out. Hannibal reined in and Jonathan caught up to them a little out of breath. 'There was something else,' he said. 'I almost forgot . . . something that I want you to tell Ruth. When I was there—in London that time with Cecily—we went to the National Gallery, I think I told you. There was an exhibition of sketches done by war artists, some a couple of hundred years old.' He paused to catch his breath. 'And there— large as life—I saw two sketches and a painting done by Harry. Couldn't believe my eyes! I asked the person in charge just to

225

be sure that it really was Harry Lambe—Ruth's Harry. They told me he's famous, and his paintings are worth a lot of money. Pity he didn't live to enjoy it. I wanted Ruth to know. You tell her for me.'

'I will.' Hannibal smiled slightly. 'I don't know whether she'll be glad or not.'

'And Nonie,' said Jonathan. 'It's all right, telling me what you did. I'm glad I know—it's always better to hear the truth.' I know it is, thought Nonie, I know, I know. She only nodded.

Jonathan stepped away from the horse. 'Cheerio, then. Cheerio Jackie.'

Jackie waved his scarf until the jinker turned out of the street.

26

Bonsoir old thing
Cheerio, chin chin,
Napoo, toodleoo
Goodbye-ee

WESTON & LEIGH

*I*t was April, and the leaves on the apple trees were turning yellow. Flora lay on a rug in the orchard, propped up by pillows, 'getting her strength back', as Ruth called it. It was taking a long time, thought Nonie, looking at her sister's thin face, the slight furrow of concentration on her forehead as she turned pages of a *Girls' Own Paper*, brushing away a fallen leaf with a limp hand. Anyway, how could you get back something you never had?

Three weeks had passed since Jonathan Cousins came home. Jackie Haggerty was still staying at Greystones, and Kester was still in town. A fox had dug under the wall of the henhouse and taken half the chickens, leaving behind a snowstorm of feathers. One or two days after that Hannibal came upon the old wombat, dead, down by the creek.

'She was old,' he said to Ruth. 'She'd had a good life.'

Ruth shrugged her shoulders, angry with herself for feeling sad. 'Everything comes to an end,' she said.

Late one morning they found that Bert Haggerty's old nanny goat had slipped from its tether and wandered away. Nonie and Jackie were sent in search of it. 'She won't be far,' said Ruth. 'Probably headed home.' They took a rope, and apples in their pockets and, climbing up the track to Dingley, found quite soon that they were following a trail of neat droppings. Conveniently, the goat had nibbled back the snares of blackberry and cut a clean path for them.

'She's a good old girl,' said Jackie from time to time, copying his father's tone. 'Good old girl, our Sweetie.'

It was easy being with Jackie. He did not talk much and when he did he seemed not to mind whether you answered him or not. They stopped half way along and turned to look down upon Greystones, clearly defined amongst the bush green of the valley by the blaze of autumn leaves in the orchard.

'That's your place, that is,' observed Jackie solemnly, pointing.

Nonie remembered standing with Flora some months back, and looking down on the roof of Greystones in much the same way. She had been uneasy with the idea of Greystones being her home then, but today when Jackie spoke she smiled at him. 'We're walking up to your place now, aren't we?' she returned.

'Our old place,' corrected Jackie. 'We don't live up there no more.'

They began to climb again. 'Do you miss your old place, Jackie?' she asked. Jackie did not answer her. He smiled at a blue wren dancing on the track ahead.

The guesthouse had remained empty. Dingley's new owners had cleared a great deal of land on the far side of the ridge and begun to put in fruit trees and nut trees. Close to the property boundary, a further area of land had been excavated and would be the site of a new house. The old house had been considered not worth living in, not even worth demolishing, with its sagging roofline and the passage of damp up the walls. After months of neglect, the garden had swelled and spilled over its neat rock borders and swathed the foundations of the guesthouse in greenery. Tree branches scraped across cobwebbed windows, a stem of ivy waved triumphantly from a chimney pot. Emptiness lay upon the place like a quilt. It deadened the birdsong, dulled the hum of insects. They walked knee deep through grass, past a jungle of yellowing wisteria, and stopped by the front door.

'No one's here now,' remarked Jackie. 'Old pianola's got tooken down to Ruthie.'

'That's right,' said Nonie.

'I like that old pianola.'

'Do you?'

'Kissie plays that one sometimes, and when I was a little tyke I could sit on Kissie's knee and play too, I could.'

Nonie looked at him and tried to picture it. 'What did you play?'

'"Soldiers of the Queen".' He grinned at her. 'I like that one. Kissie makes the roll go around and I play with my hands real gentle, but my Dad said "No" to Jim and Stan because they go too rough on the pianola and hurt it. Bang! Bang!' He raised his hands and crashed them down onto imaginary piano keys. 'Jim and Stan is dead now,' he added and looked thoughtfully at the house. 'Uncle Henry is dead and Aunt Jentah,' he continued softly, as if reciting. 'And Harry Lambe is dead, and Lily is dead too.'

Nonie was surprised to hear her mother's name. 'Do you remember them all, Jackie?' she asked.

'Got a 'ceptional memory, I got,' he replied with a lofty look in her direction. 'Quite proud of my memory, we all are.'

They walked around to the kitchen door. The screen in the outer door was ragged. The area outside the kitchen, once a clear quadrangle of well-worn earth, was cluttered with clumps of bracken. Jackie growled at it, as his father must have once done. 'Bloody bracken,' he recited under his breath. 'Bloody be the death of us, bloody bracken will.' Then he added out loud in his own voice, 'Sweetie don't eat bracken. She don't like it.'

'Where will she be?'

He did not answer her. He wandered toward the woodshed, once stacked with logs, now gaping and empty but for a few pieces of bark curling on the ground outside. More bracken grew in its corners, Jackie shook his fist at it. He rounded the side of the woodshed and Nonie followed him to the herb garden. The air here was thick with insects and there was a waft of honey. There had once been a neat path of crushed rock which ran along the centre of the small rectangular garden, but it was barely visible now. Leggy branches of silver rosemary stretched upward out of the dead sticks of last season's growth. Mint yellowed on huge stalks, a clump of parsley was heavy with seed, battered leaves of rhubarb sprawled in a corner. There were the pungent and sweet smells of sage and rose-scented geranium.

'Is this where we'll find her?' asked Nonie.

Jackie said, 'I found Jonathan here. He was crying.' Nonie felt a tightening in her chest. Jackie said, 'I come looking for him. No one else knew where, only me.'

'When?'

'On the big wedding day. We come up from town and my mum had a new hat. Beautiful hat. Just the ticket! We all got photos tooken.' He waved in the direction of the arbour.

'Lily's wedding?'

'That's right.' He beamed at her.

'Not Jonathan,' said Nonie gently. 'It was Kissie. She cried because she hated her dress, didn't she? She must have come out here crying.'

Jackie shook his head. 'Not her. Kissie never cried that wedding day. She yelled, like a common tramp, my Auntie Queenie said, and Jonathan says to Kissie, "You shut-up, you".' Jackie looked at Nonie with big eyes. 'That's bad, that is, saying that to Kissie.'

'Why did he say it?'

Jackie looked around. 'Sweetie isn't allowed to eat the rhubarb. It makes her sick. She likes parsley, she does. When she gets here she'll eat all the parsley up.'

Nonie touched his sleeve and he looked slightly startled and stepped backwards. 'Why was Jonathan crying?' she asked him.

He frowned back at her. 'Jackie? You've got an excellent memory, haven't you?'

His frown faded. "Ceptional memory,' he corrected gently.

'Why was Jonathan crying on the big wedding day?' she pressed, and then seeing the look of bewilderment on Jackie's gentle face, she realised her mistake. Jackie did not understand 'why'. 'What did Jonathan say when you found him crying? Can you remember, Jackie?'

Jackie smiled then. 'Jonathan said, "Don't mind me, old man, I'm just a silly duffer", he said to me.' He gave Nonie a confidential look. 'Him not a duffer really, not Jonathan.'

'Of course not.'

'He said, "Kissie's being a bad girl, she got nothing to scream about." He said he'd got to be best man to Paul, he said, "and it should be me marrying Lily, not him".' He lifted his head and turned slightly. 'I hear something,' he said. 'Must be our old Sweetie.'

Nonie did not look in the direction that he had turned to. She looked along the ruined rows of the herb garden and just for a second she saw Jonathan there in his morning suit with his head in his hands. Then she turned back and saw a real man, not an apparition from the past, round the end of the woodshed and stop in his tracks at the sight of them.

Jackie was standing a little in front of her, and Nonie was glad of him. The man hesitated, looked as if he would move closer, then decided against it. He raised his hand. 'I'm looking for the folk that run the guesthouse—the Cousins or the Haggertys.'

Nonie hesitated too, waiting for Jackie to speak, but he did not. 'They're not here any more. It's been sold,' she called back.

The stranger nodded. He was wearing dusty boots and a soldier's trousers and shirt, with an old brown coat thrown over the top. The brim of his digger's hat was bent and stained. He pushed it back, wiped his forehead which was startlingly white compared with the rest of his grimy, sunburnt face, then pulled it down again. He slung his pack and bedroll onto the ground and squatted down beside them.

Jackie remained silent, staring at the stranger as he took a tobacco tin from his coat pocket and proceeded to roll a cigarette. 'There used to be a bit of work up here,' the man said casually. 'Could always pick up a meal for an hour of woodchopping. I figured I'd stop by on my way through.'

'The Haggertys have moved into town,' offered Nonie. She noticed, fascinated, that the man had only three fingers on one hand, but he rolled his cigarette with ease and placed it between his lips while he felt around in his pocket for matches. 'When did you get back?' she asked.

He shrugged, ran a match along the side of his boot and lit the cigarette. 'While ago.'

Nonie moved a few steps closer till she was beside Jackie. 'The new people are putting in an orchard,' she said. 'They might give you work.'

The man was looking sideways at her through a haze of smoke. 'No,' he said, turning his head away. 'Don't need the work, just thought I'd call by, renew old acquaintances.'

'Did you know the Haggertys?'

'A bit.' He pointed with his cigarette to Jackie. 'Remember you, all right, Jackie Haggerty.' Nonie looked at Jackie, expecting a reaction, but Jackie's face was completely blank. 'Don't remember you,' continued the man, turning his attention to his boots. 'At first I thought you must be Kissie Cousins, but that can't be. She'd be a grown woman now—probably about your age when I last saw her. How old would you be?'

'Fourteen.'

He grunted. 'You don't look like her. Her hair was different, and she was fat, chubby anyhow, a butterball of a kid. Pretty with it.' He turned his face away and looked the house over. 'Gone to rack and ruin,' he observed with his cigarette between his teeth. His eyes, barely visible under the brim of his hat, screwed up as smoke curled into them. 'Kissie's married now, I suppose.'

'No, she's not.'

He turned back to Nonie and looked at her again. Nonie was aware that Jackie was making gentle keening noises and beginning to sway. He is worried about the goat, she thought, we must go and find the goat, but she found herself blushing under the man's stare and felt unable to move. 'She's a pho-tographer—Kester, I mean she's planning to be. She rides a motorcycle.'

He roared laughing at that and Nonie felt bewildered for a moment, then indignant. The man stubbed his cigarette butt under his boot, rose to his feet still laughing, and shouldered his swag. Nonie found her own feet. She pulled at Jackie's sleeve. 'Come on,' she whispered. 'We'd better find Sweetie.'

Jackie nodded and began to move away. The man called out to them. 'Kissie's brother—the brainy one who went to the university—he a photographer too?'

'He's just got back.'

'War hero, is he?'

Nonie felt offended. She flushed. 'He was like you, I sup-pose. A soldier.'

'Didn't get his hand blown off, though.'

'No.' She felt awkward and angry.

The man adjusted his hat, tipping it further forward on his face. He took a few steps away, then stopped as though another thought had just occurred to him. 'I know who you remind me of—you must be Ruthie Field's kid, from down the valley.'

Nonie answered in spite of herself. She felt Jackie's anxiety to get away like a current running along one side of her. 'Ruth Field is my aunt.'

He shrugged his shoulders. 'Don't know how that can be. Ruthie's brother was an adopted boy, blackfeller. You can't be his.'

'Her other brother is my father.'

'Other brother?'

'Paul.'

'Didn't know she had another brother.'

Jackie tugged at her arm suddenly. 'There she is!' he shouted.
'I hear her! Hear her, Nonie? Sweetie! Sweets!' There was a
bleat in answer to his call. 'She's down at the blackberries, she
is.' He headed off around the east side of the house. Nonie
turned back, unable to walk away without some acknowledgement of the stranger. She saw that he was already heading
down the drive toward the main gates. 'Goodbye,' she called,
glad that he was going. He turned back at the sound of her
voice.

'Goodbye-ee!' he called back cheerfully, without slackening
his pace. 'Goodby-ee, Non-ee! Give my regards to Butterball
when you see her!'

A little later they were leading Sweetie home down the old
track. The goat pulled ahead of them on the rope, dainty on
her hooves, but determined. Occasionally she stopped dead and
yanked backwards to reach a blackberry tip, or a young branch
of black wattle. Jackie stopped each time and waited patiently
while she ate. Once Nonie said, 'That was a strange fellow,
Jackie, that swaggie up at your old place.'

She thought that Jackie was not going to answer her, but
after a moment he said darkly, 'Don't like that one. Him a
teaser.'

Flora was waiting at the gate for them with Bosky at her
feet. Ruth was sitting on the verandah steps holding a bundle
of letters. She called Nonie over. 'You found her. Good. Hannibal has just got back with the post.'

Nonie stood at the foot of the verandah steps and watched
Flora and Jackie lead the goat into the orchard while Bosky
followed on, worrying their heels. Ruth frowned at the dog then
returned her attention to Nonie. She seemed unlike her usual
contained self. 'Nonie, I wanted to tell you—I'm very pleased—

234

I received a letter from the timber mill today. I've been waiting on it for days. They've agreed to my price to buy the property.'

'Greystones?' It was an unexpected announcement.

'The house, land, everything.' Ruth rattled the letter in her hand. 'They intend to put a rail through from the mill to town. They'll be able to keep the mill working right through the year that way. The manager will live in the house, rather convenient really.' She stopped speaking and looked at Nonie. 'You seem surprised.'

'I—I didn't know.'

'We've been talking about it for months. I thought you must have realised.'

'No.' She asked tentatively, 'Where are you moving to?'

'Us. We. We're all moving, Nonie. Together.' Ruth looked at Nonie sharply. 'We're going to move closer in. Nearer town.' She smiled. 'For so long I was so afraid of leaving. Now I can't imagine why. This place—it ruined my grandfather, and killed my mother and father, and as for me—oh well, it doesn't matter. I'm tired of living in a valley. When we find a place, I hope it will be on a hill. Somewhere with a view.'

Nonie thought that she had never seen her aunt so happy. She asked, gently, 'Auntie Ruth, did Jonathan Cousins want to marry my mother?'

The question made Ruth utterly still. Her hands, which had been agitating the letters in her lap, lay motionless. 'Yes,' she said.

Nonie said nothing. Sometimes, she thought, it is better to be silent. She waited. Ruth eventually spoke again. 'Of course it broke Jonathan's heart. It ruined his friendship with Paul. None of us could understand it.' She put her head on one side. 'What made you ask?'

Nonie sat down on the bottom step and tucked her knees up under her. 'Something Jackie said.'

'Jackie couldn't have known.'

'It's just that he remembers funny things.'

Ruth smiled distantly. 'What was he telling you?'

'He talked about the day of the wedding. He said Kester shouted and Jonathan cried.'

'Poor Jonathan,' murmured Ruth.

The cat, Henrietta, appeared from under the verandah steps and climbed into Nonie's lap. She was highly pregnant again, looking smug. Nonie shifted her knees to accommodate her. Her hands stroked the cat's full belly, felt its great heat. Nonie said, 'We can't leave the cats behind.'

'No.' Ruth sighed. 'Nor the dog, though he's more trouble than he's worth. I wish Kester would take responsibility for her belongings occasionally. Queenie is absolutely right about Kester. She was brought up thinking she was a princess, and she's inclined to treat those around her like servants.'

'I think she's nice.'

'Well of course she's nice. She's also impossible.'

From the orchard they could hear the dog yapping and Flora's and Jackie's laughter. The cat rubbed its face in Nonie's palm. Nonie said, 'Why couldn't you understand it?'

'What?'

'You said it just now, talking about the wedding.'

Ruth shrugged. 'We couldn't understand Lily's choice. Jonathan was so devoted, so loving. Paul was so . . . indifferent.' She stole a sidelong look at Nonie as she spoke, wondering if she had said too much. She was surprised to see Nonie smiling.

Nonie was thinking that of all the words used to describe her father in the year that she had been at Greystones, this word—'indifferent'—was the first word she recognised as being true to her own memory. She looked up at her aunt, still with the smile on her face. 'All right,' she said. 'Then why was Kester shouting that day? It can't have been the dress. It's too silly.' Then before Ruth could answer she knew what the answer would be. 'It was because Kester loved him, wasn't it? She was angry with him, not with the dress.' Ruth shrugged slightly, but Nonie knew that her guess was correct.

Ruth said, 'Kester was only a girl. We didn't take her infatuation seriously. Certainly Paul never treated her with anything other than indifference.' That word again. 'Perhaps that was the attraction. Lily loved him for his indifference, so why shouldn't Kester?'

'Silly thing to love someone for,' remarked Nonie with a snort.

'Quite.'

Nonie added, 'I think Ned Gannon loves Kester.'

'He always has,' replied Ruth.

At that moment, Ned Gannon and Kester were announcing their intention to be married. Ned's mother and all his brothers and sisters had arrived at the Haggertys' cottage with the couple, and during the uproar that followed, Bert Haggerty, red in the face, handed around glasses of sherry while Consie hugged everyone. Queenie, grim, said, 'Well, that's about the last straw, I suppose. We might as well all move over to Holy Rome.' But later, as she sipped the sherry that had been forced on her, she was seen to wipe a tear from the corner of her eye and raise her glass to Esme Gannon.

In the meantime, Jonathan, while joining in the excitement, counted days in his head. Forty days it might take for his letter to reach England, and ten of those had already passed; a week, perhaps, for Cecily to consider his proposal; forty days more before her reply would be in his possession. Or perhaps she would take longer to decide, or perhaps it would be thirty days before it reached England, or perhaps longer. Tomorrow, he thought, he would enquire at the post office. While he chatted to the Gannons, he counted the days over and over.

Hannibal came around the side of the house with a shovel over his shoulder. 'I'm glad you found the goat,' he said, then stood there in the shade of the house, in silence.

'I told Nonie our news,' said Ruth.

He nodded and lowered the shovel. 'I was going to dig over the bed beside the runner beans. I suppose there's not much point now.'

Ruth shrugged. 'It seems strange not to be planning the next season's crop.'

'It does,' said Hannibal. He leaned back on a wooden verandah post, his hands idle on the shovel handle.

'Are you glad, Hannibal?' asked Nonie.

He looked at her for a moment. 'Glad enough,' he said.

'And what about you, Nonie?' said Ruth. 'You'll be able to go back to school if you still want to. Do you?'

'Yes.' Nonie felt her face grow hot. She put her cheeks down to the cat's fur.

'Why?'

'I'm not sure.' But she was quite sure. She said tentatively, her face still partly obscured by the cat's body, 'Do you think it's all right for a girl to go to the university?'

There was a moment of silence. 'Of course.' Ruth tried not to sound surprised. 'There are many women at university these days, I've heard. I never thought about it, to tell you the truth, but,' she frowned slightly, 'it could be expensive.' Nonie said nothing. Ruth saw the red flush at the back of Nonie's neck. She said, 'We can ask Jonathan if you like. We will ask him.'

Hannibal said, 'What are you going to study?'

Nonie lifted her head slightly. 'If I can,' she said, 'I want to be a doctor.'

'A doctor?' repeated Ruth, astonished.

'If I can.'

'Why?'

'Because of Flora. I have to look after her.'

Ruth and Hannibal were silent. Nonie's eyes burned. Now that she had said it all, and heard the words herself, she felt choked.

'Well, there's a turn-up,' said Hannibal gently. 'Good for you.'

Ruth stared at Nonie still hunched over the cat and remembered something.

Ruth sat on a hard chair in a room that smelled of furniture wax. The nun, facing her from behind a bare desk, had given the impression of kindness, while remaining distant. There had been little religious education in Ruth's life. These women swathed in black, with only their faces showing like white saucers, their subdued voices, their dove-like hands, made her uneasy. She had arrived by train an hour before, taken two trams, and walked three blocks to finally reach the St Vincent Home for Girls. She was aware, as she sat there in a room which gleamed unforgivingly with cleanliness, that her shoes were dusty.

'Of course we are extremely pleased that the Field girls have a relative who is interested in their welfare,' the sister said. 'We chose, however, not to disclose the contents of your letter to them.' Ruth began to speak but did not get far. 'We feel that it would be wrong to build up unreasonable hope. Sister Inez is fetching them now. She will tell them that there is a distant relative here to visit them.'

'But I intend to take them with me. I wrote that in my letter.'

The nun smiled. Her white hands fluttered into her sleeves and vanished from sight. Ruth stared at the place where the hands had been. 'Yes you did Miss Field, and I thank you for your generosity, and your donation. I only ask that you meet the girls first.'

'Is there something wrong with them?'

'Flora is a good and loving child. She is, however, in poor health. I expect the news of her mother's death will come as a terrible shock to her.' The nun paused and frowned slightly. 'The older girl, Nonie—Antonia is her name—has been rather more difficult. She is unco-operative at best, sullen and wilful at worst. We have been on the brink of dealing with her severely on many occasions, but have not done so because the younger one is so

attached to her sister and we have felt that it would be detrimental to Flora's well-being. We are not monsters, Miss Field.'

She spoke the last sentence so sharply that Ruth was startled. 'I'm sure you are not,' she replied, feeling guilty.

'Her school report suggests that Nonie is clever. Rather too clever, I am told, inclined to be sly.' The white hands fluttered from the black sleeves again and perched in repose on the desk top. 'We feel that it would be a wonderful reward for Flora to be taken into a loving home. We cannot expect the same for Nonie. That is why we have said nothing to the girls. You may choose to take Flora, if you wish, and leave Nonie with us. She is nearly thirteen. We will be seeking to place her in a suitable position in the coming year. It will not, perhaps, be the best position, but with some girls—girls like Nonie who have few redeeming graces— we must be prepared to settle for second best.'

Ruth did not know what to say. Another child like Paul, she thought, God forbid! They sat for the next few minutes in silence. There was a knock on the door then, and Sister Inez entered in a whisper of black cloth, ushering two figures ahead of her. 'Here they are,' she said.

Ruth rose to look at her brother's children. She saw Flora first, an undersized child in a grey pinafore with an upturned face, Lily's eyes, a frightened smile. She looked at the other girl and saw the top of a head, a flush of red creeping up the back of her neck into her hairline as Nonie twisted away and bent her head down behind her sister. Then Nonie turned back and looked swiftly, searchingly at Ruth. In a second Ruth saw Lily's eyebrows, the line of Lily's nose, Paul's thin mouth, the jut of his chin. But the look in Nonie's eyes Ruth recognised as her own. She turned to the sister in charge. 'I will take the girls with me at once,' she said.

The heat was beginning to leave Nonie's cheeks. She raised her head. 'I never thought about it being expensive,' she said tentatively.

240

'We'll work something out.' Ruth arranged her bundle of letters thoughtfully. 'I don't know how much money will be left after we've moved.' She was still for a moment then she said, 'Of course, we have Harry's paintings.'

Nonie looked at her aunt. Ruth was looking at Hannibal. 'That's the answer,' she said. 'Don't you think? If what Jonathan told you is true—if Harry's paintings are valuable now—we can sell them, one or two anyway. How many do we have?'

Nonie turned around to Hannibal. He was smiling down at the shovel handle. 'We have six,' he said. 'And some drawings.'

Ruth stood up. 'I'm glad you didn't let me send them all back,' she said. 'His family may hate me for it, but I'll sell them back to them now. Harry wouldn't mind, would he, Hannibal, he'd think it was a fine idea.'

'Yes, he would.' Hannibal was still smiling.

'I haven't looked at them in ages, not properly.' Nonie watched Ruth jump down the verandah steps. 'Come with us, Nonie. We can decide which one we'll sell first.'

Nonie said suddenly, 'Auntie Ruth, did anyone ever call Kester "Butterball"?'

Hannibal gave a short laugh. Ruth stopped in her tracks and looked surprised. 'My goodness, yes,' she said. 'It used to make her furious—all tossing curls and stamping feet—remember, Hannibal?' Hannibal nodded and laughed again.

'Who called her that?' asked Nonie.

'Paul, of course. No one else would have dared. Coming?'

Nonie stood up feeling breathless. The cat flowed calmly from her knee to the ground. 'In a minute,' she said. 'I want to look at something.'

She watched her aunt walk away towards Hannibal's cottage, her hand resting lightly on his arm, talking excitedly. In her other hand she held the bundle of unopened letters. One of these, she would soon discover, contained a cheque for two hundred pounds. With it, a letter from a Melbourne firm of solicitors announcing that the money was the entitlement of the family of Paul Field, who had enlisted in the AIF as Jack Field Cousins, and that it had been kept in trust, under instructions, to be paid out to his family on his return from the war, or on news of his death.

Nonie walked to the gates of Greystones. She thought, if I look down the road, and he is not there, it will be all right. And if I look, and see him walking home . . . She did not finish her thought, because she did not know what to think. But when she turned her face and looked along the road that led to town, she hoped in her heart that he would not be on it. A wattlebird clacked and swooped from a nearby tree, its wings causing a movement of air which brushed her cheek. She closed her eyes for a second, startled, then opened them for another look, just to be sure. Then she smiled. Trudging towards her along the old Chum Road was a fair-haired boy, pushing a bicycle.